## LOVE LOST, LOVE FOUND

That night Nia and Brett had decided to stay in and have a meal picked up from Sylvia's. After dinner, Nia said that if she didn't get some exercise besides shopping, she was going to weigh 200 pounds before they got back to Los Angeles.

They changed into sweat suits and headed for the second floor.

"Don't go on the machines," Brett said. "Let's work up a real sweat."

"On what?"

"This." He stepped across the room and pushed open a panel to reveal a complete table tennis setup.

"Well, aren't you full of secrets?" Nia said as she picked up a paddle, twirled it in her hand and put it back.

# BOOK YOUR PLACE ON OUR WEBSITE AND MAKE THE ARABESQUE ROMANCE CONNECTION!

We've created a customized website just for our very special Arabesque readers, where you can get the inside scoop on everything that's going on with Arabesque romance novels.

When you come online, you'll have the exciting opportunity to:

- View covers of upcoming books

- Learn about our future publishing schedule (listed by publication month and author)

- Find out when your favorite authors will be visiting a city near you

- Search for and order backlist books

- Check out author bios and background information

- Send e-mail to your favorite authors

- Join us in weekly chats with authors, readers and other guests

- Get writing guidelines

- AND MUCH MORE!

Visit our website at
http://www.arabesquebooks.com

# LOVE LOST, LOVE FOUND

### Viveca Carlysle

## BET Publications, LLC
http://www.bet.com
http://www.arabesquebooks.com

ARABESQUE BOOKS are published by

BET Publications, LLC
c/o BET BOOKS
One BET Plaza
1900 W Place NE
Washington, DC 20018-1211

All Kensington Titles, Imprints, and Distributed Lines are available at special quantity discounts for bulk purchases for sales promotions, premiums, fund-raising, and educational or institutional use. Special book excerpts or customized printings can also be created to fit specific needs. For details, write or phone the office of the Kensington special sales manager: Kensington Publishing Corp., 850 Third Avenue, New York, NY 10022, attn: Special Sales Department, Phone: 1-800-221-2647.

First Printing: December 2001
10 9 8 7 6 5 4 3 2 1

Printed in the United States of America

# Prologue

Brett Faulkner stood in the hot June sun and gave the college student behind the wheel of the moving van some last-minute instructions. At six feet, three inches, he towered over the student. He was twenty-five now and had known Nia most of his life. He had told himself that this was the only adult way to handle what was happening. If Nia didn't want to be with him, he had to let her go. As a result of her decision to go back to California and try the corporate world again, they had never gotten beyond a partnership. Brett always thought they would. He thought it was just a matter of time. He was wrong.

Brett and his father were both falconers and had inspired a few of their young guests to learn more about the endangered species list. Nia and Brett had been partners on the lecture circuit, with talks and demonstrations about the peregrine falcon.

The business had fallen off, and they were about to revamp it when Nia's parents died. It was sudden and devastating and a terrible loss to everyone who knew the couple. The only thing Nia wanted now was to get out of Wyoming.

"Take it easy and don't worry about the time it

takes you to get there," Brett told the driver. "The building manager is expecting you, and he has someone to help you unload the truck."

"Yes, sir. I'll be careful. This is a great job."

"I guess so."

Brett stepped back and watched the young man pull away from Nia's house and head for the highway. He had posted the job offer on the bulletin board at the university for her. *Wanted: moving to Los Angeles, California. Need a driver for moving van. References required.* Within hours, Brett had gotten a response from Kent Hemmings.

The thin, blond student had completed his junior year majoring in business administration. He was polite and had provided good references.

He was only a couple of years younger than Brett and was transferring to UCLA for his final year. This would save the expense of an airline ticket.

"I'm from California, and I love to ski. So I picked a college where I'd see snow," he explained to Brett. "Unfortunately, my courses require more time than I thought."

"So you haven't been able to ski."

"Not only haven't I been able to ski, my dorm seems like it is a mile from some of the buildings. I thought I was going to freeze to death the first year just getting to class."

"Your California bones can't take our winters."

"That's about the size of it. I've tried, and I'm out of here."

"I want to explain something. Ms. Sebastian is going through a bad time. Her parents were killed in an accident, and she's going to be starting a new life out there."

Even as he said the words, pain shot through his

body. He didn't want her to leave, but he'd talked to his stepmother, who felt trying to stop Nia could only make things worse.

"Don't worry. I'll get her there safe and sound. Does she have any relatives there?"

"Her mentor and two friends."

"If you give me your number, I'll keep in touch."

Brett handed Kent a business card. The business was gone, but since he'd used his home telephone number, that wouldn't change. If Nia Sebastian insisted on moving on with a life that didn't include him, Brett wanted to make sure it was a safe beginning.

Brett's long legs were encased in worn jeans. His T-shirt had the name TARHARQA RANCH across it.

The ranch had been a dream of Brett's father, and for the past five years, Brett, his father and his stepmother had brought dozens of inner-city children to the ranch for the summer. It had started with only boys, but for the past two years it had been co-ed. He always thought that Nia would be there.

"People handle tragedy in different ways, Brett," his stepmother told him. "If you keep pushing Nia to share her pain with you, she's going to bolt."

*Why can't she lean on me for a change?* he thought.

Brett had made a decision about changing his life. He was going back to school. He'd been accepted by New York University Law School and would be moving to New York about the same time as Nia would be starting her job in Los Angeles.

"Are you sure about this?" he asked just before Nia climbed into the truck. He was giving her a chance to stay. If she said yes, he would have hopped in his pickup truck and caught up with the moving van. He would have gladly paid for the airline ticket for Kent Hemmings if it meant Nia was staying. But that was not to be.

"I know you think I'm just running away, but I have to do it. Trisha and I talked and I hope she can explain it to you better than I can."

Trisha, Brett's stepmother, had already tried to make him understand, but he didn't tell Nia.

"So you've said for the past month. You've made it very clear that I'm no longer part of your life."

"I'm sorry."

"Don't be." His anger took over. "This might be what we both need."

Maybe it was the comfort zone that finally made the difference. If Nia stayed, she would have been enveloped into his family. He had been exploring possibilities. He'd realized that all the things he wanted to do required more education, and he'd been planning to return to college.

Brett Faulkner showed maturity in the way he lived that hinted he had an "old soul." He'd had pain in his life from his mother's death to his journalist father's capture behind enemy lines. His father was rescued, but the result of untreated wounds left him unable to walk. How could Nia think he couldn't help her get through her tragedy? However, the choice was hers.

He didn't try to keep the bitterness from his voice. She was turning away from him at the time he felt she needed him the most. Two months before she'd lost both her parents because a tractor-trailer driver had fallen asleep at the wheel and slammed into them as they drove home late one night. They were a loving family, and Brett had grieved also. He just didn't realize how much this would change *his* life.

He understood her need to get away, and he'd known for a long time that one day she'd return to California. She had unfinished business from her corporate life. The longer she stayed in Wyoming, the more he hoped she didn't need to go back to her other life. Now someone from her past had stepped forward. Her Stanford professor turned banker, Alethia Madison.

"Alethia made the proverbial offer I can't refuse. Her assistant is resigning and she says I can have the job."

"Why is the person quitting? Maybe the job's not that great."

"The woman's husband is being transferred out of state. . . ."

"And she would rather have her husband than a career."

They had fought this battle too many times, and Nia was tired of defending herself. She was going back to Los Angeles. No matter what Brett said or did, she knew she would not be complete until she vanquished those feelings of inadequacy that came any time a man and woman broke up.

She'd never told anyone, not Trisha, not Alethia, not even her best friends. Until it was behind her, she would always feel that she had run when she should have fought.

Nia tossed her long, black hair over her shoulder. Somehow the rubber band she'd used to keep it in the ponytail had broken and the gentle breeze blew her hair all around her face. She wore jeans and a two sizes too large, worn Stanford University sweatshirt, which didn't hide the curves on her five-foot, four-inch frame.

She was six years older than Brett, but with only sunscreen protecting her face, she looked like a teenager. She had worked in Los Angeles for two years after graduation. Then she'd met a man who'd turned her life around. They worked in the same office. He was a rising star, and she was just holding down a clerical job until she could find something in international management. She was in love for the very first time. He was not in love at all, but he was an excellent liar. When Nia began pressing him for a commitment, he confessed that he was engaged. Nia had returned home to re-group. She and Brett were childhood friends, and their love of falconry had caused her life to take a different path.

Nia's parents owned a store and had expected her to learn how to run it. She thought it was the only way of life. When she began working with fal-cons and hearing Kaliq talk about the places he'd visited, a new world opened for her. She liked the idea of sand and surf and had decided that California was where she wanted to be. She'd always said that she had to go back to California and prove she could succeed in the business world but until her parents' death she'd always thought about it as being in the future. Then she began to think about the things she wanted to accomplish. Life was so fragile to her now. It could be gone in a second, and she knew that if she stayed in Wyo-ming, she would never get over the demons that told her to go back to Los Angeles and try again.

Nia had tried over and over to explain to Brett

what she was going through. He was stubborn. He wanted his way or no way. She had to admit that they were very much alike in the way they held to their strong beliefs.

"I can't deal with you right now. I'm going to California. I don't know how long I'll be gone. I don't know what's going to happen, but I have to do this for me. Now if you can't handle it, I'm sorry."

He leaned forward and kissed her cheek. "Good luck."

Nia grabbed her duffel bag and tossed it into the front seat of the truck. She'd said her goodbyes to everyone else and now it was time to move on. As Kent put the truck into gear and headed for the highway, she glanced in the side-view mirror. Brett had turned his back and was walking to his car. Tears filled her eyes and rolled down her cheeks. She didn't try to stop them. She only knew in her heart that this was what she needed to do. She believed in a force in the universe that controlled everything. If she whispered what she wanted, somewhere in the universe she would be heard and her wish granted. That was one of the reasons she felt that if Brett was supposed to be in her life, it would happen. If not, she would just have to see what else was out there for her.

*Five Years Later*

# *One*

She was fighting mad, and there was nothing she could do about the situation. In the five years since they met, Nia Sebastian and Kent Hemmings had become good friends. She'd acted as his financial counselor on a buyout of a small electronics company the year before. He and his partners had done a terrific job in turning the company around. In order to get the money they needed, they had gone public and sold shares in the company as Nia had advised them. The last time they met, she told them it was time to buy back as much stock as they could so they didn't lose control.

Unfortunately, they were too late. They didn't know that a shark was in their waters. Jared Schuyler had started buying stock and now had the five percent he needed so he could announce his takeover plans.

Nia Sebastian sat next to Kent Hemmings as she perused the papers he had brought over as soon as he got them. Her brown eyes flashed as she read the documents. Jared had made it very clear that Bryant Electronics would be the next jewel in his crown.

"I never thought he'd do anything like this," Nia

said. She handed the papers back to Kent Hemmings. "I'll bet Daphne put him up to it."

Kent ran his hands through his blond hair. "I'm between a rock and a hard place on this one," he told her. "I've got my money tied up in the house we're building, and I don't know if we could fight this off."

"How are Jeff and Paul handling it?"

"They're bouncing off the walls, ready to fight one minute; the next minute they just want to throw in the towel."

"What you need is a white knight."

"I'd still be losing the company."

"Maybe not."

Kent grinned at her. "I told them you'd come up with something."

"I need someone who would pose a threat to Jared. If he thought for a moment that he would have a real fight on his hands for this company, he might decide he doesn't really want it."

"So we would have to sell?"

"It would be your decision. You might decide to sell it, but stay on as a vice president. You might even just make it a partnership and have one more person to share the work, or you might feel like walking away. In any case, you'll be satisfied that Jared didn't get your company. I'll get on it right away."

Her administrative assistant buzzed, and Nia picked up the telephone and listened for a minute.

"I'll be right out." She hung up, and she and Kent left her office and he said good-bye to Charlotte.

Nia walked him to the elevator and Kent leaned down and kissed her cheek. "Don't forget Lisabeth and I are throwing a bon voyage party for the Nilssons at the end of the month."

"I'm not sure . . ."

"Don't even try to get out of this one. Lisabeth will come to your house and drag you to the party."

Nia slipped her hands into the double-breasted, navy pin-striped coatdress. She had several coat-dresses in different materials and colors. She'd made it her version of a business suit. It gave her the neat and pulled-together look her clients approved of. She thought about the time when she had first started. She'd tried wearing a business suit. It hadn't worked. No matter how hard she tried, her skirt would work its way around until the zipper was on the side instead of in back, or in the front. She'd found a beige coatdress on a shopping spree with her friends Julie and Bree. She wore it to a business luncheon. Sitting there and not having to worry about her blouse rising, or her skirt slipping, she actually enjoyed the meal. Nia immediately went to a tailor and had several more made.

The elevator arrived and Kent got in. Nia waited until the doors closed before she balled up her fist and yelled, "Damn!" She took a deep breath and walked back into her office.

"Charlotte, what did he say?"

"He wants to have dinner with you."

"He can keep dreaming. If he thinks threatening my friends is going to help his case, he's wrong. The next time he calls, I want you to say these exact words to him: 'Ms. Sebastian considers it a conflict of interest to talk to you,'" Nia told her.

"No problem. I'll tell him, but he gets really upset when I call you Ms. Sebastian."

"There's nothing he can do about it. When I divorced him, I legally returned to my maiden name. I'd really like to forget that I was ever Mrs. Jared Schuyler."

Nia returned to her office and sat at her desk. She powered up her computer and began to search her contact files for a venture capitalist, someone to push Jared away from Bryant Electronics. Any time there was a hostile takeover threat, the company had an option to sell it to someone else. That person was called a "white knight" for coming in and saving the day. Since Kent was the last appointment for the day, she concentrated on his problem for now. She had so much on her plate in the next few weeks. Her best friend was getting married, and she was a bridesmaid. Her other best friend was going on a long-term assignment in Hawaii. Then there was the party Lisabeth wanted her to attend. Kent's wife was sweet, but she gabbed incessantly. For what most people could say in thirty seconds, Lisabeth needed three minutes. Nia was her latest project. Nia had been single for two years and Lisabeth had decided that was long enough and she was matchmaking. She didn't consider any of the men in Nia's life candidates for long term, so they didn't count.

An hour later, Charlotte struck her head in the door to say she was leaving. "I'm all set for the surprise shower."

"Thanks for the help."

Charlotte was gone in a second. Nia took another hour before she'd armed herself with the names of prospective white knights. She would begin contacting them the next day.

As she walked through the reception area, she spotted a magazine that Charlotte had been reading. It was facedown. When she turned it over, she saw that it was one of those weekly gossip magazines. The headline was SEXY BACHELORS FROM COAST TO COAST.

There was a little picture in the upper, left-hand corner of a movie star couple who were getting divorced. She'd been the wife's financial counselor early in her career, but the husband had insisted she sever ties with Nia and use his advisor. Nia wanted to read the story, so she struck the magazine in the side of her briefcase and left to pick up her car. She hoped the woman had listened to her about finances. She'd lived in Los Angeles long enough to know that if you were getting married, you needed a strong prenuptial agreement.

The elevator took a few minutes to arrive, and by the time Nia reached the lobby level, said good-bye to the guards and walked to the garage, it was after eight. She stopped at a fast-food place and picked up chicken and a salad since it was too late to cook at home.


A short time later Nia pulled her burgundy BMW up to her driveway. As she stepped out of the car and walked to the gate, a shiver danced up her spine, and she turned to look around. She saw nothing. She opened the gate, got back in her car and drove it in the driveway.

When she closed the gate, she again got the feeling that something was wrong and still she didn't see anything. She hurried to her door, unlocked it and went inside. She quickly threw the dead-bolt lock and then chastised herself for being so foolish.

When she flipped the switch by the door, it turned on every light in her house. She'd had it wired that way just after she purchased the three-bedroom home in the Los Feliz section of Los Angeles.

Nia dropped her briefcase in a chair and the food on the kitchen table, and went straight to her bedroom and into the master bath. She stripped off her clothes and took a shower. After letting the water pound on her muscles, she felt better. The bath was stark and functional. Black and white tiles on the floor. Black shower curtains, white towels. It was so different from the rest of her house.

After her shower, she slipped on her white terry cloth robe and padded into the dining room. She pulled out her china and silver and set the table for one. When she was married, the maid always set the breakfast table for two and the dinner table for one. Toward the end of their marriage, Jared rarely shared dinner with her. He said the best deals were made hitting a few clubs at night.

Now Nia set the table for one at both breakfast and dinner. Lunch was either a business meeting with a client or she ordered in. She'd done well as a financial counselor. Until now. It was a vendetta pure and simple. When Nia first left Jared, Kent had called in a favor and got her a great deal on a condo.

Nia liked the condo but it never felt like home to her. When she mentioned it to Alethia, her mentor advised her to look for a house.

Kent wasn't surprised when she told him she was selling the condo. He was surprised when Daphne offered to help Nia find a place. The woman who had been the mother-in-law from hell extended an olive branch. She told Nia about the little house in the Los Felez section of Los Angeles.

Nia felt that somehow Alethia had engineered

that gesture, but she didn't know why Daphne agreed to look for the house.

Nia stretched out on the recliner and remembered how she'd met Jared because her mentor was his godmother. Alethia and Daphne had been roommates in college. Alethia was there on a scholarship, while Daphne came from a wealthy African-American family.

The only time they fought was over the lavish wedding Daphne had planned for Nia and Jared. Alethia had tried to intercede on Nia's behalf, and she and Daphne had almost ended their friendship. Finally to keep the peace, Nia had agreed to the spectacle. It was the first of the skirmishes she would lose to her mother-in-law. Nia ended up participating in fund-raisers, dinner parties and volunteer jobs. She hated them, but when she tried to explain that to Jared, he just reminded her that there were quite a few women in the world that would love the chance to play tennis doubles with stars, athletes and political bigwigs. Little by little Nia began losing herself until she put her foot down and refused to put off a client to go to a fund-raiser. The more she asserted herself, the more she knew that they had married for the wrong reasons.

Jared was fascinated with Nia's heritage. He considered her exotic. She was attracted to his ambition. The fascination wore off within the first six months of their marriage.

She popped her food in the microwave and walked into the living room. Nia sat back in the recliner next to the telephone. She listened to her messages. There was a call from Bree confirming she'd found a catering service for Julie's shower. Another message from Alethia saying that she had to leave town unexpectedly, but would be back for Julie's shower. Nia frowned. She'd seen her mentor the day before and they were so close to Alethia finalizing the purchase of the bank. She hoped that the trip didn't mean there was a problem.

The last call made her slam her hand down on the arm of the recliner. "Nia, why don't you just talk to me? I'm sure we could work something out." Jared's voice was smooth with what she perceived as a snicker behind it. She didn't wait for him to finish the message. She punched the button to erase it.

If she had thought for one moment Jared really meant what he said, she would have been glad to sit down and talk to him. That wasn't what he wanted. He wanted to gloat. He wanted to look her in the face and tell her that he was taking over Bryant Electronics. She knew that was what he wanted because during their marriage she'd seen him do it over and over. One night she felt so sorry for the owner. She asked Jared to stop taunting the man. Her then-husband turned on her and said he had the right.

"You asked him to meet you. You made it seem as if you were going to make a deal with him so he could get his company back. But that wasn't it. You want to humiliate him face-to-face."

"As the victor, that's my right."

That night had been the one that opened her eyes to the kind of man she'd married. She didn't like him or herself for being swept away by his facade.

The bell chimed, indicating her food was ready, and Nia snapped out of her reverie.

She put the food on her plate and began to eat. She remembered the magazine and returned to the living room to get it. Once back in the dining room, she read the article on the couple getting a divorce and was disheartened to learn that her former client had not prepared herself for the divorce. She was about to go from Hollywood's A-list to a small apartment in Studio City and was going to try to revive the career she gave up for marriage.

"I'll never do that," Nia said aloud. She finished the article, but began to thumb through the rest of the magazine. When she got to the section of the sexiest men coast to coast, each page gave an area and a bachelor. California had an actor and an entertainment lawyer. Texas had a rancher. When she flipped to the next page, her heart skipped a beat. She couldn't believe it. Dressed in an Armani suit, with his long hair pulled back into a ponytail, was someone from her past. Brett Faulkner.

# Two

It was happening again, and Brett could not find a way to stop it. He'd lived in New York four and a half years. He thought New York women were more sophisticated than the women he'd dated in the past. He thought he'd made it very clear that he wasn't interested in anything long-term. He felt badly telling her that he didn't want to see her anymore. It was always best to make a clean break. Jane had cried, and he'd felt like a heel. He was as hurt by the change in circumstances as she was. He knew she wouldn't believe him, but it was true. He didn't like hurting anyone. Brett knew that over the past few months Jane had become more demanding of his time. Jane was beautiful, a petite but curvy woman. She was also fun, talented and exactly the companion Brett wanted in a woman at this stage in his life. The only thing he didn't want was a wife.

He arrived to treat her to an evening of dinner and theater, but could tell immediately something was wrong. Her eyes were red and swollen. For a moment he thought she knew that he'd planned a special evening because the relationship was over.

When he asked why she was upset, she tossed a

newspaper at him. It was a picture of him and his uncle as they celebrated a hockey victory. Palladin Rush had coached a hockey team for years and they finally won.

"Why wasn't I with you?" Her voice trembled.

"We talked about this before," he said. They agreed that they wouldn't do family things so that their families wouldn't link them as a couple. It made it awkward for everyone when they decided it was over. In most cases it was the same as a couple who were getting a divorce. Brett had seen it happen to several of his friends and was determined it wouldn't happen to him.

"I thought we were getting closer."

"I don't know what to say. I thought we had an understanding. . . ."

"You can't love," Jane screamed. "That's your real problem. You try to pretend that you're honest about a relationship. That as long as you tell me you're not ready for marriage, you've done your part."

"I thought we discussed all of this before."

"You discussed it. I wanted to be with you because I thought I could change your mind. Don't you ever look in a mirror? Women love being with you. They find you different, exotic. There just aren't that many part Cheyenne, part African-American, rich men in New York. You go around wearing your cowboy boots and hat, and you wonder why people don't believe you."

"What does that mean?"

"You seem to be acting out a part. That's why women don't believe you. You don't know how hard this is for me. I wanted to be strong, but I'm not. I can't go on like this. I'm sorry."

"I know women find me attractive. It makes me feel good to know that a woman I want to be with also wants to be with me. I just don't understand why you think I'd lie when I said I didn't want to get involved. What did I do that made you think I would change?"

"Because someday you are going to change your mind. You are going to fall in love and want someone. I hope she doesn't want you. I hope you see what it's like."

She began to cry, and Brett didn't know how to comfort her. He went outside and removed the key from his key ring. He locked the door and then dropped the key in the mail slot. It was a sad time for both of them. She couldn't go on without a commitment, and he couldn't make that commitment.

Brett returned home. He stripped, showered and climbed into bed. He thought about the situation. He'd made it so clear that he didn't want marriage. He never understood why women didn't believe him. He really thought that he and Jane were good together. She was an upcoming actress who had gotten great reviews in an off-Broadway play. He thought she was surely more interested in her career than marriage. He really liked her. She was bright, funny and smart. He thought her ambition was the sexiest thing about the woman. He wondered what she said about him falling in love so hard and being rejected. How could he tell her that it had already happened? He'd loved Nia Sebastian with all his heart, and she'd left him. She'd married another man, and it still hurt, even though she'd been divorced and he hadn't contacted her. He was afraid of getting hurt again.

Whatever had happened to that old adage about honesty being the best policy? It hadn't worked for him. He didn't see any other way to deal with the situation. He hoped the next woman would not only believe him, but would want that kind of relationship. Why did it keep happening to him? Each time he'd tried to find a woman who had a career plan that didn't include marriage. Each time he'd hurt someone. The best thing he could do now was take a lot of time before going through this again.

# Three

Brett had a fund-raiser to attend, and he would find out if his assistant wanted to go with him.

Before when a relationship ended, he would just go back to Wyoming for a few weeks and give the woman time to cry on someone else's shoulder. He felt that if he was out of sight, then he would be out of mind. The last time he went home, he was approached by a few members of the National Brotherhood of Skiers about a ski resort, and a developer about creating a dude ranch in conjunction with the one for inner-city youth that Kaliq Faulkner ran.

The more Brett thought about it, the less he liked the idea of the dude ranch. His father's ranch was strictly a labor of love. He didn't want to mix in something commercial, but the ski resort sounded interesting.

The project would require extensive concentration, and there was no way he could do it alone. The research would be fun. He'd spend time at ski lodges all around the world and make his decision. Ana Lisa began to compile the information for him. He hadn't thought about a time frame. It was just an idea in the back of his mind. He hadn't planned on acting right away, but one thing led to another.

On a ski trip to Colorado, he'd met a few more members of the Brotherhood of Skiers. They'd spent years visiting other ski resorts and now they wanted a home base. Brett saw the project as something he wanted to be part of, and he talked it over with his assistant. She thought it was a great idea for Brett's company, The Aiyanna Group. The name was Native American for "forever flowering," which was exactly what he wanted the company to do.

At present, he was the only member of the "group," but he was looking for partners and knew that would soon change. It was time to add partners and expand his business.

The idea of owning a ski lodge piqued his interest, but he needed to take some time off and check the land and the schedule that most ski lodges maintained.

In college, Brett had been called "cowboy," and he was the only one in his crowd who had grown up on a ranch. It cropped up again with his risk-taking methods as a venture capitalist. He seemed to have the gift of finding the right company to back. Each of them had paid off and made him a wealthy man. He'd learned the financial rewards of being the money man behind businesses from his "uncle." Palladin Rush had an uncanny knack for finding the right projects. Brett wouldn't take on a venture by himself. He'd put together a consortium and spread the risk.

Brett had done quite well for himself. Just as he

had acquired his nickname, he'd also been selected as one of the most eligible men around. The fact that he raised and trained falcons only added to his mystique. He wanted to do something different. He wanted to do something spectacular. He didn't want the hype of gossip columns to make him seem less sincere about his business. He'd been put on several lists, the most eligible, the richest, the sexiest. He was thirty now, and he wanted to be on the top businessmen's list. If he could pull this resort deal off, he would be all over *Business Week* and *Forbes*.

He'd give the resort an exotic name, and since falcons had been a big part of his life, he had thought about incorporating them into the theme of the project. Brett had learned the art of falconry from the same school that his father had attended in Europe. Maybe he could do something that made people think they were like knights when chivalry meant something. He wouldn't allow the guests to use the falcons. He would give demonstrations the same way he and Nia did.

Nia. She had crossed his mind every now and then for the past five years. Sometimes it made him want to pick up the phone and call her. He needed to tell her that she was right. He also wanted her to see the person he'd become, more successful than they had ever dreamed. Back then, the endangered peregrine falcon had been important. He still contributed to the group who was keeping them safe.

For him there had been all the time in the world to develop a relationship with Nia. He didn't know he was on borrowed time. He allowed Trisha to keep him up to date. From the little bulletins he got, Nia was doing well. She hadn't remarried, but probably had a significant other. Her career was on target and she seemed to have expunged the demons that had forced her to return to Wyoming. She hadn't made it a secret that she was home because things hadn't worked out in California. In a way, she was hiding from reality. After her parents' deaths, she just decided to try big city life again. When he thought of Nia, it always seemed to be when he was ending a relationship. That had happened two nights before when Jane suggested she move in with him. Brett had never lived with a woman, nor did he let a woman live with him. He thought that made it clear that he did not want a wife. The first couple of times he did this, the women moved on and married someone else. Why couldn't Jane tell that he wasn't husband material? He couldn't understand it. He'd been truthful. He'd told her that he wasn't a long-term guy and she'd agreed that they were just going to have fun. Somewhere along the way she'd decided that they were a couple and the next step was marriage. He felt sorry for her.

*So much for the maudlin side of me,* he thought. It was time to get back to the real matter at hand, his next business deal—falconry, skiing, and romance all at one place.

He wanted it to be similar to a theme park, but for a more upscale clientele. He was sure he could create something like that in Wyoming and that it would be successful. After all, he was in the business of making companies successful.

He placed a call to his father. He wanted to give him a last chance at the idea of using the dude ranch.

"I don't want anything to take away from the children," Kaliq said.

"Dad, I understand, but this wouldn't take away from them. In fact, it might help with the expenses. The more others get involved, the more you can expand the children's section."

"I don't want the ranch to get so big we aren't giving the children individual attention. It might be better for other small camps to spring up and do the same thing."

"I just wanted to make sure you still felt that way."

"Say hello to Palladin and his family."

"I will."

Father and son had not always had a smooth relationship. Brett had lived with his mother until her death and then with his father. Kaliq Faulkner didn't give up his career as a globe-trotting journalist until after he'd been captured and lost the use of his legs. It took until Brett was twenty before they relaxed enough to be with each other. That was when Trisha Terrence came back into Kaliq's life.

When Trish married Kaliq, she gave up her world and embraced his. She was a cordon bleu chef, who now joyfully served plain meals to as many as fifteen children, ten full-time ranch hands and five part-time hands.

It was Trisha who had encouraged Brett to find out what he really wanted to do once Nia left. She didn't regard his moving to New York as running away. She called it "exploring the possibilities."

When he graduated and elected to stay in New York and only visit Wyoming, Trisha had been his champion again. But lately, with the women problems he'd been having, he'd thought more about moving back to Wyoming. That became feasible when Ana Lisa came into his life.

At thirty, Brett was still carving out a career as a venture capitalist. He'd changed quite a bit from the unsure, heartbroken person who had arrived at Palladin Rush's door. The venture capitalist he'd called "uncle" since he was sixteen had thrown his arm around him and welcomed him to New York.

So many students arrived and found that the "city that never sleeps" could ruin your health, but Palladin convinced Brett to join a gym and work out three times a week. Brett could stay in shape and have the same stamina as working on the ranch. The result was a broad chest, washboard abs and hard biceps that were well hidden under his specially tailored suits. His black, almond-shaped eyes and thick black hair were a gift from his late mother, who was part Cheyenne. He wore it in a long braid that hung just below his shoulders. His facial structure and dark brown coloring were from his African-American father. When his frame filled out, he made a dashing figure for the ladies and a menacing one for the men.

When Nia's parents were killed in a highway accident, she received an offer from her former Stanford University advisor. She jumped at the chance and left Brett and Wyoming behind. Brett waited until he heard she'd married a man named Jared Schuyler from the Baldwin Hills section of Los Angeles. From what he understood, that meant the man was not only wealthy, but also part of the city's black elite.

Deep inside, he wanted to become so famous she'd regret she'd broken up with him. That changed as soon as he heard about the marriage. He lived in a condo owned by his father's best friend, Palladin Rush. Besides Palladin and his wife, Jesslyn, he had their nine-year-old twins, Ethan and Vance, following him around.

Several of Palladin's business associates had daughters attending Radcliffe and Vassar who found Brett's background quite interesting. After all, how many of their classmates could boast that the man squiring them trained falcons and had a condo? Shortly after his first major deal, he bought a town house in Harlem.

He took intermittent trips to Wyoming to see his father and stepmother. Each time they saw him, Kaliq and Trisha knew he had come a little bit more into his own. His stepmother kept in touch with Nia and informed the rest of the family as to what was happening to her. The marriage had not worked, and she was now divorced. Brett made no effort to contact Nia. First he wanted to make a life for himself. He'd done a terrific job. He'd parlayed his knowledge of corporate law into a career as a limited-venture capitalist. He had a talent for knowing just what the market was going to do, which companies were ripe for takeovers, and how to prevent takeovers. His name was whispered around boardrooms—as someone to fear if he was across from you working out the terms, and relief if he was on your side during negotiations.

Now he'd amassed a fortune and because of that prosperity, he'd attracted some of the most beautiful women in New York. These women weren't shy about telling him what they expected, yet each woman who'd said she wanted "no strings" ended up pushing toward marriage. For the next few months he would concentrate strictly on business.

Palladin, Jesslyn, Kaliq and Trisha hoped he'd find someone and they weren't shy about telling him it was time to get serious. Ethan and Vance admired his love 'em and leave 'em life. They jumped at the chance to hang out with Brett. He loved playing "big brother."

He hated it when he tried to end relationships. He'd been honest that he wasn't looking for a wife, but that didn't stop some of the women from trying to change him. He didn't mind them trying. He just hated that when they didn't succeed he was perceived as the bad guy. The gossip columns couldn't wait to announce he'd broken yet another heart. The columnists fought over who had the juiciest tidbits about how he had ended the relationship.

Even Brett had to admit the last breakup had warranted press coverage. The daughter of a successful club owner in Harlem had stormed into his office and poured a mixture of syrup and sawdust in the CPU of his computer. As if that wasn't enough, she gave an interview to a gossip columnist. He almost sent her the bill for the new computer. Fortunately he kept tape backup of everything and was only inconvenienced, not devastated. He did try several personal assistants, but was beginning to feel like *Murphy Brown*, a sitcom of several years back about a woman whose aggressive manner prevented her from keeping a secretary. The running joke was that each week there was someone new trying out for the job. Brett's secretaries lasted about a month. His hectic schedule drove most people crazy. There would be times that required twelve-hour workdays and then dry spells where there was nothing to do.

He'd given up hope. But just when he thought he wouldn't find anyone ever, he hired Ana Lisa Murphy as his personal assistant. She was black and beautiful. Her six-foot, full-figured body indicated correctly that she was strictly no nonsense. Her name was her heritage—a Latina mother and African-American father. Brett had no designs on her so they made a perfect team. The skill of hers that Brett loved best was that Ana Lisa was also a website designer. He taught her about business and she kept all ex-girlfriends away from him. She also delighted in teasing him about his life-style.

"One day you are going to find a woman who will change your mind about a lot of things."

"I don't think so. I'm perfectly happy with my life."

"You, my favorite boss, are playing with fire and one day you will get singed."

Brett never meant to hurt any of the women he chose as companions. He was a monogamous dater. He liked the pleasure of one woman's company rather than the tedious search or brainless filling up of little black books with the names of women at his beck and call. He didn't understand why some of his friends and colleagues showed up with a different woman just to impress the others. Maybe that was a better way.

Once in a while Nia crossed his mind. He knew it started after she got her divorce and that probably meant they had some unfinished business, but he didn't want to explore that avenue. Right now, he liked his life the way it was.

He looked at the clock. It was time to get dressed and get to the office. When he purchased the four-story brownstone in Harlem, he had dome extensive renovations. First he added an elevator and then converted the entire top floor that had once housed three bedrooms to a master bedroom and bath and a dressing room.

The second floor was a state-of-the-art exercise room. Normally he worked out every day, but this last deal had kept him too busy. He, like most men, hated exercise. He did it not only because women liked his well- but not overly trained muscles, but also exercise gave him the stamina to handle a whirlwind of activity before, during and immediately after taking over a business. He thought he'd better get back into a routine quickly or he'd have to hire a trainer to force him to exercise.

Transitions were brutal on everyone. He'd even had to talk a man out of killing himself when he lost his family business to a hostile takeover. Brett had also faced people who hired him to take over a company and then tried to negotiate Brett out of the deal with a flat salary rather than the lifetime-percentage contract they had all signed. It was not the first time somebody had tried to take advantage of him, nor would it be the last. People needed the money, but hated the idea that it made you their partner for the life of the business.

After his workout, he showered, shaved and slipped on a white terry-cloth robe and went to his office. The one thing he liked most about working at home was that he didn't have to worry about how he looked. He sat down at his computer and busied himself with research on expanding Taharqa to accommodate adults.

Several of the parents had mentioned that they wanted a chance to see the ranch. A few guest cottages could be placed on the property. As long as the parents didn't interfere with the children, it could be a vacation for them also. When his father was first looking for names for the ranch, Brett had made several suggestions. His father hadn't used any of them. Instead he'd found the story of a sixteen-year-old Nubian soldier who had defended Israel and later ruled for twenty-five years. Kaliq loved telling the story behind the name each year on the first day the children arrived. Most of the children came back until they were too old. Some of the boys, who were too old to participate as campers, had applied for jobs as ranch hands.

Kaliq and Trisha had received thank-you notes from several teachers for changing the study habits of some of the children who now wanted to go to college. Now if Brett's idea worked, he could offer more jobs to the former campers. The program was a continuing success story, and only a few children failed completely and returned to the ways of the street.

Perhaps they would give the ranch a different name and image. It would have to be tied to falcons. Maybe they would aim to attract a very upscale clientele. After an hour, he saved the information to a Zip disk and locked it in a cabinet. It was time to get dressed.

Tonight he was scheduled to attend a fund-raiser with Palladin and Jesslyn Ruch. The couple was quite active in their community and this one was for the scholarship program at the private school their sons attended. Kaliq had recommended that several boys from his camp to apply for the scholarships. Palladin helped by making sure that there were enough funds to take care of all the fees associated with the school.

Brett didn't want a date, so he'd asked his assistant, Ana Lisa, to accompany him. The limousine was scheduled to pick her up first and then Brett. He didn't use the elevator, but walked up one flight to his dressing room.

The items in his closet now were a far cry from what he had worn when he first came to New York. Then he was never without his wardrobe staples of a Stetson and cowboy boots. The wardrobe served its purpose to distract and disarm people while he absorbed what the city was made of, including some of its most prestigious African-American citizens.

In his second year in law school, all that changed. He began to dress the part of an average New Yorker. When he took his first job at a law firm, he blended in well. He was on the A-list as one of the city's most eligible bachelors. His mission was to be the best and that's what he was. Now he alternated the looks whenever he felt like it.

Women knew the rules because he explained often and early that he didn't want a serious relationship. His career was his wife and mistress.

Brett tossed off the robe and stood before the full-length mirror. The frosted, sliding doors opened to reveal the small bedroom he'd converted to a closet. Everything was neatly arranged. He selected a two-button tuxedo, with a wide collar rather than a wingtip tuxedo shirt. The drawers at the baseboard of the closet held his shoes. He opted for black patent-leather, opera-style slip-ons.

He put on the shirt and tuxedo, then the tie and cummerbund, shoes and steel-and-gold cufflinks.

He returned to the full-length mirror once he was completely dressed, nodded his approval and went downstairs to wait for the limousine. When it arrived, he climbed in and greeted his assistant.

"What's on the agenda tonight, boss? I'm not complaining, but is this business or pleasure?"

"It's just a dinner dance, and I didn't want to show up alone."

"You wouldn't have to be alone if—"

"Don't start," Brett said and laughed. He and Ana Lisa had forged the kind of boss-employee relationship that was special to both of them. She had a bright mind, ran the office and understood the nature of the business. Within a year he'd asked her to call him Brett rather than Mr. Faulkner. He considered himself very lucky to have found her.

Ana Lisa wore a sedate black dress with a plunging neckline. Despite her six-foot frame, she'd added black spike-heel shoes and now was as tall as Brett. She would certainly turn heads tonight.

"Boss, do you know a Frank Cassidy?"

"The name isn't familiar."

"He called at least five times and practically begged me to give him your home phone number. He said it was urgent and had to do with a bank in California."

Brett shook his head. "I still don't recognize the name. Did he leave a number where he could be reached?"

"No, but he knew about tonight. He didn't say it, but I think he may be on the guest list."

"Maybe his face will ring a bell."

They discussed a few other business projects and soon arrived at the school. The Rushes were waiting at the entrance and waved as his driver opened the door and Brett and Ana Lisa got out of the limousine.

Other limousines were pulling up to the school. It sometimes amazed Brett how people poured money into looking beautiful and prosperous while they wrote checks for a charitable cause.

He wasn't ashamed to include himself in that group. It was the nature of the city. Palladin wore nearly the same style tuxedo as Brett's. The women were very different, Ana Lisa's dress showed the curves inherited from her Latina mother. It was the height she got from her Irish father that made it easy to carry off such a bold style.

Jesslyn, who was quite petite, chose a monochromatic look. She wore a long, fitted gown in her favorite color—blue. The side split in the dress was up to her midthigh, which gave her an illusion of height.

As they started toward the stairs, someone called Brett's name.

A thin man with a shock of white hair walked toward him. His face was red from the wind, and he appeared to be quite old. "I'm Frank Cassidy."

"Have we met?"

"No, but I've heard a lot about you from Alethia Madison. She's here to see you."

Brett turned to Ana Lisa and said, "Go on. I'll join you in a few minutes." His assistant gave Frank Cassidy a glare as if to warn him not to cause trouble and joined Palladin and Jesslyn. Palladin looked at Brett, who nodded, signaling that he didn't need him.

*Alethia Madison.* The name from the past sent spikes of ice through Brett's veins. Why would she want to see him? Unless . . . he didn't want to think anything negative.

"How can I help you?"

"It's not me." Frank turned and pointed to an older woman standing a few feet away. She was tall and what was now referred to as "full figured," not fat. She wore an ivory dinner suit with rich beading.

"Is she coming to the fund-raiser?" he asked Frank.

"No. She had another engagement earlier this evening. We're only in New York for today."

"And you are?"

"Her former lawyer. I'm retired, but she asked me to act as her escort since I live here and she's not familiar with the city. It's very important to her."

That statement was enough to tap into Brett's curiosity. He started toward the woman, but she met him halfway. She held out her hand. He took it gently. "Ms. Madison."

"Call me Alethia."

She had a firm grip and he liked it. "Alethia, it is. Why are you here, Alethia?" He made it clear that he knew she wanted something.

She smiled. "I'm here because you're the only one I would trust at this time. I need you to help Nia Sebastian."

# *Four*

He turned and stepped aside. His face hadn't changed, but there was something. The years he had not seen Nia faded away. His instinct to help an old friend would always be there. Trisha would have called him if anything was wrong. Something must have just happened to Nia.

"Is she all right?"

"Physically, yes. I'm worried about her emotional state."

Brett took a deep breath. He and Nia had been friends and partners and the time apart didn't matter.

"What kind of trouble is she in?"

"It's a long story. . . . Could we go somewhere and have a drink?"

"Just a moment," Brett told her. He walked up the stairs and disappeared inside. As he suspected, Palladin was standing by the door, waiting for him.

"Problem?"

"I'm not sure. Apologize to the ladies and make sure Ana Lisa gets home safely?"

"Of course."

"I'll let you know what's going on."

"I'll expect to hear from you," Palladin said and turned to go in.

"If it's serious, I'll call you tonight. If not, don't worry."

Outside, Alethia Madison poked Frank in the side. "He's our man."

"Careful. Don't start poking these old bones too hard."

"Frank. As I've heard the kids say, you are just pushing this retirement thing to the 'max.' Don't you see the possibilities?"

"I see you getting in a whole lot of trouble. Faulkner is not the kind of person you can manipulate and get away with it."

"Frank! You're getting soft. You don't stand up straight anymore. You don't want your law practice. There's no excitement in your life. You're going to make yourself old. What am I going to do with you?"

Frank groaned. "I *am* an old man. I want just to sit around the house I worked for and never saw. I want to watch television. I even got a satellite dish so I could watch a hundred other channels."

Alethia wagged her finger at him. "I know you like to watch those so-called reality shows. That's a sorry thing to do."

"The only thing I'm sorry about is they didn't have any of those shows around when I could participate in them."

She felt a stiff breeze. The temperature was dropping. She pushed her hands into the pockets of the royal blue coat she had purchased before she left California. March was winter in New York and she hated cold weather. It had changed considerably since she'd gotten off the plane. Coming from very warm California to wintry New York was certainly enough to shock the system. It was a total myth that a larger girth provided warmth. She was freezing, but she didn't care. She had to do something to protect Nia, and she had to do it quickly.

"What makes you so sure he'll drop everything and rush to help your little protégé?"

"I know what I'm doing. All I have to do is get them in the same city and let nature take its course."

"You think he'll really believe you?"

"Of course not. The man isn't dumb. He knows that Nia is smart enough to bail herself out of this. I think he just needs an excuse to see her again. I just wanted it to sound a little mysterious."

"Nia will kill you."

"Probably. I don't care. She's going to need someone, and her former partner fits the bill."

"I'm out of it from now on. I set up your meeting. It's your deal from here. But just a friendly warning, one day you're going to manipulate the wrong person."

"I've been around too long to worry about that. I want Nia to have a champion on her side. That's the name of the game."


While Alethia was in New York, Nia Sebastian and her best buddies Julie Taylor and Bree Carter were preparing for a girls' night out. Julie had surprised her friends only two months before by announcing she was getting married and moving to Paris. Their friendship had been forged eighteen years before in Alethia Madison's class. They became study partners and later, best friends. Julie was the fashion queen. She'd done some modeling and acting and loved clothes. Bree had struggled with her weight until her friends convinced her that she was never going to be a size four.

"Come on, we've got to stop by Charlotte's," Nia said.

"Why do we need your secretary?" Bree asked.

"I have to get a package from her."

"Do we have to get to the restaurant at a certain time?" Julie asked.

"We'll only be a few minutes late," Nia assured her.

When the arrived at Charlotte's apartment complex, Nia suggested that they all go with her. "It will only take a couple of minutes," she promised.

They got out of the car and walked through the grounds to the building. Charlotte lived on the second floor, and they walked up rather than use the elevator.

Nia rang the bell and in seconds Charlotte opened the door. "Come on in. It's in the dining room."

Nia went in first, and Bree pushed by Julie to be next. "What's the hurry, Bree?"

In another second that question was answered. Cameras flashed and people yelled, "Surprise!" Julie threw her hands over her face.

"You got me!"

"I know you thought the shower was at the restaurant," Nia said and laughed.

"I'll get you guys," Julie promised.

"We had to find a way to surprise you, and it called for a little misdirection," Bree said.

"You wretch, pretending you didn't know why we had to stop by Charlotte's house. Wait, someone's missing. Where's Alethia?"

"She said she had to go out of town for a few days," Nia said. "She wouldn't tell me anything else."

"Have you noticed that she's getting secretive?" Bree asked.

"At first I thought it was about the bank, but everything is on schedule."

"So what will happen to you after the bank opens?"

"I'm scheduling a series of financial lectures and Alethia is still trying to talk me into working with her permanently. What's next for you?"


When Brett returned, Frank Cassidy pleaded another engagement. Alethia glared at him knowing that his engagement was with a TV show about couples switching partners for a date and then telling the viewers if it was better than their current relationships. Frank paid no attention to the glare, hailed a cab and left.

Brett and Alethia found a small bar nearby and sat in the back booth. As soon as their drinks appeared and the waiter disappeared, Brett spoke softly.

"Why are you here?"

"I guess I should tell you a little about myself," Alethia began.

He knew who she was and the battles in which she'd been involved since she'd left her job as a tenured professor at Stanford to go into the private sector. She'd been a role model for black women for decades and it was big news when she opted for a high-paying job with a California bank. It was then she'd offered the job that Nia had accepted five years ago.

"I read *Black Enterprise*. I'm aware of your work."

"So, in other words, get to the point."

"No, ma'am, in those same words," Brett said and flashed a big smile. "You know we're here because you said Nia needed help. You knew that would get my attention. So let's get to the facts."

Alethia's loud laughter made patrons turn their heads for a moment and then return to their conversations.

He leaned back and waited. His black eyes never left her face as she talked. If Nia needed him, there was no question he would be there.

"Do you know Kent Hemmings?"

"We met once."

He didn't say that Kent had kept him posted on Nia for about three weeks after they'd first arrived in California. Once Brett went to New York, they had lost contact.

"Well, he's taken a little company called Bryant Electronics and done a terrific job. Nia acted as his financial advisor. Kent spread himself too thin, in spite of Nia's advice, and the company's open for a hostile takeover."

"Why does this concern me?"

"The real reason Kent is under attack is because of Nia. The man behind the takeover is Jared Schuyler."

Nia's ex-husband had also been profiled in several magazines. He'd come from a wealthy black family and was on the way to becoming a millionaire in his own right.

"What's that got to do with Nia?"

"He's trying to hurt her. He found a way when Kent bought a company that no one wanted on Nia's advice. He's turned it around, but in doing so left himself open by letting too much stock get out of his hands. He was trying to buy it back, but by that time Jared had enough stock to announce a hostile takeover bid."

"So what's it all about? He takes the company away from Kent and that hurts Nia, so, what—she comes back to him?"

Alethia shook her head. "He doesn't want her back. He wants to destroy her for leaving him."

"What can I do?"

"Take Bryant away from him. Act as a white knight or buy the company outright and keep Jared from this little vendetta. Nia is devastated. She and Kent have been friends for a long time."

"I'm sure Kent can find someone."

"There are three partners. They can't seem to agree with one another. Kent, Jeff and Paul fight among themselves. I think an offer from you would stop all of that."

Kent had been the one who drove Nia to California. He was the one Brett had instructed to take very good care of Nia. He wasn't surprised that they'd become friends. He didn't tell Alethia that he'd already committed to the ski lodge and wasn't planning on anything else for the next several months.

"Why me?"

"I believe you and Nia are still friends, even though you haven't seen each other for years."

"My stepmother keeps both of us supplied with what's going on. I've checked out Nia's website."

"Sometimes Nia can be very secretive when bad things happen to her. She's always been able to share the good times, but thinks she has to suffer alone."

"Why can't you help her? All it takes is finding a white knight to bail out the company and it stops everything. Why are you here?"

She took a long sip of her drink and pursed her lips as she seemed to be debating with herself on how much she should tell Brett. He knew it and was determined to wait her out.

After another minute or so, she explained, "I'm in the process of buying a bank. I've done my research, and the one I was after was not just any bank but one that is the heart of one of the black communities. I've spread myself pretty thin with all the deals I've had to make."

"You've called in all your favors, and you need more."

"Exactly."

Brett didn't want to tell her about his deal and that he was basically in the same situation. As with most of the wealth in the United States, it looked better on paper. Not that he would ever be considered poor and not that he couldn't buy anything he wanted at the moment, but the other deal had to be completed before he'd feel comfortable about tapping into his reserves.

"Does Nia know you're here?"

"Absolutely not. Nia wants people to think she's tough. You're right, she's looking for a white knight, but Jared and his mother and their law offices are well known in the area. They're also the people you want to be within the black community.

I want you to just be seen with Nia so it takes Jared's mind off Kent's business for a while."

"Do you really think that the idea of a man in her life will make Jared Schuyler worry? Nia could do that anytime."

"You said you read *Black Enterprise*. Well, I read the magazines that provide the best gossip. The truth is Nia has been dating men who are safe. Yes, she's having a great time. I would never say that her life is bad. It's just that these men aren't a threat to her career."

"Ms. Madison . . ." He switched to the business voice he used when he was about to say no to someone.

"Alethia, please."

"Alethia, I can't help you."

"Why not?"

"Because it's not just Bryant Electronics. You want me to step in and give Schuyler the idea that Nia and I are together. There are a dozen men you can call for this. Why me?"

"When Nia came to California, she told me how you felt and she wondered if she'd made a mistake."

"She didn't. We were in the wrong place at the wrong time."

"Perhaps."

"If I agree to come to California, it's not going to be as the person out to save the company. I'll advise and that's all."

She smiled. "And look in on Nia?"

"What if Nia doesn't want my help?"

"I can get her to pretend for a couple of weeks and you should know by then."

"It's an interesting proposition. I'll think about it."

Brett wasn't fooled by this proposition. He knew exactly what she was asking. She wanted the same thing that his stepmother wanted. She wanted Brett back in Nia's life. What he had to decide was if he wanted the same thing.

He thought about the changes he'd made in his life over the past five years. He was a very different person than the man who'd tried to keep Nia in Wyoming. He had developed a business and lived a life-style covered by gossip magazines. If he'd changed, so had Nia. He wanted to see the change.

As soon as she walked into her room, Alethia headed for the telephone and called Frank. She didn't care if she was dragging the man out of bed or away from the television. She needed to talk to someone about her victory.

"I knew it would work," she said when Frank answered.

"Not even a hello," Frank chided. "Just reveling because you've manipulated the man into doing something you want done."

"Don't spoil it. Be happy. Nia only thinks she's having fun with all those dates. She needs to settle down and, believe me, Brett Faulkner is the man."

Brett sat in his study and looked over Nia's website. It had changed since the first time he saw it. Before it was a little stark with just her picture and her qualifications. Now it was different, looser, but easy to get around. She'd held several seminars for women on pulling their finances together, and she'd done some lectures since he'd last checked the website.

He returned to the search engine and put in "Jared Schuyler" and waited. It took a few minutes but, along with other information that came under the search criteria, he found articles on Jared. One detailed his meteoric rise after the death of his father. His marriage to Nia, a mixed doubles tournament at the tennis club that he won with his mother as his partner. Another magazine had an article about a birthday celebration in April that received a tremendous amount of press coverage. He found a small article on Jared and Nia's divorce for irreconcilable differences only eighteen months after they married. The picture of Nia as she left the court stirred something inside Brett. It was her face that shocked him. She had dark circles under her eyes, her mouth was drawn into a thin line and she had a look of pain that stunned him. What had happened?

He returned to her website and took a closer look at the picture. The dark circles were gone, but there was something about her eyes. Something that made him want to take her in his arms. Something that made him want to find out more.

One more fact was clear to him. Alethia had lied. Jared Schuyler was not the kind of man who let go easily.

He felt a sudden twinge of regret. He and Nia did have unfinished business, and both of them had avoided it. Brett leaned over and picked up the telephone. He called the hotel and asked to speak with Alethia.

"I'm sure you have a plan, so fill me in," he told her.

"I want you to pretend that you're an old lover

and you want her back. I want Jared Schuyler to leave her alone."

"You think Nia will go along with this?"

"No. We can't tell her we've talked. Just come in and sweep her off her feet, please."

"I've got some more thinking to do, and I'll let you know."

Alethia dropped the telephone back in the cradle and lay back in bed. The first part of her mission had been accomplished. She'd gotten Brett's attention. Now she just had to get him to California. She didn't have any proof, but she was afraid for Nia. Jared wanted her destroyed. The men in Nia's life were considered eligible, but none of them exuded the allure of Brett Faulkner. He met all the qualifications. He was rich. He was handsome. He was tough.

# Five

Brett strolled into his office at nine-thirty in the morning and was not surprised that he had a welcoming committee. He wore a *Dolce & Gabbana* double-breasted suit, a white shirt and a plaid tie.

Ana Lisa sat at her desk, sipping coffee. When she looked up at him, she gave a low wolf whistle. "Are we going someplace special, boss?"

"That depends on a certain lady."

"Anyone I know?" asked Palladin Rush as he came out of Brett's office.

Brett whirled. "I wasn't expecting you."

"Now you know you cannot run off on some secretive mission and not have Jesslyn want me to give you the third degree."

"And what does my favorite uncle want?"

"He wants to add hot lights and a rubber hose. Let's talk."

"It's not a big deal. The woman's name is Alethia Madison. She's Nia's mentor."

"Let me guess from here. Nia's in trouble, and you're the only one that can save her?"

Brett grinned. "I hate when you do that."

The two men entered Brett's office and closed the door. Palladin was dressed in his uniform, straight-legged jeans and a turtleneck sweater. His coat was draped over a chair in the conference area of Brett's office.

"When you came to New York, you couldn't even say the name Alethia Madison."

"I think she did Nia and me a favor when she lured her back to Los Angeles. Nia needed to fight her demons, and I needed to grow up."

"Are you going to help Nia?"

"I don't know. When I heard her name and that she was in trouble, my instinct said help. After sleeping on it, I'm not too sure."

"I'm going to give you some advice and then I'll get out of your way," Palladin told him. "That's why I'm here. My instincts said it was Nia. If you start doubting your gut feelings, you're committing emotional suicide. I don't want you to do that."

"Thanks. Alethia's going to call me and we'll talk again. I'll let you know."

"I'm going to hang out in Border's Books at the Trade Center and then meet my wife for lunch."

Palladin left, and Brett sat behind his desk for a few minutes. Palladin had lived by his instincts from the time he was in the Secret Service until he did an undercover investigation of the woman he later married. The evidence said she was committing industrial espionage. His instinct said she was innocent and she was. Maybe Brett's first instinct to help was the one he should follow. He still wasn't sure, no matter what Palladin said.

He pressed the intercom and asked Ana Lisa to come into his office. He was amazed by her. At six-feet tall, she commanded attention, but she always seem to wear something that made people turn around to take a second look. Today it was a jungle-print something that matched her head wrap.

When he had first interviewed her, she was wearing something almost as wild. His instinct told him to hire her. She'd been with him one year, and he was thinking about making her a partner. She had personally found three businesses for him to rescue and all three were giving out pure profit.

She strutted into his office and sat in the chair she used when she took dictation.

"Let me bring you into the loop," Brett said. "Alethia Madison wants me to help an old friend," he told her.

"Someone from Wyoming?" she asked.

"Yes, my old partner."

"So Alethia Madison wants you to what?"

"Act as a white knight and get them out of trouble."

"Can you do that, boss?" Ana Lisa was thinking about the other deal he was handling.

"I don't know. I told her I'll think about it."

"Uh-oh," his assistant whispered.

"What does that mean?"

"It means I'm going to be running the office for a while."

An hour later, Alethia called. She was on her way back to California and couldn't have lunch with him. She wanted him to give her idea some thought and then call her with an answer.

He told her he'd think about it.

A few days later, Brett was on a plane. Not to California, as Alethia would have liked, but to Wyoming. Sometimes, no matter how much he enjoyed New York, he returned home to rethink problems, regroup from mistakes and reorganize his business.

Kaliq and Trisha were surprised because he usually called before he came to Wyoming. He pulled up in front of the house in the black Excursion SUV that he kept at his own house, about a mile from his family's.

"You should have called." His stepmother pouted as she hugged him. "I would have done more food shopping."

"What she means is that she would have pulled out all stops to fatten you up," his father said. He rolled his wheelchair over to his son.

Brett leaned down and hugged his father. "I didn't want to put anyone out."

"So you need some space to think."

Brett was always amazed at how well his father understood him. He supposed it was some special parental gift. He wondered if he'd ever have it.

The rest of the week, Brett tried to get into his old life. He began working with the falcons. Unfortunately, his old life evaded him. He didn't have the connection with the peregrines he once had. He didn't know how it had happened, but he was determined to get back to the basics. If the ski resort deal went through, he'd be spending a lot more time here.

Brett Faulkner watched as the graceful bird soared high above him, plummeted to the ground, soared again and headed for the horizon. He took off his Stetson and wiped his face. He waited for a few minutes, then climbed into his Jeep, slammed the door and headed home.

Ana Lisa calmly said she'd handle things until he got back, but he knew she was thrilled to get him out of the way so she could prove her worth. He had complete confidence in her.

No matter what he did, he couldn't get Alethia's words out of his head. Nia was in trouble.

He thought he just needed some time and had returned to Wyoming and his father's ranch. Yet nothing stopped the restless emotions he felt.

He placed the call as soon as he entered his living room and waited six rings before someone answered.

"Trish, I lost another one."

"It happens to the best of us. Don't worry about it. Come on down to the house for dinner."

"I don't think so. . . ."

"Come on. I'm making something special for your father, and you love my food."

Brett smiled at the thought of sitting down to his stepmother's cooking. The Parisian-trained cordon bleu chef created the same kind of meal she served to the people who were lucky enough to visit her Pennsylvania bed-and-breakfast inn. Although she now lived on the ranch, food was still her passion.

"I don't think I have an appetite," he said.

"I'm making scallops with mushroom and whiskey sauce. . . ."

Brett burst into laughter. "Don't do this to me. I want to feel sorry for myself."

"I know, but if you come to dinner I might see fit to give you a nice wedge of vanilla cheesecake for dessert."

"You are a cruel, vicious woman. Give me twenty minutes to get presentable."

Brett knew why he was losing his falcons. It had nothing to do with his skill. It had everything to do with Nia Sebastian. Ever since he'd learned that she was a free woman again, she'd crossed his mind often. When Nia's parents had been killed in the highway accident, she couldn't or wouldn't let Brett help her to get through her pain. They had said some cruel things to each other the last time they spoke. He'd accused her of running away when things got tough. She'd said he needed to grow up. Now he could admit they were both right.

Nia had run back to the corporate world of Los Angeles and he'd gone in the opposite direction, to NYU law school. He'd loved New York. He even worked with a falconer who used the falcons in New York to force birds out of the sky at Kennedy Airport during takeoffs.

A year later she'd married and less than two years after that she'd divorced her husband, but had not returned to Wyoming as Brett thought she would. New York had been a pleasure and a curse. He loved school and he had a busy nightlife, but now at thirty he was ready to settle down. He missed her. He wanted her. He hadn't known how much he missed Nia until he stood on that mountain and watched the falcon fly away to a new life. It was time for him to do the same, but he wanted that new life with Nia Sebastian. When they had been together, he never lost falcons. What bothered him the most was he didn't care the way he should.

\* \* \*

Trisha Terrence Faulkner turned to her husband. "Brett lost another falcon."

"He's lost his touch," Kaliq said bluntly. "He's not comfortable with the falcons, and they know it." Kaliq turned his wheelchair to face her. "It may be a permanent thing."

When Kaliq had been trapped behind enemy lines, his legs were broken and no medical attention was provided for him. By the time his best friend could rescue him, he'd lost the use of his legs. That wasn't enough to stop him. Kaliq Faulkner had never been one to sugarcoat anything. He believed in facing the truth and getting on with life.

"It's time Brett found out what he wants."

"Don't say that. It's happened to all of us." Trisha remembered when she'd first learned about falcons. The peregrines would never be domesticated. The birds could decide at any time to fly away and never return.

"Not to Brett. He had a special touch with them."

"So what are you saying?"

"It may be time for him to walk away." Kaliq saw the pain cross his wife's face. "It might not be forever."

"He's been running away in some manner ever since he and Nia broke up."

"I don't think going to NYU law school is running away." Kaliq pulled his wheelchair up to the table.

"Brett and Nia were so good together."

"She married another man."

"Well, she's not married anymore, and Brett

wasn't ready for a serious relationship then. They just shared a love of falcons."

"You are such a romantic. You want him to go to California and bring Nia back so they can start over."

"I think they could make it now."

"Why are you, Jesslyn and Alethia so sure about something like this?"

"Women know."

"Nia has a full social life and so does Brett. Neither of them has been sitting around waiting for the other to come back."

"I think they're just fillers. If they weren't, one of them would have found someone forever."

"I think you're going to be very disappointed. I can see your wheels in motion. Don't say anything to him. He'll just do the opposite of whatever you suggest."

Trisha blew her husband a kiss. "Exactly."

Later that night, as they polished off the last of the cheesecake, Trisha took a deep breath and turned to her stepson. She wanted to phrase it properly because she didn't want him to rebel.

When Trish and Kaliq met the second time, she was being stalked. She came to Wyoming to hide. The man followed, and they had to fight for their lives. During that time she and Nia had talked quite a bit. Trisha knew about the man who had broken Nia's heart. She also knew that Nia had made some mistakes, but so had everyone.

"I think you need a vacation. You're still getting calls from those companies who want you on their legal team. I know eventually one of them is going to lure you away."

"You think if I go away for a while, my falconry skills will return."

"Maybe."

"Where would you suggest I take this vacation?"

"Trisha!" Kaliq's voice took on a warning quality.

"I think you should go to the Bahamas, see some old friends and talk to a couple of those firms."

Brett shook his head. "I've been thinking about taking a few days while we get this resort deal together. I'm going to try California. Only it's not a vacation. I've been asked to help an old friend."

"How?" Kaliq asked.

"A woman is planning a big move, and I've decided to join her team. I'm going to talk to her about it."

"Don't put too many irons in the fire, now," Kaliq warned.

"It's similar to something that I worked on in New York with Palladin."

Kaliq and Palladin Rush had been friends since their days at Harvard. Both men were a little disappointed when Brett opted for a radical move. NYU rather than their alma mater. But since Palladin lived in New York, it was an easy transition for Brett.

"This is more in line with a hostile takeover, and it seems interesting."

"Is that the only reason, son?"

"No, Dad. I still have a couple of loose ends to tie up. I think it's about time."

"That's good too," Trish said, then gave Kaliq a sweet "I told you so" smile.

# Six

"Nia, promise me when you get married again, you won't let your fiancé have anything to do with selecting your wedding gown. I can't believe I let him talk me into this straitjacket."

"Oh, I don't see marriage in the near future, but I'll try to remember that."

Nia helped her friend change from the ivory lace gown, which had several tiers. Although it was a beautiful dress, Julie had always hated frills and that was why she considered the dress a straitjacket. She'd always kept everything in her personal life as simple as she could because her professional schedule had become more and more frantic as her career expanded from modeling to becoming a news reporter.

Unfortunately, Jack had seen her on the cover of a bridal magazine years before he met her, and that image had been carved in his mind as the perfect bride. Julie would rather have run off to Las Vegas and get married by an Elvis impersonator than have a big production wedding, but to please Jack, she'd agreed to a monster ceremony and reception.

Jack was the one man who could accept Julie's beauty as well as her brain. When they met, she was about to leave the modeling world after being a part of it since she was eighteen. She was now desperate to use the MBA she'd received from Stanford University so many years before. A news series she had done on models was successful enough to catch the eye of a media mogul, who hired her as an anchor on a weekly news program. Jack was one of the people she'd interviewed. Now they were married.

"Nia, don't get misty on me. I don't want to hear that you eloped with the best man."

Her friend's voice brought her out of her trance and back to the moment at hand.

"You're a very lucky woman, Julie," she said. "Don't worry about me. I'll be fine." Nia brushed back a few strands of black curls that had escaped from the French twist hairstyle.

"Just think, in a few days you'll be strolling on a Parisian street looking for a house to buy," Bree said. "Imagine, your husband's company sending him to Paris for two years. How romantic can you get?"

"I expected rivers of tears from my overly dramatic mother. She'd given up hope that I would ever find a husband."

"She even cried at my wedding," Nia said. "I should have been the one crying, then."

It had been a bittersweet time for Nia. Not having her own parents, Nia had adopted Julie's parents. Not even their cautions could have stopped her from marring Jared. He had been so different from the other men in her life. He seemed to be what dreams were made of, but turned out to be a nightmare.

Almost as soon as they married, the loving-husband

facade vanished and in its place a tyrant appeared. She knew Jared was prodded to act by his mother.

Daphne Schuyler had been the typical mother-in-law-from-hell until after the divorce. Then she seemed to find all the reasons that Nia was a wonderful person. She was constantly calling to see if Nia needed anything.

Nia had made so many mistakes, including the way she'd run from Brett Faulkner and into a disastrous marriage with Jared Schuyler. By the time she had come to terms with life, it was too late.

Her girlfriends had been there for her after the divorce, but they couldn't stop her from plunging into a series of doomed-before-they-got-started relationships. It was as if she'd lost touch with common sense. It was only recently they had breathed a sigh of relief, for now she was seeing men who made her happy, not crazy.

Lately, they confined their talk to the wedding, but it had drifted to the present circumstances. Jared's takeover of Bryant Electronics had been the main topic. The last conversation was during the fittings for their gowns.

"The man needs to get a life," Julie said.

"He needs to get a woman," Bree suggested.

"Marlene's in love with him," Nia said.

Jared's secretary was a little timid. She'd never worked for anyone but the Schuylers. First the father and then the son. She'd gone from someone in the secretarial pool to an executive assistant. She had an encyclopedia for a mind. Jared didn't know how lucky he was to have Marlene.

"No. That little mouse."

"Bree, give her a break, she's sweet. When Jared

and I were married, she went out of her way to be nice to me."

"She's still a mouse."

"What she needs to do is get with the program. Get sexy. Hang out," Julie said.

"Get a real man and forget about Schuyler."

Nia and Julie exchanged looks. Bree had gone through several makeovers in her own life. Currently she had reinvented herself as a photojournalist and was leaving for Hawaii on an assignment.

"I know one thing. I've had it with his nonsense. I'm going to find a white knight for Kent, and I am going to make sure that he has a lot of other things to worry about besides me," Nia said.

"Like what? How are you going to do this?"

"I have a few ideas about the person I want as a white knight. As soon as this business is over, I'm going to march into Jared's office and punch his lights out."

"Now you're talking," Bree said.

The more she thought about that conversation, the more Nia knew that was exactly what she was going to do. She actually had visions of tossing Jared out of the boardroom, then giving her best impression of a Serena Williams's tennis serve with Jared's head as the ball.

Nia was comfortable discussing the demise of Jared Schuyler. She was not comfortable when the topic changed to Brett Faulkner.

Julie and Bree tried to convince her that she and Brett should try again. Every time Nia talked to anyone in Wyoming, they pushed her to see Brett.

It wasn't going to happen. She told them over and over. Nia loved Los Angeles, and Brett thrived in Wyoming and New York, as incongruous as that sounded. Their interests were still too far apart, she told them. Her friends were romantics and didn't believe her. Nia was going to Wyoming on business and the questions from her friends centered around possibilities.

"Are you going to see the cowboy?" Julie asked.

"No, I understand he's got a deal going and is very busy right now. Don't you think the other men in my life are quite terrific?"

They had to agree. Nia did attract the most fantastic-looking guys. She just didn't keep them around long enough for her friends to hear wedding bells.

After meeting Brett once, her friends forever referred to him as "the cowboy." Julie and Bree had grown up in Los Angeles. They were amazed and curious that Nia and Brett had African-American fathers and mothers who were part Cheyenne.

Her friends knew that Nia had failed on her first attempt at corporate life and returned to Wyoming, where she and Brett raised falcons. They even had a run on the lecture circuit, encouraging people to help preserve the species, as Wyoming had done for many years.

Nia remembered how Brett had tried to keep her in Wyoming after her parents had died. The more he tried to help her get through her grief, the more she felt she needed to go back to California . . . alone.

A few months later, when she returned to Wyoming, she learned that Brett had moved to New York and was attending NYU. His stepmother, Trisha, had tried to convince Nia to contact him, but at the time Nia felt the breakup was best for both of them. She returned to Los Angeles and later married Jared Schuyler. The marriage lasted eighteen months. Nia couldn't help thinking about how different her wedding had been from Julie's.

Nia's wedding had bordered on a coronation. Daphne had pulled out all the stops, even though Nia had wanted something more intimate. Luckily, her girlfriends had been there to help her through it.

Nia couldn't invite Trisha to her wedding. They were friends, but in a way Nia still felt guilty about Brett. She knew Trisha always hoped they'd get back together.

"Now you aren't going to get into any trouble while we're gone, are you, Nia?" Julie asked.

"I'll try not to."

"Pay no attention to her," Bree chimed in. "Find a fabulous man, have a good time and be ready to tell us lots of interesting stories. Of course, I'll hear them before Julie and tell you which ones to share with her."

"Don't even try to keep me out of the loop. The first thing I'm going to do when we find a house is get a new computer, and e-mail is the way to go for us. I'll have that done by the time you get back, Bree. Imagine taking a whole month's vacation in Hawaii."

"Hey, did you catch Alethia's moves?" Nia asked.

"She's tiring out some young guys. We'd better hurry and get back to the party," Bree said.

Alethia Madison had been their mentor since the first year they were at Stanford. She was a tenured professor whose classes were always filled by the end of the first day of registration. Right after their graduation, she'd moved into the private sector and Nia had become her administrative assistant.

Alethia was now in the process of fulfilling her dream to own a bank. She had never felt that banks understood African-Americans and she was planning to have a bank that catered to the African-American community.

By the time Julie's mother came to check on them, her daughter had changed into her travel outfit and was ready to throw the bouquet. "Come on, baby girl, your husband's waiting."

Julie, Bree and Nia smothered giggles. All of them were pushing forty and Julie's mother still called her "baby girl."

Julie had deliberately refrained until now so she could decide which of her friends she would target. She caught Nia's arm and waited until her mother and Bree were well in front of them.

"I'm going to throw the bouquet to Bree. I need you to stand in front of her and when I throw it, jump out of the way."

"She'll kill you. She says she has no plans to marry in this lifetime."

"We all said that."

"I think she really meant it. She won't allow any relationship to develop."

"Well, maybe this will make her change her mind."

Julie stood on a chair with her back to the guests. "Here's to the next bride," she said as she turned slightly and threw the bouquet.

Just as Nia tried to step out of the way, Bree nudged her forward. As she tried to keep her balance the bouquet landed in her outstretched hands. The crowd cheered. Nia caught Julie winking and knew she'd been tricked. "I'll get you for this," she said to Bree. "Don't believe that old wives' tale. I am not going to be a bride again."

"Don't fight it, girl," Bree told her. "There's some truth to those old wives' tales."

The music started and Bree was off dancing with one of the groomsmen. Nia joined Alethia at her table.

"I thought you weren't too anxious to get married again," Alethia teased.

"Don't start. Julie and Bree tricked me into catching it."

"Are you sure?"

"Positive. You aren't getting rid of me that easily."

The best man pulled Nia onto the dance floor and while they moved to a driving beat, Nia saw an older man trying to keep up with Alethia. The music stopped and Nia stifled a yawn as she thanked her dance partner and returned to her table.

"I'm going home," Nia announced when Alethia returned.

"You promised that you were going to let go and have fun for a change," Alethia scolded. "We're going to be swamped with work for the next few months."

"I'll have fun next time. I've put in too many hours."

"I know, but it's Julie's wedding."

"She's already left. I'll see you Monday." Nia leaned forward and kissed Alethia's cheek.

Nia wondered how the older woman had more energy than anyone in the room. The woman had a killer schedule and still had time for fun.

"I thought you'd come home with me and we'd sit up until dawn talking and planning."

"I think you have me mixed up with your buddy Daphne. You two like that sort of thing."

Alethia shrugged. "We aren't that close anymore." When she saw Nia's frown, she added, "Don't think it's your fault. We just grew apart and she wanted things to be a certain way and I wanted things to be a certain way."

"You mean you're both too stubborn to compromise."

"Something like that."

Nia still felt responsible that Alethia and Daphne were no longer best friends. Alethia had introduced Nia to Jared Schuyler and, despite his mother's objection, they had fallen in love and gotten married. When Nia ended the marriage, Daphne said that it was Alethia's fault for even introducing them. "She isn't right for Jared. I tried to help, but when the bloodlines aren't right, it doesn't work."

The bloodlines she referred to were Nia's. The Schuylers came from the Baldwin Hills section of Los Angeles. They were part of the African-American elite. Alethia and Daphne had met at Spelman College. Daphne had married well, as she was expected to do. She didn't consider Nia worthy of Jared. Throughout the short-lived marriage, Daphne constantly tried to change Nia's way of dress, friends, and even her career. Jared soon joined his mother in pressuring Nia to leave her job with Alethia and join Daphne in her social circle. Nia refused. She knew exactly how she wanted to see her career develop. Her mother-in-law took this as an insult. It was the first of many battles Nia had fought with Daphne and Jared.

This added more stress to Alethia and Daphne's

friendship. After Nia's divorce, she and Daphne got along better than during the marriage.

"I'll take a rain check on the all-night thing." Nia couldn't share the other reason as to why she wanted to go home. Weddings made her think about her mistakes in the romantic department. She loved her career. She just wished the men she was attracted to could deal with it.

"I'll forgive you this time, but the first thing Monday morning we will sit down and talk about your future," Alethia told her. "Let's get out of here."

"Don't let me spoil your fun. Stay and enjoy."

"Are you kidding? It's time for me to stop pretending I can keep up with these forty-somethings."

"You mean all that dancing was an act?"

"Child, my life is an act. I've got to look as if I can handle this next deal. It's a big one."

"You're finally getting your dream. I'm glad I'm going to be part of it."

"The neighborhood needs a people-oriented bank. Everything will be fine."

"From your mouth to God's ear."

Weddings had a way of making Nia think about what could have been. What if she'd married Brett and stayed in Wyoming? She would not have experienced the last five years of working with Alethia. How would marriage stack up against being a part of real change when Alethia bought a bank that catered to the neighborhood?

Although Kent wasn't part of the neighborhood, they kept in touch. She'd attended his wedding and now she was looking for a white knight to save his company.

Once he announced that he'd acquired enough stock to make a run at the takeover, not a day went by that Daphne and Jared Schuyler weren't in the newspapers trying to convince everyone that they had the best interest of the company at heart and things could only get better under Jared's administration.

Nia was at her wit's end with this and she had the wedding to help Julie through. Now that the wedding was over, she could really concentrate on finding someone willing to jump into the fray.

Misty rain had begun to fall. An hour later, by the time she pulled her burgundy BMW into her driveway, it had become a steady tattoo on her windshield. She decided to leave the car in the driveway rather than put it in the garage. She threw the car into park and fumbled in the backseat for her umbrella. Then she remembered she'd used it a few weeks before and had forgotten to put it back in the car.

She stepped from the car and threw a small crocheted wrap around herself and walked down the driveway so she could lock the car inside the fence.

As she closed the driveway gate, she noticed a tall man headed her way. He had an oversize black umbrella to shield him from the rain. For a moment, she thought she'd conjured him up by thinking about him so often earlier. As he came closer, she saw his black pinstripe Armani suit. That was a far cry from the jeans and shirt he'd always worn. New York must have had a positive effect on him, she thought.

Nia had always loved fashion and studied what

everyone was wearing. She'd arrived in California very different from the college students who were actually on campus.

Of course, it didn't take her roommates long to get the fashion-conscious teenager on the right track. New York must have done the same for Brett. Nia knew he had lived with Palladin and Jesslyn Rush while he attended school. She'd met the couple at Kaliq and Trisha's wedding. Palladin was definitely a great role model in business and fashion.

Brett's movements revealed broad shoulders and a more muscular frame than she remembered. His long, thick, black hair was pulled back from his face, and tied at the nape of his neck. The years had been more than generous to him. His once-boyish face was now chiseled into a maturity she hadn't thought possible. He stopped in front of the gate and smiled before saying, "Hello, Nia. It's good to see you again."

"What are you doing here, Brett?"

"I think it's time you finally came to your senses and married me."

# Seven

"Why are you here, Brett?" she repeated. She managed to keep the tremor out of her voice.

His declaration didn't faze her. Marriage was definitely out of the question for them. She'd sealed their fate the second she became Mrs. Jared Schuyler.

Almost every woman had a man in her past. A man who fulfilled a fantasy she'd created in her mind. Jared had been a mistake, but so had Brett, at the time. If she'd stayed in Wyoming, perhaps they could have had a good marriage. But now that she'd experienced so many things in Los Angles, she didn't know if she wanted to give them up and she was sure there would have been a nagging doubt if she hadn't found out that she could survive very well on her own.

Nia was happy with her life, her friends and especially the men in her life. She was never in need for an escort. However, her true happiness came from her success as a financial advisor. She didn't know a bigger thrill than to see her suggestions put into action and the reward of seeing them turn a company around.

Her reputation was growing, and she didn't need

any distractions. Brett Faulkner certainly fit the category of distraction.

She wasn't surprised he knew where she lived. She sent the Faulkners a Kwanza card every year. She was surprised that he would show up unannounced and acting as if she'd been waiting for him.

"You don't really think you can shock me by that ridiculous statement? Why are you here?"

"Don't you think we should go inside before you put me through the third degree? We've got a lot to catch up on. I'm not sure you want your neighbors to hear it."

Most of her neighbors were in bed. This was a quiet community and most people traveled a long distance to get to work, so they went to bed early. There were several up-and-coming actors in the area. A couple had told her how unglamorous it was to have to be on the set at five A.M.

Like in any neighborhood there was a gossip. Someone who was retired and didn't have a life, other than checking out others. Nia was sure they were being watched, but as long as there was no loud arguing, she and Brett would seem unimportant if they chose to stay outside. Still, she knew it was better to go in.

"You're showing your city ways."

"What's that supposed to mean?"

"No small talk, just up-front questions." He spoke to her as if they'd been separated for five minutes instead of five years.

She laughed in spite of her plan to be so cold he would leave her alone. "Maybe that's why I fit in this city."

Did he really think he could just stroll back into

her life? He was in for a rude awakening, she told herself, but deep inside she'd actually felt a flutter when she first recognized him.

Brett brushed by her as he entered the gate and stood so the umbrella shielded them both from the rain. She locked the gate and gestured to the side of the house rather than the front door.

She was stunning. Even with rain pouring down on her, he could see her large, dark, expressive eyes. A slight twinge made him aware they both had changed so much and memories were sometimes better than the real thing. Despite what Alethia had told him, Nia didn't appear to be in any trouble.

As they entered, Nia flipped the switches on the main panel and her house was flooded with light. The mud room seemed smaller once Brett entered it. He put his umbrella by the door so it could dry. She could see he wasn't going to go away easily and she had to admit she was curious about him.

"Why don't you wait in the living room while I change?" Nia suggested. She indicated the direction while she disappeared into her bedroom.

Brett studied the small, well-appointed living room. Soft gold walls and mahogany trim gave the room a comfortable feeling. She'd opted for lamps rather than overhead lighting.

The long, over-stuffed beige sofa sat in the middle of the room, while two dark brown recliners faced a large armoire. He walked over to it and opened the doors to reveal a large-screen TV and several racks of videotapes. Her taste in viewing was as eclectic as ever. She had everything from romantic movies to horror.

"I don't think you'll be here long enough for a movie."

Brett turned and smiled at Nia. She'd changed from her bridesmaid's dress into a gray business suit and now into a large pastel sweatshirt and white leggings. She looked more like a college student than a woman helping a community get a bank.

Trish had supplied Nia with few tidbits about Brett, other than that he had recovered well from their breakup and had decided to go to NYU law school. She knew about his successful career and although Trisha had never mentioned it, weekly gossip magazines had told her about his love life.

For most of his life what Brett wanted he got. Nia was his one failure. Was he back to remedy that because he wanted her or did he want revenge?

Whatever it was, the real reason Brett Faulkner had reappeared in her life would eventually come to light. Nia couldn't think about turning him away. Once the initial shock wore off, she was curious enough to want to talk to him.

*He only mentioned marriage to throw me off,* she told herself. She stepped back and let him in.

She indicated the foyer closet and he put his hat on one peg and the slicker on another.

"Would you like some coffee?"

"I'd love some. Why don't you point me toward the kitchen?"

"Straight ahead and to your left," she said. She wondered if she needed the coffee laced with a stiff shot of brandy to get rid of the chill that she suddenly felt.

Somehow she had known that she and Brett had

unfinished business. She'd expected them to eventually meet and settle the account. Then they would go their separate ways, free to find love.

Fifteen minutes later, they were sitting in front of the fireplace in the living room, sipping strong, black coffee—hers with three sugars, just the way she liked it.

"How did you find me?"

He looked at her for a moment and she wondered if he would be as honest as he'd been when they were partners. His black eyes met her golden-brown ones. "I guess we can start with that. You and Trish exchange Kwanza cards every year. I've known your address for some time."

"So why now?"

"I have some business to take care of out here and I decided this was a good time to pick up where we left off."

"So what was that line about marriage?"

"We never quite got to that stage in our relationship, but I always though that we would, until you ran away."

"I didn't run away. I was going through a lot. . . ."

Brett leaned forward and took her hand. "I remember. You were in such pain when your parents . . . the accident had an effect on all of us. I didn't know how to help you. What could I have said?"

"Nothing."

He was right. She had been inconsolable. She had to heal herself first and by that time, she and Brett were leading different lives. She threw herself into the job Alethia got her with the bank.

"I know you tried, but we just never had a time

when one of us wasn't getting over a broken heart."

"Except for now. I haven't had anything serious for a while and neither have you, so this might be our time."

She didn't have to ask how he knew about her love life. Probably the same way she knew about his. Only he didn't know that she had grown comfortable being alone. He was in for a rude awakening.

"Why did you decide to go to New York?"

"I thought about following you to L.A., but at the time I was so angry because you wouldn't let me help you. My father's best friend and his wife came to visit during the time I was sulking and he recommended a big change. I had been accepted at Harvard and NYU."

"And you took his suggestion? That's odd. No one could ever tell you what was best for you."

Brett laughed and showed strong white teeth that reminded her of his father. Kaliq Faulkner had never let anything stand in his way. Even though he'd been confined to a wheelchair, he had never lost his courage or his sense of humor.

"You remember. I thought I knew it all until I took his advice. You may be top dog wherever you live, but New York can cut you down to size."

"What do you mean?"

"At first I tried to blend in. I thought I was dressing like any other New York college student. I didn't even have to open my mouth before they picked up that I was a fish out of water."

"What did you do?"

"I stopped trying to blend in. I wore my boots, my jeans and my Stetson."

"What happened?"

"I felt good about me and it showed. I never had a problem after that."

"So what did you learn from that?"

"Attitude is everything. I know you think I mentioned marriage to get your attention and maybe there was a little bit of truth to it. I know what I want and things are different now."

Nia gave him a tentative smile. "I was surprised at your choice of degrees."

"Why?"

"Corporate law seems rather timid for you. I would have expected high-profile criminal cases were more your style."

Brett's eyes scanned the room and then looked back at Nia. "What makes you think that corporate law isn't as high profile and bloodthirsty as criminal? I once was involved in a case that seemed very mild on the surface. It was a family-owned firm and when we sat down to negotiate, they were so angry they couldn't talk to each other. I was working for the family attorney. The father and daughter were trying to force the son from the first marriage out. I heard someone yell duck, but I was too slow. I woke up in the ambulance. One of the family members had hit me with a lamp she was throwing at her brother."

"She?" Nia began to laugh. She couldn't stop. She could just see Brett trying to explain that he'd been decked by a woman.

"You can laugh all you want. I spent the night in the hospital under observation."

"What happened to her?"

"She and her brother decided to team up and they bought their father out."

A lot was different about this Brett Faulkner. Nia saw a man who once took himself so seriously, but now could laugh at his mistakes.

"So you turned to venture capitalism."

He laughed. They weren't trying to catch up on each other's lives. They were simply stating that they already knew what was happening.

*He's stronger, less opinionated but more secure than I've ever seen him,* Nia thought and she liked the new man. Would they have a chance now that they were older, or should they leave well enough alone and stay distant friends? She never expected to be in this dilemma. How could she be enjoying a conversation with this man as if days instead of years had passed?

"Nice place. Have you lived here long?"

"I bought it about a year ago."

"That would be about the time your divorce was final." It was exactly that time and he knew it.

"I . . . I guess so. My former mother-in-law found it."

Daphne had heard about the house before it had been listed, and Nia made the offer. Within days she'd moved from the condo.

"You two still get along?"

"Actually better now than when I was married. I don't think I was what she expected. She didn't want me for a daughter-in-law. She kept trying to determine a niche for me and I kept doing the opposite of what she wanted."

She wasn't sure that she was really what Jared Schuyler wanted either. Alethia's godson had been the golden child of society. Not one day went by without some mention in the society column. At first she thought he was different. He encouraged

her to have a career. He never complained about
the long hours. She suspected that his mother
didn't like her, but it seemed natural that Daphne
would be concerned about whom her son chose.
It wasn't until after their marriage that she realized
Daphne always gave in to whatever Jared wanted
and he always wanted what annoyed his mother the
most. Once Daphne accepted Nia, she was of no
use to Jared. He began coming home late and
hanging out on weekends with his buddies. Nia
never suspected him of cheating, but they grew further and further apart. Daphne had been furious
when Nia mentioned divorce. That would happen
only if Jared wanted it, not because his wife wanted
to leave him. "No one leaves my son," Daphne spat
at her. "He decides when it's over."

Nia had packed her things and moved into her
condo that had a concierge. Daphne was furious
when she was refused admittance because she was
not on Nia's list. After the divorce, Daphne called
to apologize and even assisted Nia in cutting
through the red tape to buy the house she now
lived in.

"Don't you ever wonder what would have happened if we had gotten married? I think we had
something very special. Maybe if we'd had more
time, it would have been different. That's why I
had to see you," Brett said.

If he told her that Alethia had asked him to
come to California a month ago she would have
exploded. From what she'd said about her relationship with her mother-in-law, it was obvious she still
hated anyone suggesting what she should do. It
made her do the opposite. That was probably why
she was in trouble. He'd find out what was going

on and fix it. Then they would see if they wanted to be together again.

"Maybe not, Brett. Sometimes people only think they're right for each other. When did you develop this need to see me again?"

"A few months ago, I woke up one morning after a successful negotiation and wanted to share it with you."

"Why me?"

"I want you back. It's as simple as that. We lost something important somewhere, and I know we could get it back if we were together.'

"I don't think so."

"Don't worry. I'll be around to give you plenty of time to get used to the idea."

"What do you mean you'll be around?"

"I have some business out here. I don't know how long it will take."

"Oh! Are you planning—" She stopped talking.

"Am I planning *what*?"

"Doing what you venture capitalists always do. Cutting in on someone's dream and taking over."

He grimaced. "You have a pretty low opinion about what I do. Just remember these companies are in trouble when I come in. You may think that all I supply is money and I get a cut of what they make. Well, they wouldn't be making anything if I didn't keep them in business." He hadn't meant to climb on a high horse, but he wasn't going to let her make what he did sound like something short of illegal.

She looked away. She didn't know why she had said it. She knew too many people in that field. It was true that there were a few cutthroats, but there were also a lot of people who did exactly what Brett described. They helped the dream continue.

As he leaned forward to pour himself another cup of coffee, she caught a glimpse of the belt circling his waist. The intricate cut of falcons in flight. She'd had it made for his birthday. She was surprised he still had it.

Nia and Brett had always talked about their dreams. At one time they even shared one, but after the lecture circuit dried up, and people found a new "ecology cause," their beloved falcons didn't count. Kaliq and Trisha took up the fight and Nia had read articles on them from time to time.

"How's your father?"

"Stubborn as ever. He was a little crushed that I didn't want to take over the camp if he ever retired. He understands that there are things that I have to do for me."

She yawned just as he finished his sentence. "Sorry. I'm not bored, just tired."

"Maybe it's the letdown. Knowing you, it's been hectic preparing for your friend's wedding and now it's over."

"I still have to get ready for the bank's opening. It's not that I'm kicking you out but . . ."

"You're kicking me out. I understand. You need your rest. Do you need an escort to the bank opening festivities?"

"Are you going to be in California for a while?"

"I might."

She walked him to the door and retrieved his hat and rain gear. "Good night, Brett." She ignored his question.

He took her hand as they walked out the door. The move was so natural. Just like old times. She didn't pull away. Brett took that as a measure of hope.

"How long are you going to be here?"

"I don't know. It depends on the deal that's in the works."

"So how did it feel to go off to New York and live? Do you feel successful?"

"I've had some good days." He smiled, let go of her hand and leaned back. "How about you?"

"I could say the same. Alethia's been great. I . . . I'd like you to meet her."

"I . . . I've already met her. She asked me to help Kent Hemmings with a little problem."

"Can you help him?"

"I don't know. Most of my money is tied up in another deal. Alethia reached me a few weeks too late. I might be able to find someone who can help if the project is worth saving."

He didn't give her time to respond. She was still speechless as he took her hand and held it near his lips. "Good night, Nia. I'll call you tomorrow. I'm sure you know a great place for us to have dinner. Pick something outrageously expensive and off the beaten path. You don't want prying eyes labeling you as my new love just yet. Then you can decide if you're going to let me take you to the bank festivities."

He was gone before she had time to tell him no.

# Eight

Travel was both the boon and bane of his success. He'd stayed in so many hotels he could tell instantly if he was going to enjoy his stay. By the same token, he could spot bad service the minute he walked into the hotel lobby.

As always, the first thing he checked on was the latest time he could order food. For most people that wasn't on the top of the list of what they wanted, but Brett knew takeovers could mean negotiating late into the night. If the kitchen closed early, he would need to pick something up before he got back to the hotel.

If his choice this time was any indication, he should have a very successful trip career-wise. He still didn't know how he was going to keep a casual demeanor with Nia. Tonight she'd been wary of him and that was good.

He, on the other hand, wanted to take her in his arms, as if only five days had passed instead of five years. His original "best case scenario" had been that Nia would realize they belonged together and he wouldn't have to work too hard to convince her to come back to Wyoming.

If the resort deal went through, and he was positive

it would, his base of operations would change from New York to the resort. Ana Lisa would handle the New York office—if she didn't decide to go into business for herself. If she chose her own business, he would close the New York office. Alethia had insisted that Nia would be ready to move on, once the bank deal was secure.

After breakfast the next morning, Brett called his trusted assistant. The telephone rang several times before she picked it up. Her voice was breathless as if she'd been running very fast.

"Are you just getting to work?"

"Uh-huh. I was just putting my key in the lock when I heard the phone ring."

This wasn't like her. She was always in the office on time. "What's going on?"

"Don't you dare take that tone with me after what I've been through. A water main broke and traffic got rerouted. So that meant the subway wasn't running and I was pushed onto a shuttle bus and then we got stuck in traffic."

"Sorry. I just wondered . . ."

"Well, don't wonder—ask!"

Brett took a deep breath. He was on the edge and didn't know why. Ana Lisa was right, he just should have asked.

"Ah-hah!" she yelled. "I know what's wrong with you."

"Yeah, what?"

"You saw her."

"Who?"

"Brett Faulkner, I've worked with you too long. I

can tell. You saw that woman who's been haunting you."

"How do you know someone's been haunting me? I'm fine."

"You were. Now that you've found her, everything will change."

"I'm sure we could go another couple of rounds with me wondering what you're talking about, but I need some information. Get me everything you can on Bryant Electronics in California."

"Will do, boss."

He didn't like it when she called him "boss" that way. It always felt as if she knew a secret about him and didn't want to share. He was a little wary. He'd never mentioned Nia to anyone but immediate family.

"One other thing, what do you mean about a woman haunting me?"

She breathed an exasperated sigh in her most dramatic delivery. "You hired me to run interference with your different problems, including women. I've known for quite some time that the only women who last anytime in your life are dark haired, smart and very independent. That could only mean that a woman from your past who fits that description broke your heart."

Brett roared with laughter. "You have the most convoluted way of figuring out problems of anyone I've ever known. Never mind my love life. Get me that info as quickly as possible."

He hung up, but her words stayed in his head. There *was* a woman who haunted him. The women she described could have been Nia's sisters. The only thing that really separated Nia and the women was that she was so much more independent. When

Nia left, he thought it was an unfavorable trait.
Now, he knew it was the one quality he would always like in a woman and that quality might always
keep them apart. He finished breakfast, took a
shower and dressed.

When he arrived at the bank, workmen were still
carving out offices in the open space. He asked for
directions. Besides the directions, he was given a
bright yellow hard hat. Hammers were pounding; the
buzz of a saw came from the rear of the construction
site. He spotted Nia huddled over the plans in another area. Because of the noise, she didn't hear his
approach. He called her name, and she jumped.

"Sorry, I didn't meant to startle you."

"What are you doing here, Brett?" She tilted her
hard hat back on her head and stared at him.
She'd asked him that the night before, and he'd
given her that idiotic line about marriage.

"I came to take a beautiful woman to lunch."

"Forget it. I'm busy."

"You are beautiful, but you're not the woman,"
he said.

Before Nia could answer, Alethia appeared. "I
like a man who's on time," she said.

"No man would dare keep you waiting. It's your
town, so where are we going for lunch?" He took
Alethia's arm. As they started out, he turned and
winked at Nia. She put her head down and began
studying the plans again.

Nia fumed over the fact that she had allowed
him to get to her. The plans were in front of her,

but she'd been staring at the same spot since Brett and Alethia left. Her anger built with each thought of her mentor and friend having lunch and excluding her. After he'd suggested that she come to her senses and marry him, she'd assumed he'd begin some type of pursuit. Now she believed he'd just said that to throw her off balance and it had worked. It wouldn't the next time. She had to find out why he was having lunch with Alethia. Something was going on and she was deliberately being kept in the dark. She wasn't going to take it. Brett Faulkner would not find it so easy to walk back into her life. She would . . .

Her cellular phone rang, pulling her away from her plans for revenge. "Hello," she answered abruptly.

"Nia?" The sweet voice of Lisabeth Hemmings, Kent's wife, was on the other end.

"Lisabeth, how are you?"

"I'm fine. I know you career women are busy so I'll get to the point. I'm giving a party and I want you to come."

Lisabeth had never had a full-time job. Her family believed that women should marry well and do charitable things. She was the epitome of a southern belle and loved it.

"I don't know. . . ."

"Now, I just won't take that for an answer. The Nilssons are going to Europe for a few days. I want you to meet them. Then we can decide when to go to the beach house. I want you to get one of those 'before' pictures in your mind. Then just wait and see what I can do with it."

Nia shook her head as if Lisabeth could see the

movement. She felt responsible for the financial problems the Hemmings were having.

"I know that business is important, but you have to slow down sometime So come to the beach house. It's a cocktail party, so come over about seven."

"When is it?"

"Saturday night. Bring a friend. Here's the address."

Nia scribbled it down and murmured she'd try to make it. She really didn't have time for this, but Kent was a friend, and if she didn't, Lisabeth would call the next day and in a hurt voice ask why she hadn't come to the party. Maybe she could get an escort to take her to the party, for a few minutes, and then leave.

When Alethia and Brett returned from lunch, they spent a few minutes in her office. He came out of the office and found Nia sitting at her computer, still working on the project.

"I was going to ask you to have dinner with me, but I have to do something for Alethia."

"How long have you two known each other?"

"Not that long. Why?"

"She seems to trust you and that usually takes a long time."

"Well, maybe we were friends in a past life."

"Yeah, right!"

"How about dinner tomorrow night?"

"I don't know. . . ."

"I insist. I'll pick you up about eight."

"Okay."

As Brett was leaving, Nia's administrative assistant

came in. "Is that your friend from Wyoming, Brett Faulkner?" Charlotte asked.

Charlotte wore a black Chanel suit and black, high-heeled shoes. Her makeup was perfect, and many times Nia wondered how she managed to look the same when she left the office as when she came in, no matter how hard she worked.

Her administrative assistant had been gathering information in Nia's office and bringing it over to the construction site. Nia had been reluctant to hire Charlotte, who was just out of Harvard with an MBA. She was sure after a year Charlotte would have the experience she needed to move on. She'd been with Nia for two years and didn't show signs of any discontent, yet.

"Yes, and how did you know about him?" Nia knew that everyone connected to the project was aware of Brett. They probably knew exactly who he was, and while his reputation was legendary in New York, he hadn't done any business deals in California.

"You know how it is. Someone tells someone, who tells someone else, until you can't remember where it came from."

"Don't let rumors get out of hand. He's only here for a few days."

Charlotte smiled and put several folders on Nia's desk. "These are the people you asked me to check out. None of them seem like white knight material. They seem to want to take over businesses, build them up, sell them and get out."

"Well, keep looking. Kent's only chance is for someone to bail him out, but not destroy his company."

"Isn't Mr. Faulkner in a position to do that?"

"Unfortunately, no. His money is tied up in another deal, but he's here at Alethia's request to lend moral support."

"I've got to get back. See you later." Charlotte hurried out.

That night Nia was surprised to get a call from her ex-husband, asking her out. Since the divorce, Jared had tried to prove to Nia that she needed him.

She showered and applied her makeup. Then she stepped into the gray beaded, form-fitting dress that came almost to her knees. She slipped her feet into silver sandals and selected a tiny silver handbag that was just big enough to hold her driver's license, a couple of credit cards, some money and a lipstick, the same shade she was wearing.

She wasn't really dressing for a date with her ex-husband. Her goal was to show him that she was just as successful without him. She wanted him to know that she was happy, healthy and that she didn't need him to take care of her.

Jared had selective memory when it came to her needing him. She'd had a business in Wyoming with Brett and had supported herself quite well before Jared came into her life. He always chose to forget that part. She knew he was attacking her clients to bring her business to its knees. Then he would either want her to come back to him or be destitute.

When he picked her up, he seemed like the proverbial cat that had swallowed the canary. He had a secret and he wasn't going to tell her. He drove to the restaurant. It was one his family used so often that the staff knew all of his likes and dislikes. They were escorted to a private dining alcove.

"Nia, I couldn't help but notice that your house is rather small."

"You always mention that and I told you I wanted it that way."

"I can't believe you'd really want that. I think you're a little sorry you didn't ask for alimony."

"I didn't need it."

"What if I told you there was a way the takeover of your friend's firm could go away? I have some papers that could let him off the hook."

"What do you mean?"

He sat back in his chair. "Now I have your attention. You know that your friend would lose his frail little wife if he loses this business."

She said nothing, but Jared was right. Lisabeth had never wanted for any material thing in life. If Kent had to start over, it would mean a struggle—one that Kent was up to, but Lisabeth would crumble.

"Show me the papers."

"We haven't ordered yet. I'll give them to you after dessert."

Nia stood up and stepped away from the table.

"Where are you going?"

"Home."

Jared's jaw clenched tight. "Sit down. I'll give you the damn papers."

Nia took her seat and waited. Jared called the waiter and ordered drinks for both of them. When the waiter left, he reached into his inside jacket pocket and pulled out the papers.

The waiter brought the drinks and, as Nia brought hers to her lips, Jared caught her hand.

"Don't you think we should toast this moment? It's probably our last intimate dinner."

She paused.

"To battles won," he said.

She said nothing, nor did she touch her glass to his. Instead, she set the glass down and began to read the papers.

"Don't act as if I'm some stranger," Jared said. "Just sign and let's get this over with."

"Jared, you know I never sign anything without reading it."

"It's a simple form. All I want is to end all of our partnerships."

"I'm not signing anything without reading it." Her voice had developed an edge.

"Never mind—" He reached across the table and grabbed for the papers.

Nia pulled them from his reach and stood. "I think it's better that we communicate through our lawyers."

She walked out just in time to see a taxi pull up and some people get out. She signaled to the driver and he nodded. As the couple got out, Nia got in and closed the door.

The taxi pulled off before Jared could reach her. She had given her address and was halfway home before she realized she was still clutching the papers. She began to read them. The first paragraphs talked about some property they'd purchased but, as she recalled, the prenuptial agreement took care of that. If the land were sold, she'd get fifty percent.

Did he really think she would have signed this? Hidden beneath lots of legalese was a section that stated he could buy her out for one dollar. The area the land was in was building, and Nia suspected he'd had an offer. One he didn't want to share.

By the time she reached her house, she was in a rage. Jared had decided she could be bought, but he needed the right price. If she gave up the land for Kent, what would he find on her other clients? All Jared Schuyler wanted was control of her life. Even if they weren't married.

Jared had pulled up by the time she reached her front door. He ran up the walkway.

"Nia, listen to me. We need to talk about this."

"No, we don't. You have some nerve. Your offer is nothing but blackmail."

"It's a business thing. I'm giving you a choice." He grabbed her hand and she tried to twist away, but couldn't.

"Really! What will you offer the next time? How many parcels of land do we own? When will you pull another one of these papers out of the hat to use to trade for something else you want?"

"I guess I'm going at it the wrong way. My zodiac sign is the ram and—"

"I don't care what your zodiac sign is."

Nia and Jared both turned to see Brett standing there. They had been arguing so intensely they hadn't seen him come in the gate.

"This is not your concern," Jared said.

"Take your hands off the lady and get out of here."

"Don't try to give me orders." Jared glared at him and then turned back to Nia. "She's my wife."

"No, she isn't."

Brett's hand shot out and caught Jared by the back of his heck and squeezed. Jared pushed his shoulders up and tried to shrink away from the pain. He couldn't. Brett pulled him and he followed until they were out of the gate.

"Get out of here Schuyler."

Brett released his hold and gave Jared a slight shove.

"Don't think we're finished," Jared yelled. "I'll always be around, and one day we'll settle this once and for all."

Brett walked back to the gate. "The best thing for you to do is to stay away from Nia. I'm not a happy camper when she's upset. It could cause you serious professional and bodily harm."

"Is that your version of a threat?"

"I don't make threats. I make covenants."

The men held eye contact until Jared turned and hurried to his car.

# Nine

They went inside. Nia's shaking fingers fumbled for the light switch. She and Brett sat in the living room.

"Would you like some coffee?"

"No, thanks. What was that all about?"

"He said he needed my signature on some papers and then he got really bent out of shape when I insisted on reading them. We argued and I left the restaurant and took a cab."

"Did you read the papers?"

"Yes. We own some land and he wanted me to sign it over to him."

"How do you feel about that?"

"I didn't take anything from him when we broke up. This property is something I actually gave money for him to make the purchase."

"Were you having money problems?"

"No. I just wanted a little independence, and I insisted on paying for half. It's the beach house in Malibu. I haven't been there since I started this project with Alethia."

Her gut feeling was that he had a buyer. Originally, they had agreed to share the house. They hadn't completely furnished it and that was going to be her job. He would maintain the pool and the grounds and they would work out the time-share arrangements. Although they had been divorced for two years, that part was still open.

"You do realize that sharing that property ties you to each other."

"I know. I just haven't been ready to use it or sell it."

"Jared was pretty upset."

"I can't believe him. We haven't had much contact since the divorce. Now, every time I turn around he's there."

"I guess it's natural."

"Natural?"

"Men get very territorial. I'm considered a threat."

"He knows about you."

"How much does he know?"

"He knows that we were very close."

Nia had never been one to confess everything, but shortly before their marriage ended, Jared became increasingly demanding about her previous lovers. Although she had not slept with Brett, he seemed to be Jared's target.

"After you were put on that magazine's sexiest men in the U.S. list, he even recruited Daphne to pump me for information. I mean it's a little disconcerting when a man tells his mother everything."

Brett remembered the article. "The reporter told me the article was for the business section and it was going to be called 'A Different Path,' about alternate career routes."

"You must have been livid when you got a copy of the magazine."

"Not at first. Somehow my home number got in

the article instead of my office number. People started inviting me to parties, graduations, weddings. That was when I got angry."

"You were a celebrity."

"No, I was single. Every one of the invitations came with a suggestion that if I didn't have a date one could be arranged."

"They tried and you never know. Jared wanted to know about your cabin in Wyoming. The reporter said it was a great place for a romantic getaway. He wanted to know if I felt the same. He never believed we were just friends."

"Then he's going to be a problem. He thinks that I'm here to rekindle our relationship."

"And you're not?" The moment she said it, she was sorry. She and Brett lived completely different lifestyles. It would never work, but the question made her sound desperate.

"Of course, I am," Brett said. "He has every reason to worry and so do you."

Nia folded her arms across her chest and stared at Brett. "Why?"

"We never explored the depths of our relationship."

"Maybe we only thought we should be together. It didn't hurt that we lived in kind of a deserted area and we were partners."

"It was fun for a while."

She remembered how easily he handled the falcons. Whenever he stood on a hill, he looked like a medieval knight. "How many falcons do you have now?"

"One."

"What happened?"

"I lost my touch."

She shook her head. "I can't believe that. You were too good."

"Not anymore. I don't even want to work that hard again. I think the time for me and falcons has passed."

She knew that wasn't true. He'd spent so much of his life with the birds. There was a connection. He probably came back to the ranch, grabbed a falcon and forgot that he'd been away from them. Then again, maybe New York had changed him so much that the birds knew. She felt her throat closing as tears formed in her eyes.

"I think you'll regain that feeling," she whispered.

"It's not that important anymore. I have a replacement and that's good enough."

Brett started for the door, but Nia caught his arm.

"I need a favor."

"Just ask."

"I have to go to a cocktail party, and I need an escort."

"Will Jared be there?"

"Not at this one, but he's not why I need an escort. Our hostess drives me crazy. Kent's wife is one of those bubbly-all-the-time people. I can't handle it."

In the next few minutes, she told Brett about Lisabeth Hemmings and her unflagging view that the world was just fine and only a few people were suffering. Those people probably wanted it that way. Lisabeth's father had started with nothing and built a fortune, so anyone could do it.

"So my job will be?"

"Don't let her monopolize me. She likes me, but

we don't have anything in common except we both own properties in Malibu."

Brett gave a low whistle. "Malibu?"

"Yes, but hers is right on the beach. Mine is walking distance."

"That still sounds good. So Lisabeth Hemmings is viewing the world through rose-colored glasses, huh?"

"More like blinders. She's a real 'Muffy/Buffy' type, but she is so nice and so sincere, you can't help but like her—then she just keeps talking and talking."

"You and Kent have been friends for a while. Didn't you know he liked that type?"

Nia shook her head. She'd met several of the women Kent had dated. They were all very nice and very smart. She and Kent had attended the last concert a favorite singer was giving. She'd said that she was going to retire several times, especially after a bad review.

They somehow ended up backstage and Lisabeth was there. She and the singer's daughter had gone to school together. Lisabeth was strikingly beautiful. Her blond hair was naturally curly and hung to her waist. She was slender, but nonathletic. After Nia and Kent had been introduced to her, she began talking, and she never stopped. Nia found it annoying. Kent found it charming.

Kent took one look and demanded an introduction. At first, Nia thought his attraction would pass, but day by day he spend more time with Lisabeth. She was sweet, but just a little too chatty.

Nia snapped back to the present when Brett asked, "What time do you want me to pick you up?"

"About six. We should get there about seven and be out of there by eight."

"I'll see you tomorrow."

They got up and walked to the door. She opened it and he stepped outside. He leaned down and fitted his mouth against hers.

She offered no resistance to the warm, dry kiss. It was something comfortable between friends and she liked it. She stepped away, and he pulled her back into his arms and kissed her again. This time it was pure passion. He held her against his body as he tasted her. Nia moaned and it brought them both to their senses. He broke off the kiss, but held her tight until he was back in control. He released her and stepped back.

"I think this would be a good time for you to go inside and lock the door."

"Why?"

"Then I won't ask if I can spend the night."

A flippant remark came to mind, but she knew he was sincere. She knew that if he asked, she would say yes. That could only lead to trouble. What she really wanted was for Brett to use his influence and maybe his money to stop Jared from taking the company away from Kent.

She smiled and wondered which one of her neighbors was watching them. The men she went out with were not the kind to have a raw, passionate moment. They were safe. That's why she dated them. Brett, on the other hand, was dangerous. She'd have to watch herself, so she wouldn't be crushed when he went back to Wyoming.

"Good night, Brett."

"Good night, Nia. See you tomorrow."

She then did exactly what he suggested. She

stepped back inside and closed the door, and he didn't move until he heard the dead bolt click into place. His long strides carried him to his SUV, and he climbed inside. For a moment he felt someone watching him. Then he saw Nia's light go out in the living room. He started the car, then took a deep breath as an idea raced through his mind. What Nia needed was a chance to see Wyoming again. Only this time it had to be something special. He'd take her to the resort. He smiled at the idea of being with her in the log cabin he'd claimed once the negotiations started. His dad and his uncle, Palladin Rush, both had log cabins. Palladin's was a magnificent structure on a Pennsylvania mountain. Kaliq's was a sprawling ranch style that gave him easy access in his wheelchair. Once Nia saw his selection, he knew she'd want to move in and change it. It was a bachelor's delight. That was the very thing that made women want to trap him. Since he'd been in California, he hadn't had a problem with the women he was dating in New York. Although several had the means to follow him, none had. Brett took one last glance around Nia's house before he turned on the lights and drove away.

Jared Schuyler stood in the shadows. He watched them enter the house and waited for them to leave. He almost gave himself away when he saw them kissing, but controlled his anger. At least he hadn't spent the night, Jared consoled himself. He was too far away to hear anything more than Brett saying he was going to see Nia the next day. How could she betray him like this? They would still be married if he hadn't gotten so angry when she said the marriage was over. He never thought she would really divorce him, but she did. It was a mistake, and he knew that one day she would realize it and come back to him. He'd been sure of it until this Brett Faulkner appeared. He also knew who was to blame for that—his godmother, Alethia Madison. It didn't matter. He wanted Nia back, and he was going to get her. He'd find a way to move the other people out of the way. Jared strode to his car, got in and sped away.

The next night, Brett was right on time when he rang Nia's doorbell. He wore a black silk suit and crisp white shirt. He let out a low whistle when he saw her.

Nia wore a pink-and-purple print, stretch mesh dress with spaghetti straps. It hugged her curves and emphasized her tiny waist and full hips. Her pink high-heeled sandals matched the tiny purse she carried.

Brett was speechless for a moment. Tonight she had pushed the executive back, and she was simply gorgeous.

"I'll have to find more cocktail parties to take you to if you promise to look like this."

They elected to take his SUV. The slinky dress didn't allow much room to move and when they reached the vehicle, Brett surprised her by just sweeping her up and putting her in the car.

When she sat down, the tight skirt slid up a couple of inches. He said she shouldn't worry about it, but Nia worried about everything. She wanted to look sexy and carefree, but in the back of her mind she feared that whoever was after her would be at the party. She knew that Brett would protect her; she was just sorry he had to do it.

By the time they arrived, the party was in full force, just as Nia had hoped. The Hemmings lived in a condominium complex in Beverly Hills. The people wandering around the apartment consisted of Kent's business acquaintances, a few minor celebrities and Kent's partners.

As soon as they entered, someone appeared with drinks and finger food. The CD music in the background was close to Muzak.

Nia introduced Brett to the partners first. Lisabeth came over and pulled Nia aside for what she called "girl talk."

This left Brett the chance to get to talk to the men a little. It was not the time to go into a detailed discussion, just the preliminaries.

Paul Kenner and his wife did not meet the Hollywood stereotype. His girth prevented anything he wore from fitting properly, but his mind was why he was on the team. Paul had been the leader of his study group in college. He was the one who could break down problems to the least common denominator.

Kent, of course, was the golden boy. He'd been born with a silver spoon, and he seemed to expect things to go right all the time. This glitch with the takeover had hurt him the most.

It was Jeff who seemed to have a chip on his shoulder. He was the one who had founded the company and his bitterness that they were on the verge of losing it rankled him so much he couldn't hide it.

"So are you going to be the one to save the day?" Sarcasm dripped from each word.

"I don't know. It might be throwing good money after bad." Something about Jeff didn't sit well with Brett. He was a Harvard grad, but never had any contacts.

"Ha! That's the name of the game—money. If I had enough of it, we wouldn't be here now."

"What does that mean?"

"I would have the business without partners," Jeff said.

Then he walked away and threw his arm around a woman Brett assumed was his date. She didn't fit in. She was more flash than substance. The multiprint dress seemed to be painted on her. It was at least twelve inches about the knee. Jeff didn't seem to notice how she looked: he knew that no one wanted her at the beach house.

After Brett had talked to each of the men briefly, and he knew that Jeff had founded Bryant, he decided Paul was the one who saw the possibilities of the company and Kent had the money to back up their purchase. Together they were a good team, but didn't seem to know that.

He hadn't told them that he could not be their white knight. He'd told Alethia and yet she still wanted him to meet the men. Now he knew why. Bryant Electronics wasn't a prize. It was a tool.

Jared Schuyler didn't want the company because he had a grudge against any of the men. Kent was Nia's friend, but that wasn't the whole story. Jared would do a lot of damage with this takeover. The partners would start pointing fingers at one another, Nia's reputation as a financial advisor would be suspect and Kent and Nia's friendship would probably end. Brett would have to ask her about the other men in her life. Did any of them have financial problems? Anything that Jared could lock onto to convince them that Nia was not a woman they needed so he could push them out of her life?

The one thing he did not do was keep an eye on Nia. He spotted her with Lisabeth and knew he was in trouble. He walked over and took her hand.

"Hi. We haven't had a chance to talk too much, but I hope we'll see each other again. Maybe we can have dinner together. Just the two of us . . . I mean the four of us," Lisabeth said.

Brett could not believe the woman had said all of that without taking a breath. She tossed her blond curls as she gestured. He looked at Nia, who smiled sweetly and turned away.

Alethia arrived and moved around, chatting a few minutes with each person until she reached Brett. She was a commanding figure in her brightly colored African garb.

"How do you like California so far?"

"I'm beginning to find my way around," he said, deliberately not answering the question.

"It'll grow on you."

"Maybe." He followed her to the balcony.

"Can you untangle this mess with Kent's company?"

"I don't know. I told you that I had other plans."

Alethia glanced around and made sure no one else could hear. "Jared has to be stopped."

"Why don't we get to the truth? You're a banker. There are a hundred guys out there who could walk in here and force Jared out. You picked me because of Nia."

"Her reputation—"

"Her reputation has nothing to do with this. Why me, Alethia?"

She bit her lower lip. "I need you to protect Nia."

"From?"

"I don't know."

"I don't believe that. You aren't the type to panic."

"No wonder you're so good at your chosen profession. You read people very well."

"Most people."

"I'm sure that's a conservative statement." She paused again. "People think that Nia knows everything that I do. She's my protegée, not my confidant."

"So what do you want me to do?"

"Just hang around and act as if your personal relationship has been rekindled."

"That won't be hard," he said, smiling.

Alethia gave a hearty shout. Others at the party turned and stared at them. "You devil. I thought you two had some unfinished business."

"We'll see."

# Ten

Brett was getting used to Alethia calling him on some pretense so he and Nia would have to be in the same room. He was a little surprised that it was a tennis club. He was even more surprised to find out that Nia still had her membership in the sleek club; she'd preferred outdoor sports, like riding.

Crenshaw Tennis Club had everything that Brett wanted to add to the ski lodge. He checked out the state-of-the-art equipment. He walked around just taking in the sights and making mental notes about the things he liked. He wanted to take notes and pictures so he could show the designers what he was looking for.

The lounge was for adults and their guests. Each area was formed by the arrangement of the furniture.

The members had everything at their disposal—exercise equipment, delicious meals, a full-service bar. If he lived in Los Angeles, he would have rushed to join this club. The membership fees were as high as he expected them to be.

"Brett. Over here," Alethia's voice boomed out.

He wandered over and joined Alethia, Lisabeth and Nia in the split-level dining room. They were munching on pancakes and omelettes. The club had all the amenities and then some. The view of Los Angeles was fabulous in the daytime and must have been spectacular at night.

"What's going on?" he asked.

"We're just planning a charity tennis party," Nia said. "I had a very good game, today, even though I lost."

"Sorry, I missed you. I was putting together a strategic move for Bryant."

"You should have been here earlier. Daphne and Jared put on quite a show for everyone."

"They just kept pushing until they got it. They both swing a mean racquet," Lisabeth said.

Brett took special note of the staff and how they would be the ones to carry the torch. If they could get an excellent customer-service crew, then that would be another feather in their cap.

Alethia tugged at his sleeve. "I've called your name twice and you were in another world."

"My apologies."

She stood up and took his arm, "Would you escort me to the health juice bar?"

"Of course. We'll be right back," he told Nia.

"Bring me one of those orange concoctions, please, Brett."

"Okay."

A few minutes later, instead of going to the juice bar, Brett and Alethia stood near the men's locker room. From the mirrored panels above the window, Brett could see anyone entering or leaving the locker room. They waited a few minutes and then he saw Jared and they went into their act.

"Alethia, I don't know when I've seen books like

these. I don't know what Kent was thinking when he let it get this bad."

"As long as Jared doesn't know what's going on, we're okay."

They kept talking but knew Jared had heard enough. He was too greedy not to take the bait.

They were laughing as they got back to Nia. She looked up. "Where's my drink?"

"Sorry, honey, I forgot. Let's get out of here and I'll buy you a drink."

Nia lifted an eyebrow, got up and took his hand. They were leaving when they came face-to-face with Jared. He saluted them with his tennis racquet and then joined his date for the evening.

When they got to the SUV, Nia tripped when she went to get in. "I am so tired I can't see straight," she said as she made it on the second attempt.

"What's going on?"

"It's been one of those days. I had two clients who just drove me crazy."

"I think I have just the thing for you."

"What?"

"I'm not telling."

Nia drifted off to sleep and didn't wake up until Brett was helping her out of the SUV.

Once inside, Nia wanted a quick shower and bed, but Brett pulled her toward the guest room. He helped her out of her clothes and got a bath sheet for her to lie on as he poured a bit of oil in his hands and began to massage her neck and shoulders. His strong hands moved up and down her back.

"I know you're sleepy, but you need this so you don't wake up with any pain."

"If you tell me you learned massage because of

an old girlfriend I'm going to kill you," she mumbled.

"Then I won't tell you," he whispered in her ear. He massaged her for a few more minutes and then told her to take a hot shower and climb into bed.

She slept soundly and the next morning she awoke feeling wonderful. She stretched and knew Brett had been right.

"I guess you're wide awake now." Brett stood in the doorway, wearing nothing but a robe.

"Yes. I guess there was something that you wanted to tell me last night. So I'm awake now. Go for it."

"It wasn't what I wanted to say. It was what I wanted to do."

He crossed the room and sat on the bed and took her in his arms. He feathered kisses across her face and her neck. He'd held her tight as he pried his robe from his body so he could feel her skin pressed against his. He groaned and she was caught up in the mood, knowing he wanted her as much as she wanted him.

They were too smart and too experienced to let excitement rule them. The pocket of his robe held the silver foil of protection and prevention. After that they could relax and let nature take its course.

They lost track of time as they shared their passion. They passed through dimensions as each tried to please the other more. It was love freely given, for neither knew if this would be the only time.

The next time Nia awoke, Brett was sound asleep. She watched him as his even breathing continued. She slipped from the bed and padded to the bath. She stood under the shower and thought about her biological clock. It was ticking louder and louder, but was Brett ready for fatherhood? She didn't think so. She'd find out when they agreed to stop using protection before they made love.

She dressed and went into the kitchen to prepare breakfast. She cut up some fresh fruit for herself and began preparing bacon, eggs and grits for Brett. She put the eggs on the side and would wait until Brett came to the table.

Nia felt rather than heard him a few moments later. She turned and he was standing in the doorway. "How would you like your eggs?"

"Scrambled."

"Coming right up."

He ate silently.

When he finished, he looked up. "Where are we going?"

"What do you mean?"

"Nia, we need to talk. We need to see where this relationship is going."

"Where would you like it to go?"

"Something more permanent."

"Where would we live?"

"What's wrong with Wyoming?"

The mere suggestion that she return to the state of her birth turned her cold. She had moved on in life and never wanted to go back. The answer to her question told more than she wanted to know. She couldn't hide her feelings and he caught on immediately.

"I take it that was an unacceptable answer."

"You take it right. I'm building a career here. I don't want to leave."

"You keep getting hurt here. That's why you came back to Wyoming the first time. Then you marry and that doesn't work. Now your ex-husband is trying to ruin one of your clients."

"I know what you're saying. If bad things keep happening to me, why do I stay? Because bad things can happen anywhere, and I love Los Angeles. You live in New York. Did you know that there are people who don't want to live there?"

"Of course."

"If I went back to Wyoming, it would kill me."

She didn't tell him the rest of it. She didn't tell him that she had enough of men dictating to her on how she should live. Her business was thriving and her reputation would withstand this problem with Jared *because* he was her ex-husband.

Nia didn't know how to explain it to him. At the moment she was too angry to try.

# Eleven

Later that day, Nia sat and thought about her love life. She had only dated one other man when she and Jared were having trouble. It was a big mistake and one that she never repeated.

Her first date after separating was with Joe Lucas, a man who had been helping Alethia get the bank rolling. Since he was new in her life, she didn't let him pick her up, but joined him for drinks and conversation to see if they were compatible.

Nia quickly regretted her decision to see the man. He complained about everything. The bar seemed to be catering to a boisterous crowd when Nia and Joe arrived. They sat at a little table in the back of the room and hoped they wouldn't be disturbed. The conversation started out nice, with the usual probing about their jobs, families and future plans.

Nia couldn't put her finger on what disturbed her, but she didn't want to start tearing the man apart when she knew so little about him. The prawns were delicious with the tangy remoulade sauce.

She'd learned that he was in the process of training and he considered this a big problem with his life-style. The sat and greeted friends arriving, and several of them stayed a little while, snacking on shrimp and catching up on old times.

This was the first time she'd been out with a man she'd met through business. Alethia had always warned her about mixing business and pleasure. But Nia had no intention of being one of those women who couldn't get back in the saddle again and thought that every man in the room was just trying to get drunk. It was normal during Happy Hour to watch patrons get so drunk that they forgot their bosses, projects and deadlines. Nia didn't want to see that side of the people she had to work with daily. She hoped Joe was different.

Joe began telling Nia about the tension that had caused him an ulcer at an early age. "I don't let the tension out enough."

He was speaking softly and Nia leaned forward to hear him. He draped his arm across her shoulder. "Why don't we go some place and let me relieve some of this tension?" he asked. "You wouldn't want me to have a heart attack."

Nia shoved his arm from her shoulders and sat up. He laughed. "Uh-oh, I guess I stepped on your toes."

"Joe," Nia explained, "when I said I wanted to come here and talk, I meant it."

"Why is it I am always attracted to people who are going through bad times? I thought we could have a test drive," he said and leered.

"You're an idiot."

He backed off and glared at her. "Come on, baby, you're not Miss Innocence."

"We were supposed to get to know each other, not . . . this," Nia said.

She was getting furious. She'd been through this so many times. "Maybe we should leave."

"I want to get you all to myself and show you how compatible we are." He gave her what he thought was a sexy grin, but to her it was another leer.

"Sorry, I have so many projects, I just don't have time to get away."

As they reached her car, she was suddenly thrown against it and Joe was running his hands under her clothes. She fought back with a fierce attack on his face.

He bent her back to the car and pressed his lips on hers.

They wrestled against the car for a moment. His mouth was slightly open and he tried to kiss her again. She tried to use her arms to make him stop, but he was determined to show her that if she kissed him, she'd want him as much as he wanted her.

"Stop it. What's the matter with you?" she asked.

"Why can't I have just a little kiss?" He sighed.

Nia pushed him away and started walking back to the restaurant. He ran behind her and grabbed her. They wrestled some more until one of the bar's bouncers, who was taking a break, grabbed Joe and turned him around.

"Okay, buddy, that's enough."

"Hey, don't touch me. Do you know who I am?"

"You're the guy going home in a taxi. That's who you are!"

The bouncer weighed close to three hundred pounds and Joe didn't stand a chance.

Nia breathed a sigh of relief when Joe didn't try to challenge the bouncer. He called a taxi. Joe stood there waiting and didn't look at Nia.

"Do you need a ride, miss?" the bouncer asked.

"No. I came in my own car."

"Smart move. Allow me to walk you to the car."

She wasn't afraid of Joe but there was no sense in taking chances.

Nia threw herself into work and decided relationships were out of the question. Until Brett walked back into her life. Then all bets were off.

# Twelve

On the drive back to Los Angeles, Brett leaned over and took Nia's hand. He didn't ask her anything, but he just seemed to know she needed to know he was there for her.

"What's the matter with you?" she said after a long silence.

"Nothing." He didn't want to answer that question. He was so much of the problem.

"It has to be something. Why do I always mess things up? I walked away from you and married Jared. I put together a deal for Kent and now he may lose his company. I . . . I don't know what's next."

"Honey, it's not you. When you left, I felt betrayed until I realized that you knew what you wanted and I didn't. You didn't just run off to California. You had very definite plans. You also had plans for Kent and, believe me, if you hadn't set up that deal, Jared would never gone for the company itself. He wanted to hurt you."

"But he'll hurt other people," Nia said.

"No, he won't. I haven't played my trump card yet. This will work out. I promise."

He held her hand all the way back to the house and she felt so much better.

Once inside the house, Brett rushed Nia. He couldn't let her go. He brought her hand to his lips and kissed her fingertips. How could something so simple make her want more than if he'd placed a really passionate kiss on her lips?

Nia couldn't believe how that made her feel. He had not kissed her and still flickers of desire coursed throughout her body. She didn't know anymore why she allowed this when they needed to talk about Kent's business.

"I thought you were beautiful, but now seeing you here tonight, it makes you absolutely stunning. What I really like about you is that you never tried to conceal your ambition."

"Ambition?"

"Yeah. You are determined when you want something. I pity the man who gets in your way."

"I think you can say the same for yourself. You arrive without warning and believe me, I noticed you were all man."

He laughed. "I think this mutual admiration society should retire."

As soon as they got to the bedroom, they took off their clothes. Nia undressed without the slightest interference from Brett.

She watched him strip and reveal his strong, gorgeous body. They slowly teased each other, even though the passions searing through their bodies made their eyes shine desire. They lay on her bed.

With bold hands, she ran her fingers over Brett's chest and marveled at the ragged little breaths she heard him take. Her hands continued touching him and waiting for him to return the favor, but he wouldn't, until he'd added protection. Safe sex was great sex.

It became a little love war over who could rouse more emotion. She slowly examined the rest of his body with her hands and her mouth, until Brett finally pulled her to him and began to reciprocate with sensuous movements. His fingers bit into her skin, his mouth possessed hers. The bed became a tangle of pleasure as they made love. "Brett," she finally gasped.

He felt victorious as he sank into her. They moaned their pleasure and finally collapsed on the bed.

How could she tell him that she had never known this kind of pleasure? Nia luxuriated in the moment and pushed all the bad out of her mind.

Somehow they managed to get under the blanket and fall asleep in each other's arms.

When she awoke early in the morning, she didn't want to move as she replayed every sensuous moment of the night before.

The telephone rang. Nia glanced at the clock. It was four-thirty. It must be important. She grabbed the receiver and mumbled a greeting.

"I know it's early, but it can't wait," Alethia said.

Nia sat up and felt a cold sweat start. "What is it?"

"Not 'what,' but 'who.' Jared Schuyler is having you investigated, and it's going to hold up my bank."

"Calm down. I know how important the bank is to you."

"You don't know what he's saying about you."

"Actually, I do know. He threatened he'd ruin my reputation if I left him. I told him to go ahead and spread lies. It wouldn't look too good on the nightly news. He's running everything with money from his inheritance. A scandal would take it all away. A little something in the will, he told me. We'll work it out."

"That's just what he's doing. He's my godson. I thought I knew him."

"He's a wimp and a bully. We just need to find someone to stand up to him."

"I want you to find out why he's doing this. Go see him and—" Alethia's voice broke. "All I ever wanted was to one day have this bank."

Nina felt Brett sit up and she knew he'd heard most of the conversation. He took the phone from her and spoke softly to Alethia.

"Whatever he's doing, we can counter. Try to get some rest."

"Brett . . . I'm so sorry . . . I didn't even think about you being there."

"Don't worry, but don't let it happen again," he teased.

Alethia laughed. "You're a good man, and I'm so glad that Nia has you."

They said good-bye and Brett put the receiver down. He let out a string of low epithets and then apologized to Nia.

"What's he doing?"

"The thing about people who pull skeletons out of the closet is that they forget their own skeletons."

"I know. Alethia used to tell me all the bad things she and Daphne used to do."

"Like what?" He pulled her into his arms and lay down.

"One time a professor was coming on to Daphne and she didn't want him, but he wouldn't stop. They put sugar in his gas tank."

"It might stop the car, but not those advances."

"Well . . . the car was a Mercedes Benz."

Brett laughed. "Why are you women so vindictive?"

"It cancels out a second request."

Now that she was calm, Brett put a little distance between them as they talked. Finally, she drifted off to sleep again.

Brett felt it was time to fight fire with fire. Jared was threatening Kent's company with a takeover, but dangled the idea of ripping the company away in front of Kent. He was after Nia, and Brett was, not about to let that happen. As he watched her sleep, he knew exactly what he had to do.

He took a short nap, then got up, showered, brushed his teeth, shaved and got dressed in casual clothes. He was going to pay a visit to Jared's office.

He went to the kitchen and prepared a sumptuous breakfast. The aroma of freshly cooked pancakes became too much for Nia and she dragged herself out of bed. She took a cool shower to wake herself up, then performed her morning ablutions and got dressed.

By the time she reached the table, Brett was working on his second batch of pancakes.

"Greedy gut," Nia scolded. "You couldn't wait for me?"

"Sorry, honey, I have to eat and run," he explained. "I've got quite a bit to do."

She waited for more information, but when none was forthcoming, decided that maybe she didn't want to know what was going on.


He went back to his hotel and examined a folder that Palladin Rush had sent by overnight express and read his uncle's instructions.

Brett then arrived at the law offices of the Schuylers a little after ten A.M. He'd been fighting back a grin ever since he had read the folder. Talk about fighting fire with fire. Marlene was seated at the reception desk. She wore her trademark bifocals and a drab print dress.

"What are you doing here?"

"I need to see Jared."

"Why?"

"It's a man thing."

He watched as the poor woman didn't know what to do. Finally, she hit the intercom button and spoke with Jared.

"Are you sure?" he heard her say. Then she looked up and grimaced. "If you'll follow me, Mr. Faulkner."

She led him to Jared's office, and when she opened the door, the man he wanted was seated behind the desk. Marlene looked at both of them quizzically and left.

"So what can I do for you?"

"Let's keep the game where it belongs."

"What do you want me to do? Rip Kent's company from under him and end his pain? I don't think so."

"Alethia thinks you're interfering with her bank."

"No, just her assistant."

"I would hate to do something along those lines to you. It could prove embarrassing."

"What could you possible have?" Jared was enjoying the game he was playing.

Brett opened the manila folder he was carrying and dumped six pictures on the desk.

"What's this?"

"You really shouldn't try smear campaigns if you have something to hide."

Jared stared down at six beautiful black women. "You . . ."

"I want you to stop the game playing or something from your past is going to go very public. Do we understand each other?"

At that moment Daphne burst through the door. "What's going on?"

She saw the pictures and gasped. She looked to Jared for guidance. He shook his head.

"Well, I think we understand each other, so it's time for me to leave. Good-bye, Ms. Schuyler, Jared."

Moments later, Brett was out of the office and wishing he could be a fly on the wall to hear what was going on. He went back to his hotel and spent some time talking to Ana Lisa and then to Palladin.

Ana Lisa informed him that the ski resort was going full steam. Instead of being excited, he felt a knot in his stomach. The ski resort was in Wyoming and Nia had told him in no uncertain terms she was not planning to return there.

After last night, he felt they were getting really close again. Maybe if he took her to the resort and she got a full view of the place, she would change her mind.

# Thirteen

Brett felt great until he walked into Nia's house and saw her grim face. She asked him to come into the dining room. They sat down and Nia looked troubled.

"What's the matter?"

"You're the matter. Alethia called me to thank you for making Jared apologize to her."

"I didn't. Daphne must have done that."

"But what did you do to bring it on?"

"Nothing."

"Brett . . ."

"Okay. I did apply a little pressure on the advice of my uncle."

She slammed her hand down on the table. "Brett, what did you do?"

"I simply took the photos of his ex-girlfriends and dropped them on his desk."

She was angry and curious at the same time. "So?"

"That's it. I dumped the pictures and let him draw his own conclusion."

"That's all?"

"He must have a guilty conscience about one or all of these women."

Nia sat there and could not believe what he'd done. "What did the women tell you?"

"Nothing. I never met them."

Nia burst into laughter. "You bluffed and he bought it."


Even hours later, the thought of the way he'd made a threat without knowing anything or saying anything brought a smile to her face. Jared had backed off from Alethia, but he'd never let Kent go.

Brett thought they needed to get away from Los Angeles. It would give Jared a false sense of security and Brett time to convince Nia that she would love the wide open spaces again. Alethia was on his side and encouraged Nia to go with him. She finally relented.


Kent had given Brett directions to Paul's cabin. As they passed steep cliffs and wide rivers, it gave Brett a sense of comfort. He glanced over at Nia, who had fallen asleep more than a mile back.

They finally came to a tiny cabin. "Wake up, sleepyhead," he called. Nia stirred just a little and began to check out her surroundings. She couldn't believe she'd let him talk her into this wilderness trek. She'd done enough of that growing up.

The sky grew dark and it began to rain just as they pulled up to the cabin door.

She got out of the SUV and, after Brett had checked the cabin for any unwanted visitors, they began to unload everything into the cabin. They worked through the rain. The weather report came on the car radio and said there would be more of the same for the next day.

"When we get back," Brett said, "I'm going to pack a survival kit in our cars. You never know when you might be trapped somewhere."

"You don't think we're going to be here longer that the weekend?"

"No, I don't and neither does the weatherman."

After they got everything into the cabin, they changed clothes and began putting things in order. Nia had changed to shorts and a T-shirt as soon as they didn't have to go back outside.

The cabin took on a cozy mood. They ate a simple meal and went to bed early. After making love, they curled up in bed and drifted off to sleep.

Nia smiled to herself as she thought about her trip to the drugstore just before they left Los Angeles. It had been quite a while since she purchased condoms. After all she couldn't leave it all up to Brett. What if he forgot? What if he ran out?

The next morning they found out the weatherman had been wrong. The sun came out and chased all the rain clouds away. They got dressed and had breakfast.

Nia and Brett put on swimsuits and walked a half mile to the river and took a dip. It was as if they were the only two people on earth.

Things had become so intense in L.A. that this was just what the doctor had ordered. The only thing that worried Brett was giving Ana Lisa complete control, but it was time, and she was trustworthy.

Brett and Nia returned from the river and snugged comfortably in bed. His face was next to hers as they talked about their favorite things.

Then they made love again. He worked his lips over hers and she wiggled to get more comfortable. She slipped her arms around his neck. He hadn't shaved, and she found the slight stubble sexy. Their kiss went from playful to searing. Slowly, they took turns pulling off items of clothing. Brett slipped Nia's T-shirt off and cupped her breasts in his strong hands. Then he slid one hand down her body, exploring until she thought she would explode. He eased off, not letting her get any further and began again, only to retreat and take her to the peak of passion until he could no longer stand it.

Late the second night, she had finally talked to him about her parents.

"I know it's silly, but if I'm not there, I can almost feel that they're still alive. But the minute I get off the plane now and someone other than my dad picks me up, it's as if it just happened. I can't handle being in Wyoming."

"Do you think you ever will?"

"Maybe, but I'm not going to try right now."

The last morning Nia was up earlier than Brett and had breakfast prepared for him. He showered and came into the kitchen, wearing nothing but the towel tied around his hips.

Nia, on the other hand, was completely dressed and giggled when she turned and saw him. "I'm sorry, sir, but this restaurant doesn't serve naked men."

"Are you saying that my towel doesn't count?"

"No, sir. It doesn't."

"So if it doesn't count, I guess I could take it off completely?" Brett's hand went to the knot at his waist.

"Don't you dare!"

"Why? It isn't as if you haven't seen it before."

Nia felt her face grow hot. She was blushing—at her age. "I don't believe you're doing this to me."

"Well, what will I get if I obey the laws of your restaurant?"

"What would you like? I mean . . . I mean . . ."

"I would like you to take a trip with me."

"Where?"

"Wherever I say."

"Well . . ."

"Come on, you're not going to get a better offer than that."

"Okay. Now go put some clothes on."

Brett's laughter could be heard all the while as he dressed.

They had agreed on three days and they had been the best three days she'd ever spent.

It had been so different from anything Nia had experienced and she kept running it through her mind as they drove home.


In Los Angeles, everything was the same. Jared would continue to taunt Kent and everyone knew that one day he would make good on his promise to take it all away. No one else wanted Kent's company.

Unfortunately, Ana Lisa called Brett and insisted he come back to New York for a cocktail part. The man had been one of Brett's biggest supporters when he started out, and he was getting married for the fourth time, but acting as though it were the first.

Although they had only been back in Los Angeles for a couple of days, Nia agreed to accompany Brett to New York again. She secretly wanted to see the man in his natural surroundings.

Who would show up at a party for a fourth go-round? Everyone on New York's A-list, or at least it seemed that way. Nia had expected to see ten or twenty lost souls with nothing better to do than attend the celebration. But when the elevator doors opened to the fortieth-floor penthouse, she could see people dancing, drinking and having a great time. Why did she think that New Yorkers were more sedate than the wild Hollywood crowds she had seen?

Nia touched an uneasy hand to her dampness-frizzed hair. She was happy to have Brett navigate her through the whole thing.

"Uh-oh," she whispered as she accidentally spilled her drink, when she was bumped from behind.

"Don't worry, I'll introduce you to anyone you want to meet." Brett, who figured the "uh-oh" was an exclamation of delight, put his hand lightly in the small of her back and moved her forward.

He leaned down and whispered, "Aren't you glad you came? Doesn't it make you wish for lots of space?" He thought about the Wyoming resort.

"It certainly does," she said as she thought of the trip in California.

Every woman seemed to be wearing clingy, slinky black silk to show off her body, toned from hours spent in the gym.

The only thing Nia regretted was that she didn't have enough time to explore the neighborhood surrounding Brett's gorgeous town house in Harlem. He'd hustled her out and into a cab and toward Fifth Avenue so fast that it had made her head spin. She'd demanded that he let her out of the taxi so she could walk a little, but Brett had ignored her protests. He hadn't talked her into coming here; he'd shanghaied her.

Still Nia had to admit, if reluctantly, that being here might have its uses, now that Brett had given her so much. There were more business contacts just in the hallway than she'd ever imagined a person could find in one place. Brett was exchanging hellos, handshakes, hugs and kisses all the way in as they moved slowly towards the host.

"Brett, great to see you," the host said.

"You too, Thad." Brett smiled. "I'd like you to meet Nia Sebastian."

"Miss Sebastian, oh yeah. The lady who lured him out to California. Now I understand." He leaned down and kissed Nia. "This is my fiancée, Brandi."

Nia was a little taken aback to learn that Thad had been involved in an ugly divorce less than a year ago. If one was Rich, there was always someone else.

"Nice to meet you both," she said.

"Catch you later," Brett said, taking Nia's elbow and guiding her to another group of people. Before they reached an alcove, Nia had met about fifty people.

"You didn't warn me about this," Nia said.

"I thought you L.A. types were used to crowds."

There was a yell and suddenly a tall, fair-skinned woman threw herself into Brett's arms.

Brett introduced Nia and Crystal and didn't notice the glares. Crystal obviously thought Brett was her property.

"Brett, darling, I'm so glad to see you," Crystal cooed. "I though you were going to call me when you got home."

Nia felt her face turning hot. She'd been dismissed totally and completely as only a woman can dismiss another. But since *she* was the woman with Brett, that was all that mattered.

When the woman left after kissing Brett on the cheek, he turned to Nia. "I want to explain that before you make more of it. She's the daughter of a client and fancies herself in love with me."

"I don't have a problem with her."

"Thanks, sweetheart." He placed a soft kiss on her lips before going off to talk to another business acquaintance.

Who was she kidding! She really felt the urge to pull Crystal's hair to see how much was real. Then she chided herself for being possessive.

She wasn't going to fall into that trap. Besides, they were leaving the next day.

# Fourteen

Instead of flying back as Nia thought, Brett asked her to spend some time in his world. She'd been dying for a cook's tour of his four-story brownstone. She knew something about Harlem. Most people did. If they hadn't pulled out maps and history books on their own, they certainly did after former President Bill Clinton decided to have his offices there.

They started on the top floor where the master bedroom was. She screamed at him when he told her about the elevator that extended through all the stories.

"You let me walk up all those flights of stairs, and I could have just popped in a private elevator?"

"When I bought the house, it didn't have that elevator. I gave you the real feeling of a Harlem brownstone."

She narrowed her eyes. "You'll pay for that."

Seeing the house through his eyes reminded her of the first time she had looked at her own little house. It had only been on the market a short time. Her first inclination had been to buy something more modern or maybe a condo, but one look at the house and she had to have it.

Nia refused to even tour the exercise floor. "A man has to take me as I am or get out of town."

They called California to talk to Alethia and Kent. There was a calm that they didn't understand. Alethia did give a rather cryptic comment about bearding the lion in his den and that she had a lot to tell them when they returned.

Later that night, Brett remembered what she'd said. "Do you think her friendship with Daphne helped smooth the way?"

"I hope so. I always felt I was partly responsible for the breech."

"Sometimes it is difficult. Alethia thinks of you as her daughter and wants to protect you. Daphne, of course, wants to protect her son."

"They encouraged us," Nia told him.

"Sure, but Daphne thought you'd conform to her standards and Alethia thought that Jared would conform to hers. Sometimes divorce is the best thing that could happen."

"I hate to do this, but I have some work to do. Could you entertain yourself for a while?" Brett asked.

"I'm dying to see what films you have. I'll be in your little movie theater."

On her way to the home theater, she heard a key in the lock and stopped. The door opened, and Nia found herself staring up at a tall, stunning woman with a multicolored head wrap.

"You must be Ana Lisa," was all that Nia could say.

"Ah. You are right and you must be the pretty little thing that has my boss in Windsor knots."

"Watch that. I may have to find a new assistant," Brett said. He was halfway down the stairs so he must have been expecting her.

"If only you could. No one but me is brave enough to challenge you." She turned back to Nia. "If he's giving you trouble, just call me and I will put him in his place."

"One day, I'm going to find a man who will make your knees turn to jelly," Brett promised.

"If I can resist you, I can resist any man."

The next moment Ana Lisa enveloped Brett in a bear hug that made Nia pray she didn't break any bones.

"I just want to drop these papers off and remind you about the party for the Rush kids."

"I forgot." He turned to Nia.

"I guess we're going to another party," she said. "How do you ever get any work done?"


Nia had only met Palladin and Jesslyn Rush when they came to Kaliq Faulkner's wedding. They were a terrific couple and very much in love. She caught them embracing once, and it was as though they were newlyweds. Exactly what she wanted.

They were always doing something and then they would just take off for a vacation alone. Now that their sons had been accepted to an exclusive boarding school, they were celebrating. The twins were a handful but Nia liked them. She wanted children but she couldn't imagine how it would be to have twins running around.

While Brett loved his father, Palladin was Brett's idol, which was the reason he had stayed in New York. But lately, Nia noticed he'd been talking about Wyoming a lot. She didn't know what would happen with them, because she couldn't live there.

The limousine was scheduled to pick them up at six, and they had to hurry to get dressed.

The frosted-glass, sliding doors opened to reveal a small bedroom Brett used as a closet. Brett pulled out several different tuxedos before deciding to wear his favorite style in a different color than black. He selected a gray, two-button tuxedo, and a wingtip tuxedo shirt. The drawers at the baseboard of the closet held his shoes. He opted for gray hand-tooled boots. A fashion maven might faint, but he liked it.

He dressed, checked himself in the mirror and went in search of Nia. She had refused to dress in the same room, saying that she wanted to surprise him. He knocked on the door. There was no answer. He knocked again. Finally, he opened the door and called out her name. Still no answer.

He turned on the light and there she was. He was speechless for a moment as his eyes took in the full look.

Nia wore a red dress with very strategically placed designs. She reminded him of the actresses of the 1940s—sleek, sophisticated and blatantly sexy. Even the red sandals were sexy.

"I hope you're quiet because you like it?"

"I'm speechless because I like it. You know this feels like déjà vu. I was going to some function with Palladin when I met Alethia."

"I was really upset when I heard she came to see you."

"I guessed that. Maybe we'll run into her lawyer. He's the one who actually approached me. I think his grandchildren go to the same school."

"Frank?"

"Yes."

"I've met him a few times. He adores Alethia, even though he pretends he doesn't."

After the party, she could only remember that Jesslyn Rush was a dynamic woman. She even challenged Ana Lisa.

"Can you believe these petite people? Not as big as a minute and giving orders," Ana Lisa said and laughed.

New York seemed to be one social whirl, but Palladin had told Nia that it took a lot of hard work to make it seem like fun.

# Fifteen

The next morning the telephone rang a little past seven A.M. Brett decided to let the answering machine pick up the call until he heard Alethia's voice; then he grabbed the receiver.

"We're here," he said, interrupting her as she started to leave a message.

"I thought you might have the phone turned off," she told him.

"What's the problem?" asked Nia as she lay next to Brett, but never opening her eyes.

"Let me put you on the speaker," Brett told Alethia. "What's going on?" he asked.

"Daphne's been hospitalized. I was with her and she . . . collapsed."

"Oh, no," Nia gasped. "It was her heart, wasn't it?"

"I'm afraid so," Alethia answered.

"How bad is it this time?" Nia asked.

"They plan to keep her overnight, but she'll have to take it easy for the rest of the week. I was calling to tell you that you didn't have to rush back."

"Thank you," Nia said. "I hope she gets well soon."

They said their good-byes and Brett switched the telephone off. Then he turned to Nia.

"You knew about her heart?"

"Yes. When I was married to Jared, Daphne used her condition to manipulate everyone."

"She doesn't have a bad heart?"

"Oh, yes. She takes nitroglycerin tablets. When I was married, I used to think she only had these attacks when she couldn't get her own way. They never seemed to happen any other time."

"Do you think she's faking?"

"Not this time, because Jared is doing quite well. Daphne only seems to have an attack when she's losing a battle."

"Would Jared suddenly pull out and say he didn't want the company because of this?"

"It wouldn't surprise me. He's done it before, but only if it was something he and Daphne both agreed on. He pulled this same thing with another company. An ex-girlfriend started up a business and he went after her as soon as she took it public. It caused enough anguish to break up her marriage and then he just pulled out."

"What did she do?"

"She got a divorce, went to New Mexico and started up again. I hear she's just fine except . . ."

"It cost her a husband."

"I guess it made Jared feel good."

Brett sat up and puffed his pillows against the headboard. "I see. Do you think if—"

Nia shook her head, interrupting him. "No. It wouldn't work."

"You didn't let me finish the sentence."

"Brett Faulkner, I know how your mind works.

You were going to ask that if Kent and Lisabeth pretended to break up, would that stop Jared."

He grinned sheepishly. "I hope my clients can't read me that well."

"I've known you a very long time."

"True."

"Don't worry, darling, I won't give away any of your secrets."

"So what do you think? Do you want to stay in New York a few more days?"

"I'd love to."

"I'm going to the office for a few hours. Do you want to come along?"

"Not really. I have some work to do also," she explained. Nia had her laptop so she could link with her other computer and see how her clients were doing.

"Do you mind if I use your phone?"

"Of course not. Use my office," Brett said as he bounded from the bed and headed for his dressing area.

A half hour later, he was back, fully dressed and ready to leave. He bent over and kissed Nia. She opened her eyes and smiled.

Nia got up later, showered, slipped into a short terry-cloth robe she always took with her and went to the kitchen. She fixed herself a quick breakfast of eggs, toast, and a cup of coffee. She returned to the bedroom and dressed in jeans and a sweatshirt, then padded barefoot to Brett's office. The room was decorated the same way as the rest of the house. Earth tones, no frills, very masculine. She sat in the chair behind the desk and hooked her laptop into his telephone and went to work.

After a couple of hours of tracking investments

and business deals, she was satisfied that her clients were all in good shape. All except for Kent.

She then checked out Brett's home theater. She browsed the tiny, black, loose-leaf notebook that was a guide to all the movies he had available. Nia was surprised at how many she'd missed in the past year. She bypassed those to watch an old Morgan Freeman foreign film, *The Red Violin.* She was happy to see it had subtitles instead of dubbing. She hated movies that had characters' mouths moving at the wrong time. It was a beautifully crafted movie, where the star was actually a violin passed from century to century and how it affected its owners.

After it ended, she thought about another, but realized that she hadn't eaten since breakfast and it was now almost three P.M.

Brett came home just as she felt her stomach growl. They prepared a meal together and when they finished, he told her he had to make a courtesy stop at a party for one of his business contacts later that evening.

"You go. I really don't want to do anything right now. I think I've been running on adrenaline for so long I thought it was natural. Now that I've actually stopped, I feel exhausted," Nia said.

"Are you sure you don't want to come with me?" he asked.

"Positive."

"I really hate to leave you here alone."

"Stop being a worrywart. You take care of your business. But tomorrow, I want to become a high-maintenance woman."

"What does that mean?"

"It means that there will be no business meetings, parties or office hours. You are going to show me your city."

He kissed her breathless, then said, "You have a deal, beautiful lady. Okay, but just a little hint—if you really want to relax, check out that little room." He pointed to a door that Nia hadn't paid much attention to. She'd thought it was a closet and never looked inside.

After Brett left, Nia's curiosity lured her across the room as if it were a physical force. She had to find out what Brett meant, so she opened the door. When she stepped into the tiny room, the lights came on. He had one of those sensors that detected movement and automatically turned the lights on.

She found herself in a small bathroom that had a shower, and another structure that resembled a large wooden box with a lid on it. The floor was completely covered in marble tile and had a drain in the middle. She walked over and lifted the lid on the box to find a Japanese soaking tub. She knew a few people in California who swore by them, but she'd never tried one. Now was as good a time as any to rectify that little glitch in her education.

Nia turned up the water heater on the tub to reach a level between 100 and 107 degrees. One did not bathe in the soaking tub. She looked on the shelf above the tub and found some mineral packets. They weren't as good as hot springs water, but would have to do, she thought as she opened a packet and dumped it into the tub. Real hot springs water was good for rheumatism, high blood pressure, diabetes and other illnesses, her friends had explained. The true Japanese bath would have had large bowls of hot water to rinse your body, but Nia circumvented that by rinsing off in the shower and then climbing into the tub. This was the place to meditate, relax and recover from exhaustion or stress.

Nia was able to sit on the bench so the water came up to her neck. She closed her eyes and allowed her body to become accustomed to the hot water and then got out of the tub.

She sat on the little stool by the tub and applied a generous amount of liquid soap to her body. Her hair had been tied back almost the same way Brett wore his. Now she took off the rubber band, loosened her hair and shampooed it. Then she stepped into the shower and rinsed all the soap off and got back into the soaking tub. Half an hour later, she emerged from the bath, feeling more relaxed than she had ever before. Nia wrapped herself in a large bath sheet and applied night cream to her face. There were no thoughts racing through her mind about Brett, Kent's business or any clients as she stretched out on the bed. She glanced at the clock. It was eight P.M. She drifted off to sleep.

# Sixteen

In California, it was five P.M. and Alethia was returning to the hospital to see Daphne. When she walked into the room, she wasn't surprised to find Jared sitting by the bed.

"How is she?" Alethia whispered.

Before Jared could answer, Daphne said, "She's just fine. She's awake and she wants to go home. She's sick of people talking about her as if she doesn't exist."

"I see you've returned to normal, Daphne," Alethia said.

"Why don't you go find out what the doctor is planning for me, Jared?"

It was a request to get him to leave the room and they all knew it. He smiled, stood up and left.

"How are you really feeling, Daphne?" Alethia asked as soon as Jared was out of earshot.

"I'm fine. I just got a little upset over betrayal by a friend."

"I didn't betray you. I just know that you can stop this nonsense with Jared any time you choose."

"I trusted you with a secret and now you're using it against me."

"You didn't trust me. I was the only one who would come to your rescue."

Daphne pressed the button to raise the bed to an upright position. Her eyes flashed and she barely opened her mouth when she spoke. "You accused my son of being vindictive and spiteful as if he were a child. He's a very competent business-man and you know it."

"I wonder if you know it?"

"What's that supposed to mean?"

Alethia came closer to the bed. "Jared can run Schuyler and Schuyler, but you won't step aside to give him a chance. If you did, he wouldn't be run-ning around strong-arming Kent."

"So he can fail? Look what happens every time he's allowed to use his own brainpower. Look who he married!"

"How dare you—"

"Oh, don't get defensive. I know she's your little protegée and you're so much alike. She was wrong for Jared."

"Oh? I think it's more that Jared was wrong for her."

Daphne glared at Alethia for a moment, then burst into laughter. She continued to laugh until Alethia joined her.

"Oh, Alethia, we are such a pair. You're as pro-tective of Nia as if she's your own and I dare any-one to try to hurt Jared."

"I can't believe how we come out kicking and scratching."

The grin left Daphne's face. "The only differ-ence is that I haven't resorted to blackmail."

"I don't think of it as blackmail. I think of it as a state secret that will never get out as long as Jared doesn't try to destroy Nia. This little situation with Kent is something from which she can recover."

"One day I won't be able to control him. One day I won't be around to protect him. Then what are you going to do?"

Jared and the doctor walked into the room and heard this statement.

"Now, Mrs. Schuyler, don't you worry. The tests came back and you're fine. In fact, you can go home in the morning."

"Did you hear that, Mother?"

"Yes, dear." Daphne's smile returned. "I'll enjoy being home and pampered."

"A few more days of bed rest will work wonders."

Alethia grimaced. "I guess everything is settled. I'll drop by to see you in a couple of days."

"I'll walk you to your car," Jared said.

Alethia had parked in a very well-lit area. They said nothing on the way there. Alethia opened the door and Jared held it while she got in. He closed the door and she let the window down when he tapped on it.

"I just want to tell you that I know you and my mother go back a long way, but I don't think you're friends. Mother and I have talked about a lot of things. I know more than you think. I don't want you around her anymore."

"What if she doesn't agree?"

"Just convince her that it's healthier for you to stay away from her."

Jared turned and walked back to the hospital. Alethia couldn't move for several minutes. He had actually threatened her. She couldn't believe it. Daphne thought she and Jared were of the same mind and now she would have to tell her about the threat. She couldn't let him get the upper hand or he would find a way to destroy Nia.

When Nia awoke, Brett was lying next to her, still asleep. She vaguely remembered him coming home. She couldn't remember ever feeling so free as she had when she slipped into bed after her soak.

Nia rolled over and stretched. She felt marvelous. Now she could spend some time with Brett without thinking about Kent's business. She still felt that Daphne's attack could have been self-induced. In a way she hoped it was. She didn't want anything to happen to her former mother-in-law; she just wanted the madness of Jared's revenge to stop.

Her movements awakened Brett. "Good morning. You were knocked out when I came in last night."

"It was your secret weapon that did it."

"It's great, isn't it? One of my clients turned me on to it. He and his wife could not believe how few we had in New York. You know in Japan they still have communal baths."

"I don't think I'm ready for that yet."

"Nia, I don't think we'll be that open ever."

"So what's on the agenda today?"

"The Empire State Building. We'll take a little tour and have lunch with my uncle and aunt."

They dressed, had breakfast and headed for the subway. It was the easiest way to travel around New York.

"What if I didn't have you as a guide? How would I get around by myself?"

"As long as you know where you are and where

you want to go, New York City Transit has a twenty-four-hour number."

"I guess every large city has something like that for tourists."

They got to the Empire State Building just after eleven A.M. and walked around to the different shops before going to GiftBaskets Inc. The tiny shop was busy, as usual. Lena, Jesslyn's sister, was manning the cash register. Several college students were putting baskets together.

"Hi, Aunt Lena," Brett said.

"Hey there. I heard you were coming down and bringing a lady friend." She stepped from behind the counter and Nia's eyes widened. Lena wore a short tight dress that hugged curves that everyone wanted. Her three-inch heels brought attention to a great pair of legs.

She gave both Brett and Nia a bear hug. The woman was as strong as she looked. "Come on back. They're in the office," Lena said.

They followed her down a narrow hall and she rapped on the door. "Are you guys decent in there?" she asked as she opened the door. If they hadn't been "decent," she hadn't given them much of a chance to correct that.

"Hi, come on in," Jesslyn said. "Don't pay any attention to my sister—she's the insane part of the family."

"Well, I'm not going to be insulted anymore. I'm going back to work." Lena whirled and was gone.

Jesslyn saw Nia's face. "Don't tell me. He didn't warn you about Lena."

"No. He just mentioned she was your older sister."

"She's harmless, we think," Palladin said. "Except when she thinks her little sister is in danger."

Years before, Jesslyn had had amnesia and thought she was Palladin's ex-wife. He went along with it, as he felt it was the best way to protect her. Lena had warned him that his plan had better work or he would answer to her.

"Let's go. I'm starving," Jesslyn said.

"I have reservations at The Bayou."

The foursome headed uptown to the restaurant that served fabulous Louisiana cuisine. Brett, Palladin and Jesslyn had eaten there many times. Nia loved the food and the company.

After lunch, they parted, and Brett and Nia decided to catch a movie each had wanted to see. Then they had an early dinner and went home. Nia read several financial magazines that Brett subscribed to. He called Kent to see how the partners were pulling together, but wasn't happy when Kent told him the last meeting had dissolved into a finger-pointing fight instead of coming up with a game plan.

"I think Jared is calling in a lot of favors to make sure he's the only one around wanting Bryant," Kent said.

"I wouldn't put it past him, but I promise we won't lose this one."

# Seventeen

The next day, Nia settled into Brett's office as if she'd been doing it for years. She loved its extravagant surroundings. The rich mahogany cabinets, which ran from the floor to the ceiling, looked like panels until one saw the strategically placed door knobs.

She wore an oversize T-shirt and leggings as she plugged in her computer. After three hours of strategic planning for one client, she switched to the financial records of another. This one had ignored her advice and tried a get-rich scheme. Now the money he'd set aside for his daughter's college fund was several thousands of dollars less than it should have been. It wasn't the first time a client had gone against her advice and lost money. The daughter was adorable, and was working so hard to get good grades. Yet her father's salary put her out of the running for scholarships. Now his squandering good money could mean that she would have to give up on an Ivy League school. Nia promised her that if she couldn't get enough back into the college fund, she'd show the girl how to attend another college and then transfer in her senior year to the Ivy League school she really wanted to get her degree at. That

was what many Harvard, Yale and Princeton gradu-
ates had done: take three years to save up tuition,
maintain good grades and then transfer into one of
the top schools. The degree would still come from
Harvard, Yale, or wherever.

After Nia did some restructuring, she faxed the
plan off to her client. When she got back to Los
Angeles, they would sit and talk about everything.

Nia stretched and remembered how good she
had felt after using the Japanese tub. She made a
note in her personal planner to check one out for
herself.

She went to the kitchen to see what she wanted
for lunch. Once Brett knew they were going to be
in New York, he'd called a special service that he
used and had them stock the refrigerator.

Nia prepared a roast-beef-and-tomato sandwich
on whole-wheat bread. While she sat at the dining
room table, drinking cranberry juice and nibbling
on her sandwich, she thumbed through *Black Enterprise*, to see what other financial advisors were
doing.

After lunch, she returned to her laptop and
worked on plans for a few more clients. She
wouldn't be with the bank forever.

Brett called during the day to check up on her.
He was coming home in an hour and bringing tickets for a popular Broadway play.

"How did you manage to get tickets? I heard
they were sold out for the next four months?"

"I did a little arm twisting and a little threatening."

"Oh, yeah, right!"

"Okay, so I did a little begging and calling in
favors. It worked, didn't it?"

"Brett, are you trying to say the end justifies the means?"

"Don't put words in my mouth. Just wear something pretty."

"See you in a few minutes," she told him.

Nia headed for the bathroom as soon as she hung up the telephone. She stripped to the skin, turned the water on and blended it to the correct hot-and-cold mixture she preferred. She selected an unscented soap, wet her hands and rubbed the soap until she had a good lather going. Then she stepped into the shower. Ten minutes later, she stood in front of the closet which Brett had told her to put her things in. She selected a short, above-the-knee, black skirt and a black, one-shoulder top. The combination was perfect as she added black stockings and high-heeled black sandals.

She put the clothes on the bed, sat at the night table and carefully prepared her makeup.

She hadn't brought many clothes with her, but had chosen her color scheme well: red and black with a few multicolored scarves. Brett arrived as she was putting on the last of her makeup. She had her lipstick poised to put on the first coat, when Brett walked in the door.

He showered, shaved and changed to a navy Armani suit and met Nia in the living room. Then they were off to the theater. Nia loved the musical and told Brett she couldn't wait to add the CD to her collection.

They came home and made love.

# Eighteen

The next day, Nia decided to go shopping. She couldn't imagine anyone coming to New York and not doing any shopping.

At a Ralph Lauren shop she found stretch-canvas sailor slacks in bright red and a navy-and-white, off-the-shoulder top.

The she found a terrific boutique just off Fifth Avenue. The dresses in the window were sleek and sophisticated and she loved everything she saw, but she needed only one. Unlike the stories she had heard about lazy sales clerks, Nia found one who helped her find several dresses in her size.

After trying on five, Nia decided on a pink, spaghetti-strap gown with a diagonal hem.

Then it was off to find the accessories. She chose silver sandals and a tiny pink purse that could only hold mad money.

In another store, she found an elegant black dinner suit with a white scarf blouse. As she moved from store to store, she thought about her mother and their shopping trips. They were always painful. Her mother had been less than thrilled at being saddled with an energetic daughter and made that very clear. They were never close and most of the happy times she remembered were when she went shopping with Trisha, Alethia and her best friends.

Still, though she had a good time looking around and navigating the New York streets, she began feeling a little nostalgic for Los Angeles. It was a city that she felt she would always love.

They were going out again. She suspected that Brett just wanted to keep her busy. He hadn't told her where they were going, just hinted that it was some place fancy with a lot of history. She slipped on the black dinner suit.

Brett didn't get home until late and had to rush around the house to get ready. He selected a gray Armani suit, with a pearl gray shirt and black accessories. Moments later, they were in the limousine.

Her face registered shock when she realized they were at the fabled 21 Club—a restaurant that had gone from a speakeasy during prohibition to a class-A supper club.

Once you had needed a password to get through the doors. Now you needed to be famous in the world of show business or art or make reservations far in advance. Many stars ate here and many more people wanted the chance.

As they entered the room, Brett knew that all eyes were on Nia and he felt a surge of pride and a hint of jealousy.

Brett and Nia dined on oysters on the half shell, and seared gulf shrimp with black-eyed peas.

"So, now that I've left you alone a few times, are you afraid of the city?"

"Not anymore. But I wouldn't want to live here."

"Why not?"

"I think that every city has a heartbeat for someone. Mine is Los Angeles. I think yours is Casper."

"The ski lodge might not be in Casper."

"Maybe not, but can you say it won't be in Wyoming?"

Brett shook his head. "It will be in Wyoming. I can't deny that, but what happened to you? Why don't you like Wyoming?"

"You know my mother and I fought all the time. I spent more time with your family instead of mine. I loved my parents dearly but they were happy with their lives. I wanted something different."

"I fought with my father a lot and look how we turned it out."

"Sometimes I think it's different for a girl."

She paused and began eating her food. She had said too much. He might begin to read between the lines and she didn't want him to have that much information just yet. In fact, she wasn't sure she ever wanted him to know all about her.

"Come on, don't get philosophical on me."

"I just think that girls need those mother-daughter talks. I didn't have too many of them with my mother."

"What about the ones you want to have with *your* daughter?"

"I hope they are memorable, fun and that she accepts my advice, since I will be older and wiser."

Brett laughed. "What do you think you'll get?"

"A little brat who thinks the world revolves around her and I'll be frantic."

"So you want a little girl?"

"It might be nice, but a little boy can be just as good."

Brett smiled as images floated through his mind. Images of Nia being pregnant, images of them as a family. He wanted that for them. But how were they ever going to settle the logistics?

For him, everything they had done since they came to New York had been as if they were married. They lived in the same house, slept in the same bed and planned their lives together. He couldn't understand why that was the case in the city neither of them planned to live in forever.

# Nineteen

Brett called for the limousine while he was paying the bill. On the way out of the restaurant, they ran into Crystal again. She had her arm looped through the arm of a distinguished-looking man. She smiled and nodded to Brett, but the smile faded and her eyes sent daggers to Nia.

When they were in the limousine and on the way home, Nia asked him about the young woman.

"I went out with her a few times, but she got very possessive very quickly. I tried to keep it friendly, but she pushed for more before I was ready. It was an ugly breakup."

Nia knew that Crystal was out of his life and she would not return.

She was sleeping soundly when a clap of thunder made her bolt upright. She saw lightning flash and looked over at Brett. He was still asleep. Another powerful blast of thunder and she accidentally let out a scream. She wasn't usually afraid of thunderstorms, but she imagined being in a strange city may have influenced her.

The scream woke Brett up and he realized that

Nia was a little nervous. He pulled her into his arms and she put her head on his chest and drifted back into a relaxing sleep.


At eight the next morning, they were sharing a breakfast of freshly squeezed orange juice, croissants and several different marmalades.

The bell rang and Brett asked Nia to answer it.

"Nia Sebastian?" the delivery man asked.

"Yes."

"Please sign here." He held out his clipboard.

She signed and then the man handed her a dozen roses.

"Very cute," she said when she returned to the dining room. "Making me pick up my own flowers. Where can I put them?"

"Any place you choose." He handed her a vase with water, which he'd obviously gotten as soon as she went to answer the door.

Nia decided to keep the flowers in the bedroom and she placed them on a table where they would be the first thing she saw in the morning and the last thing at night. She knew they wouldn't last, but had a feeling they would be replaced before they died.

# Twenty

Nia received a call from Jesslyn Rush, who asked her if she'd like to come down to the shop. She jumped at the chance to learn more about Brett's life in New York.

"I have been meaning invite you out, but Palladin and I have a pretty full calendar."

"Thanks. I'll be there in a couple of hours."

When Nia got there, Lena was working on baskets and someone else was working the cash register. He was very different from the college kids that Nia had seen before. This man was incredible. His black hair was cut very close to his head and, when he smiled at a customer, Nia could see a dimple in his left cheek. His white shirt had the collar turned up and the top button was undone. When he stepped from behind the counter, Nia saw that his long legs were encased in tight jeans that hugged his muscular thighs. Before he returned to the cash register, she saw him stare at Lena for a long moment.

She smiled as she thought about it. Lena had a very handsome admirer.

Lena waved her over and they chatted for a moment before Jesslyn came out.

Then Nia and Jesslyn went outside the Empire State Building and had lunch.

"What was Brett like when he came to live with you?"

"A little bitter. No, I take that back. He was *very* bitter."

"What did you think of me?"

"At first I wondered where your brain was. How could you just leave that way? That lasted until the first day Brett was in my home. I realized that he was demanding too much from you. If you had stayed with him, I doubt if either of you would have grown if you hadn't been brave enough to go to California."

"I have been worried that Brett may have been difficult. . . ."

Jesslyn laughed. "No more so than his father or his uncle."

They talked a little more and Nia found herself wanting to belong to this family—but at what price? Would she be willing to give up her career in Los Angeles and reestablish it in Wyoming? Even after talking to Jesslyn, Nia didn't want to start over.

That night Nia and Brett decided to stay in and have a meal picked up from Sylvia's. After dinner, Nia said that if she didn't get some exercise besides shopping, she was going to weigh 200 pounds before they got back to Los Angeles.

They changed into sweat suits and headed for the second floor.

"Don't go on the machines," Brett said. "Let's work up a real sweat."

"On what?"

"This." He stepped across the room and pushed

open a panel to reveal a complete table tennis setup.

"Well, aren't you full of secrets?" Nia said as she picked up a paddle, twirled it in her hand and put it back. She continued the process until she chose her weapon.

"This is what I need," she told him.

They stood at opposite ends of the table and began. They played several games and didn't really keep score. The idea was to work up a sweat and get their metabolisms to burn off the calories.

# Twenty-one

The party was in full force by the time the limousine dropped Nia and Brett off. The Rushes were celebrating the new contract with the school program. They had added several new subjects to the school curriculum and although most of the students saw it as more work, the parents saw it as an improvement long overdue. Nia and Brett joined the other couples dancing in the living room.

As they danced, Brett thought about the first time he met Alethia. It was for the fund-raiser whose results they were now celebrating.

In attendance were several neighbors who were long-time friends of the Rushes. Brett pointed out the Rothsteins. He'd told her all about their son and his menagerie of exotic pets. The Rothsteins had been there for as long as Jesslyn. Hunter Rothstein was ten when he began collecting all sorts of weird animals. His worst pet was a boa which drove his mother crazy. Now, at twenty-four, he was the tall, blond hunk who had recently picked up his MBA and was surrounded by several young women vying for his attention.

"I love seeing kids grow up," Brett said.

There seemed to be an inexhaustible supply of

food, and the drinks ranged from soft beverages to strong liquor, which was closely guarded to make sure none of the underage crew got into it.

Later, as they mingled, Nia wanted to get away for a moment. She walked out on the balcony and found Lena Owens.

"Oh, I'm sorry. I—"

"Don't be sorry. You needed to get away from the crowd too?"

"Yes. I don't do well at parties. Weddings are fine, but parties scare me."

"Nia, I can't believe someone from Hollywood doesn't love to party."

"Well, I'm not from Hollywood and believe me Los Angeles is not all party."

"What do you do?"

"I'm a financial advisor, but right now I'm helping a friend as she takes over a bank."

Lena raised one eyebrow. "A bank?"

"Yes. She's going to own a bank."

"That's great. I never found out what I wanted to do until I had to take over the shop for Jesslyn. I found out I absolutely loved it."

They talked for a while until Brett popped his head out and sighed. "There you are. Have you been out here all this time?"

"All what time?" Lena asked. Then she glanced at her watch. "Oh, my God. We've been out here for two hours. I've got to find my date."

Brett shook his head. "He left an hour ago."

"Oh, no. I'll take the subway."

"No, you won't," Nia said. "We'll give you a lift, won't we?"

"Fortunately for you, Ms. Owens, you are one of my favorite aunts. Come on, let's go."

Lena handed Nia her business card. "Call me. We'll do lunch."

They waited until she was safely inside before heading to Brett's.

"You and Lena really hit it off."

"She's terrific. She's like the sister I never had."

The next day, Nia went to the Empire State Building by herself and had lunch with Lena. They sat in a booth, ate pizza and talked some more. Lena seemed to have answers for everything, or a flip remark that made Nia laugh. She knew that sooner or later, Daphne would regain her strength and they would be summoned back to California. But for now, she would enjoy her new friend.

Once Brett knew that Nia was comfortable traveling around by herself, he could take care of as much business as possible in the week they would be in New York. He was a bit surprised that it was Lena and not Jesslyn that Nia became friends with.

"I'm beginning to love New York," Nia told Lena. "Not that I would want to live here. Sorry, but I really love Los Angeles."

"I can't imagine living someplace where you need a car to do anything."

Four days in New York and something was going every night. No wonder they called it the "city that never sleeps," Nia thought.

# *Twenty-two*

Nia was surprised that she had bonded with someone who was so different from herself. She was meeting Lena for their last time, at least for a while. They were walking around the Empire State Building and decided to stop in at Border's Books Café.

They claimed a vacant table near the window, went to the counter and got coffee and scones. They sat at the table and looked out at the people scurrying about, as New Yorkers do.

"I want to ask a question," Nia said. "But I want you to know you don't really have to answer it."

"Honey, those are the questions that most need answers. Go for it."

"Why aren't you married or with a significant other?"

Lena stared out of the window for a moment and then turned to Nia. "I've been asked that before. Usually I respond with a line I heard in a movie. 'The last time someone asked me to marry him, I didn't know it was going to be the *last* time someone asked me to marry him.' See, it makes you laugh. It just doesn't tell you the truth. I would love to get married. I would love to even have a significant other. It's just that I won't settle for anything less than what I really want."

"Even if it means losing someone you love?"

"You can't be the only one in love in a relationship. If the man isn't going to meet you halfway, why should you do all the giving?"

"Depends . . ."

"Depends on whether you want to settle or be alone. Which doesn't always mean being lonely."

"Brett wants to have this great place in Wyoming, a resort. But I don't ever want to live in Wyoming again."

"Nia, now it's my turn to ask a question you don't have to answer. Why not?"

Nia bit her lip. "My parents were killed in a car accident. They were coming home one night and a drunk . . ."

"Too much pain."

"I . . . I was cleaning the house and I found some papers. Papers that I didn't know existed and never got to ask my parents about."

Lena waited until Nia had calmed down. "You don't have to tell me."

"Lena, please don't tell anyone. I found out that I was my father's child, but not my mother's."

"Oh, my God."

"My father had an affair with another member of my mother's tribe. She chose not to raise me and they made a deal."

"Are you going to tell Brett?"

"No. He'd just go off on a tear and try to find out all the information and truth. I don't want to know the truth."

"And you're afraid that living in Wyoming will change things for you."

"Totally. If I'm there, I'll keep remembering and I don't want to do that."

"I understand. As long as you stay away, you can even imagine they're still alive. My advice is to do what your heart tells you. Besides, men don't have to know everything."

Nia burst into laughter. She wiped her eyes with a napkin.

As she rode the train, she checked her cell phone and saw she had two calls from Alethia. That could only mean trouble. She'd call as soon as she got home.

When she walked in the door, Brett was waiting for her. He enveloped her in a big hug and a deep, passion-filled kiss.

"I thought you'd still be in D.C.," she told him.

"Hey, as soon as that deal was finished I hopped on a plane."

"I'm glad you did."

He kissed her again. Then she closed her eyes and slipped her arms around his waist.

"I got a call from Alethia on my cell, but she was fading out. So let me get back to her before—"

"She left a couple of messages on my phone also. Duty calls. I can guess that's going to be the reason."

Alethia seemed unsettled when they reached her. "Sorry, guys, it's time you came back to get this settled."

"You sound pretty anxious," Nia said.

"I think this is going to be quick and painless and then we can all go back to our real lives."

By the time Nia finished the conversation, she was feeling as good as Alethia.

They were lying across the bed. Brett pulled her

across his body until she was on top of him and Nia made a vow. She was going to enjoy every moment she spent with Brett and, when it was over, she would have known the best kind of love. Something that some people never experienced. She and Brett had been very careful no matter how they felt. Protection was second nature to them. If she got pregnant, it would take out all the possibilities. A child sounded good to her, but if she and Brett didn't stay together, that would not happen.

She forgot about everything else and just reveled in the kisses that Brett trailed across her face, her neck, as he gently stripped the clothes from her body. His fingers tracing the contours of her breasts, her rib cage before he took off his clothes and they lay together. He eased her legs apart and settled his body between them. It was an age-old dance they had done so many times and yet each time seemed like the first. Each time they learned something new. Something more they could please each other with. Nia moaned as he moved over her.

When the passion left, they were still holding tight to each other. But Nia wondered if passion was all they would ever share. They lay in the darkness for a long time before Nia spoke.

"Do you keep secrets from me?"

"Secrets? Like what?"

"Things that happened in your life. Bad things. Embarrassing things."

"Ah . . . probably."

"What if it was really important and I didn't tell you?"

"Honey, it's a fallacy that men want to know everything, the same way it's a fallacy that they want to tell you everything. Unless it's that you don't love me, I don't have to know. Now, that said, do I win the brass ring?"

"You win the whole ball of wax."

The morning they were leaving, Frank Cassidy came to see them. The man appeared to be more relaxed than the last time Brett had seen him. They were sitting in the living room, drinking coffee, when Frank began to talk.

"I need to talk to you about Alethia," he said. "I need to tell you about her life before she was a teacher.'

"I know about her past," Nia said. "She and her family didn't get along and they still don't talk."

"That's the story Alethia would have you believe," Frank said. "It was more than that with the Madisons. Alethia was a dreamer and her family were hardworking people who didn't believe in dreams. Alethia has a dark past. They couldn't understand and she retreated into a fantasy world. One of her teachers saw the promise and tried to talk to her family, to no avail."

"But she left anyway."

"Yes, with the help of the teacher she did. The teacher let her live with her, but the woman was sickly and died before Alethia graduated. That's why Alethia was a teacher and why she had favorites."

"So what's the dark past?"

"Alethia and Daphne decided that they needed rich husbands. They had plans to meet as many rich single men as Daphne's old crowd could produce. One of them got pregnant."

"One of them? You don't know which one?"

"She wouldn't tell me. Daphne married the rich man and when Jared was born, both Alethia and Daphne were together and hadn't been seen for months."

"Are you saying that Jared may be Alethia's son?"

"Yes. Or maybe not, but something happened when they went away. When they returned, they were very close until you married Jared. When you return to Los Angeles, get Alethia to tell you the truth. Secrets can only lead to trouble."

"We'll do what we can," Brett told him.

Frank left and a few hours later they were on the way to Los Angeles.

# Twenty-three

Nia and Brett had fallen into a pattern of trying to schedule business appointments at the same time so they could be home together. It seemed odd that Brett had only been back in California three weeks. She'd go out and meet her clients, and he and Kent would get together for strategy meetings. Since Jared's partners had pulled out, the dynamics had changed, but the scuffle went on.

Brett would check in with Ana Lisa to see how things were going, but the only iron he had in the fire was the ski lodge with the brotherhood of skiers. It would take them a few months with this deal. It was just too big and they wanted to cover all the bases as far as his business was concerned. He was still working with Kent to prevent the takeover.

Brett had whipped up a stir fry and a salad. They were sitting at the dining room table.

"How did you learn to cook this?"

"I took a course."

"Really. Why?"

"I just thought it would be fun."

"And?"

"You know me too well. I was seeing a woman who was taking the course."

The phone rang, and it was Alethia asking them to come to her house that night.

"She wants to talk to me, you and Jared. I don't think she wants Kent involved yet."

"I don't believe this," Brett said.

"Why not?"

"I think she has something that will blow up the deal or she's grasping at straws. In any case, she wouldn't involve Kent."

"Don't be so cynical. Miracles happen."

"Not this time. He's not going to give up on taking Kent's company. He's hellbent on revenge, and no one is going to stop him except a white knight." Although he didn't tell Nia, Brett had one trump card he could play. If it came down to it, that's what he would do.

"Are you sure you want to go to this meeting?" Brett asked. "This great movie is coming on tonight. I heard the review and I'd really like to see it."

"Tape it."

"Okay and we'll watch it later tonight. I hear it's very sexy and we might get some ideas."

Nia stood up and walked behind Brett's chair. You don't need any more ideas."

He turned and pulled her into his arms and held her for a moment. "You are making it very difficult for me. Let's call her and say we can't make it."

"I don't know why Alethia wants us all together. I trust her. Maybe she thinks that we can settle this and go on with our lives. I mean she is Jared's godmother."

"Well, let's get the show on the road." He released her, and they headed for the door.

It was easier to take Nia's car rather than Brett's. While the SUV covered a lot of ground, it would not fit in the parking spaces at Alethia's condo. That was true of most condo parking lots. The drive was short and for the most part silent. She and Brett didn't need to keep a conversation going anymore. That pleased her and frightened her at the same time. She was getting accustomed to being with him. She stretched out, put her head back on the headrest and closed her eyes.

Nia didn't want to say anything to Brett, but she was more than a little uneasy. She knew Jared's temper, but she also knew that if he lost control, Brett would stop him.

They were the first to arrive. Alethia opened the door and Nia gasped.

Alethia wore a black, form-fitting, knit dress that came to her knees. This was a very different woman from the one who had nurtured three young women through some rocky times.

"I feel under dressed," Nia said as she ran her hands down her jeans. "What's this all about?"

"I had to do a presentation for a couple of people and I've had this dress for ages."

"Give it up. You just want to look good for Brett."

"Stop being fresh."

The bell rang quickly several times.

"I'm calling it my peacemaking outfit. I think we can bury the hatchet." She hurried off to answer the doorbell.

"I just hope no one tries to bury the hatchet in my back," Brett whispered.

"Come on, behave."

Jared was the next person to arrive. He nodded

at Brett and Nia, but made no attempt to shake hands.

Nia didn't think it was starting well, but she was amazed at how they would all agree to listen to Alethia, even when they weren't even talking.

Jared pulled Alethia down the hall and turned his back on Brett and Nia. She assumed he was afraid they would be able to read his lips.

After he spoke with her, he went to the telephone. Nia assumed it was to tell his mother if it was safe to come in.

Alethia came over with an odd expression on her face. "I need to talk to you," Alethia said to Brett. "Let's go on the terrace."

Something delayed Alethia, and Brett went outside to wait for her. He stood in the dark and looked out onto the city. There was something about looking at a big city at night. The lights seemed to wash away all the dirt and crime and pain that most big cities held. Brett turned and stood in the shadows, watching Alethia's other guests. He watched as Jared leaned close to whisper something in Nia's ear. He didn't like the man as it was. The last thing Jared needed to do was make Brett angry enough to break up his little tête-à-tête. He watched Nia put her plate on the table and reach for a drink as Jared caught her hand. Brett opened the screen door but, by that time, Alethia was there, coming out on the terrace.

She followed his gaze. "Don't worry about that. I won't keep you too long."

He turned and stared at her. "I find that I'm very territorial where the lady is concerned."

"I've noticed that. I thought you two were *pretending* to fall in love."

"I never agreed to that little game plan of yours."

"Brett, what are you saying?"

"It's very simple. I'm going to marry the lady."

Alethia laughed out loud and her body shook. "Hot damn! When are you going to make the announcement?"

"There's one little thing that's in the way right now."

"Really, what's that?"

"I have to ask her and she has to say 'yes.'"

The doorbell interrupted them. Alethia opened the door and Daphne strolled in. She nodded to Brett and turned to Alethia.

Alethia laughed again. "Come on in. There's no sense in us making plans. You've already taken care of everything."

They walked off the terrace and found Jared had left Nia and was now waiting for Brett.

"I hear you've moved into my wife's house."

"She's not married to you."

"So you think you're pretty smart. You come here with your New York ways, telling everyone that you're going to get Hemmings out of this jam. Well, if you do, you can kiss that ski resort good-bye."

"What's that supposed to mean?"

"It means that you spread yourself too thin. I did some checking. You can't save Hemmings and join the consortium to buy that land in Wyoming."

Brett laughed. "You really shouldn't eavesdrop. You hear the wrong information and you do something foolish."

Jared was noticeably shaken. He had listened to Brett and Alethia and told his other partners that he didn't need them for this deal. They had already put their money elsewhere. "You bastard!" Jared yelled and lunged for Brett, who sidestepped him and let him fall on the floor.

Daphne rushed to her son's side. "Why did you attack my son? What kind of animal are you?"

Brett ignored her and went to Nia. She looped her arm around his waist and looked down at Jared. "What happened?"

"As if you didn't know," Jared growled.

"I don't understand." Daphne helped Jared to his feet.

"I'll tell you, Mother." Jared turned to her. "My sweet godmother and Nia's stud put on a show for me."

Brett started forward, but Nia tightened her arms around him. "Don't."

"I'm confused," Daphne said.

"It was all an act. I told you what I overheard. Alethia and Faulkner knew I was there. Now, I've got to hold on to Bryant with my own money."

Daphne's face crumpled, tears flowing down her cheeks as she approached Alethia. "How could you do that to him? He's your godson, for heaven's sake."

"I had to stop him. I tried to talk him out of it, but he wouldn't listen."

"So you hid and let him hear that conversation. So he could lose everything. Well, he's not going to. You think you're so smart, Alethia Madison. I'll show you how smart you are. If I have to sell my house, I'll see that Jared has the money to rip Bryant Electronics right out of Kent's hands."

"It's too late. You can't win this one."

"Yes, I—" Daphne's face paled. She clutched her heart. "My medication."

Nia ran to the sofa and got Daphne's handbag. Before she could open it, Jared snatched it away. He searched and found the bottle. Daphne put the pills in her mouth and slumped down to the sofa. After a few minutes, she was well enough to leave.

But as she reached the door, she turned to Alethia and said, "You will regret your betrayal. My son will win, and you will be very sorry."

Brett went along with the Schuylers to see if they needed any more assistance.

While he was gone, Alethia began to cry. "I couldn't let him destroy you."

"Are you okay?" Nia rushed over and threw her arms around Alethia. "I thought you two were friends again."

"We are, honey," Alethia said. "I'll call her tomorrow, and everything will be just fine. She's just angry because I . . ." Alethia wiped her eyes and began to laugh. "It's a little trick she played on me when we were in college. I guess it was so long ago she didn't remember."

Brett returned to find Nia and Alethia sitting on the sofa. He'd heard enough to know that there had been some kind of breach because he was helping Kent.

"What the hell was that about?" Brett asked.

"Nothing."

"Don't tell me nothing. I saw the look on both of your faces."

"Brett, please let me handle this. I'm a tough old crow. I don't care what Daphne says."

"Do you want me to stay a little while?" Nia asked.

"Absolutely not. Go on home. I've got some work to do."

Reluctantly, Nia and Brett left her alone.

"I feel so badly for her," Nia said. "She got all dressed up and was prepared to talk to you and Jared, but he's such a jerk. He wouldn't even listen to what she had to say."

"Then Daphne didn't help much. I hate to say this, Nia, but Daphne and Alethia are lying about something. I don't think she ever planned for us to sit down and talk. There is more to this than either of them is willing to admit."

Alethia stood by the window and watched them get in the car. As soon as she was sure they were on the way home, she picked up the phone and dialed.

"I'm really thinking of ending all of this turmoil. I'm warning you, Jared."

"Don't threaten me. I will take over Kent's company, and I will destroy Nia's reputation. It will be smooth and legal, and there's nothing you can do about it."

"That's where you're wrong. I can end everything." She slammed the telephone down. "Wait until tomorrow," she said aloud. She stormed into her bedroom and began stripping off her clothes. She stopped and pulled out her handbag and rifled through it. "Oh, no!" She put her clothes back on. "I know what I have to do."

She locked her condo and hurried to her car. She got in and gunned the motor. As she headed for the bank, she never looked in her rearview mirror to see that she was being followed.

Alethia arrived at the bank and the guard let her in.

"Can you believe I forgot the report I have to make comments on tomorrow?"

"I can understand you being nervous. I have to say, ma'am, I'm happy to see a strong black woman doing this. Perhaps some more of our people will take up the fight."

"I hope so. Don't worry about me. It will take me a few moments to do what I have to do. Just pretend I'm not here. I'll find you when I need you."

She went into her office and used her key to open the desk. Her office was still unfinished. They hadn't put in the security camera yet, but that would be done before the bank had its grand opening. As soon as the guard disappeared, she went to another cabinet and unlocked it. She pulled out a diskette, and breathed a sigh of relief.

"Gotcha! I thought I lost you. Can't give out the original, but this copy will do."

She glanced at her watch. Just a few more minutes.

# Twenty-four

After they left Alethia's apartment, Brett drove back to Nia's. He kept glancing in his rearview mirror. He couldn't shake the feeling that they were being followed. The only person he could think of was Jared. Alethia was wrong. She said that Jared wanted to hurt Nia but didn't want her back.

Brett knew he did. He remembered how Jared stood silently with his arms folded across his chest. He'd only stepped forward when he realized his mother was sobbing from Alethia's verbal attack. He was impressed by Alethia's smooth way of handling Daphne Schuyler.

"Your mentor is quite a woman," Brett said. "I told her I was going to marry you."

"You aren't serious." Nia laughed. "I can't believe you told Alethia you were going to marry me."

"I told *you* we were getting married." He smiled at the memory of standing in the rain and watching her face when he said it. He'd told his father it would be something outrageous. He didn't know where it came from, but it had worked.

"I have never seen such arrogance. I had half a mind to make you really suffer and then tell you

I wasn't interested in you anymore," she told him.
"I tried to make you jealous."

"You think you didn't?" he asked in mock horror.

"Not nearly enough. I crumbled."

"You made me beg."

"Good for me." Nia had never been in control
of a relationship. When she and Brett were partners, he called the shots. She always let the situation get to the point where she ran. She'd run
from Brett, and she ran from Jared.

They were home. She had a fleeting thought to
call Alethia. Brett may have been fooled by the
tough talk, but she knew there was a lot of pain
behind the outburst. She would call her in the
morning.

She stepped from the car and felt as if she'd
been struck. The heat was so fierce she thought of
it as a physical barrier. The weatherman said there
was a storm brewing, but so far there was no sign
of the rain needed to reduce the temperature.
They'd had a couple of brief showers that day, but
that only made the heat worse.

They went inside and Nia turned to him "Are
you going back to check the street?"

"What do you mean?"

"All the way home, you checked the mirror as if
you're looking for someone." Nia stepped toward
him. "What is it?"

"I didn't want to say anything." He was annoyed
with himself for being so obvious. "I got the feeling
someone was following us."

"Are you going to check the street?"

He nodded. He went out the back, and Nia stood in the doorway watching him. He returned with a sheepish look on his face. "Nothing. How safe are the locks on your doors?"

"Extremely. I knew once people saw a single woman coming and going from this house, I would become a target. I took a self-defense class, not that I remember anything, and I learned about locks." She closed the door and flipped the door guard over.

"Were you afraid of anything in particular or anyone?"

Nia looked down and away. She shook her head. Brett didn't push the issue. Instead, he looked at the clock. "Hey, we're in time for that movie."

She welcomed the subject change. "I set the VCR."

"Now we don't have to waste the tape." He went into the living room and turned on the TV.

He stretched out on the sofa. Nia joined him. She sat down and leaned against his chest. During the first fifteen minutes, they laughed at almost every line.

"I can't believe this," Nia said. "I thought it was supposed to be so dramatic."

"That's the last time I trust a fill-in critic."

"Fill-in?"

Brett shook his head. "She was filling in for the regular reviewer."

"She?"

"Come on, Nia, are you saying that I took her advice because she was pretty?"

"Was she?"

"A little."

"Then, Brett, I am saying that you took her advice because she was pretty. I'm glad I didn't waste my tape."

They tried to find something else, but nothing interested them. They were trying to decide whether they should go to bed or look at a tape from her video collection when the doorbell rang.

Nia looked at Brett and shrugged. He pulled the curtain back and then opened the door. Two men came into the living room. There was something about them that said "cop." Then they introduced themselves as detectives.

Brett identified himself and felt his blood run cold as he looked at their stern faces.

"We're looking for Nia Sebastian."

Brett stepped aside and the detectives came into the living room and looked around. Brett introduced Nia.

"Ms. Sebastian, we are working on a homicide case."

"What's this about?" Brett asked.

"Are you a close friend of Ms. Sebastian?"

"Yes, I am."

"She may need you. We have some bad news." The policeman turned to Nia.

Brett moved to her side and caught her hand.

"There was a robbery at the Freedom's Song bank."

"But we aren't even opened yet," Nia said.

"Someone must have thought when the safe was installed this morning that money was in it."

"Does Alethia Madison know?" Nia asked him.

The look on the detective's face told it all.

"Was she hurt? Can I see her?"

"I'm sorry, ma'am."

The she remembered. They were working on a homicide. "What happened? We just left her."

"You were at the bank?"

Brett stepped closer to Nia. "No. We had a meeting with Alethia at her apartment about two hours ago," she said.

"Did she say she was going to the bank?"

"No." Tears began to stream down her face. "We weren't supposed to meet until tomorrow."

The detectives began to question them about Alethia, their friendship with her and her enemies.

As the truth dawned on her, Nia began to scream. Then she collapsed. She would have certainly hit the floor, but Brett swept her into his arms.

"I'm sorry, ma'am. Ms. Madison was found by a security guard who was making his regular rounds. She had been beaten to death with a blunt instrument."

"Oh, my God. Oh, no. Oh, no."

She held on to Brett and sobbed.

"How could someone get in the bank?" Brett asked.

"Apparently Ms. Madison opened the door. She was obviously expecting the person. There was no sign of a struggle. The meeting took place when the security guard was in another part of the building. He says there was no noise."

"That makes you think that she wasn't afraid?" Brett asked.

The next few days were blurs to Nia. She functioned. She made the calls to Julie and Bree. She accepted condolences. She went through her normal routine during the day, but at night she cried in Brett arms.

Frank Cassidy flew in from New York. He was not only Alethia's lawyer, he was her friend, and this left him in a state of shock. He had spoken to Alethia earlier the day of the murder and she seemed really happy with her life.

Julie had flown in from Paris to be with Nia and Bree. The three women clung to one another for support. Fortunately for them, Alethia had all of her papers together. The police took as much evidence as they could.

"She didn't want to be a problem and you were like her daughters," Frank told them. Once the newspapers reported the circumstances of Alethia's death, Nia's phone began to ring. Charlotte handled the calls.

Students turned out in force. They were shocked by the reports that she was beaten with a blunt object. Nia, Julie and Bree handled everything. Brett was never more than a whisper away. For Nia, it was an excruciating loss. Alethia had become her second mother. Alethia was someone whom she could depend on. Someone who was always there. Now she would never share anything with her again.

The police had questioned as many people as they could. But Brett knew that every day that passed without an arrest was a sign that the crime would not be solved. Of course, the people who confessed to every crime came into the precinct with elaborate stories of what had happened. Then the rumors started. Alethia Madison must have borrowed money from the mob or a loan shark and couldn't pay.

Before the funeral, Brett started getting up early and going to get the paper before Nia saw it. He perused it while she slept. When she awakened, he would tell her to avoid reading the paper if it held something that would hurt her.

The day of the funeral there was so much coverage. Nia, Julie and Bree were as much family as Alethia had. Nia held on to Brett, Julie held on to Jack. Bree had someone holding her hand, but Nia didn't get a chance to meet him. When they walked away from the grave site, he was gone.

Daphne came to the funeral, her face covered with a thick black veil. She hugged each woman. Jared was by her side and the florist had delivered a huge wreath from the church.

Daphne took Nia's hand. "This is why you shouldn't fight. Now we won't have a chance to make up. Call me if any of you need help," she said and disappeared into the crowd.

That night, Nia received a call from one of the detectives. He had heard about the statement Daphne made and wanted to know about the fight. Nia told him it wasn't important, but he insisted. She told him the whole story. He thanked her and said he'd call back when he got something concrete.

Nia dropped the receiver in the cradle and turned to Brett. "Do you think he's really going to question Daphne over a spat?"

"They're probably grasping at straws, but you never know. Jared came close to threatening her."

"I didn't tell him about the threat, just about the argument."

As Frank requested, Nia had arranged for a meeting in her office the day after the funeral. The lawyer began by announcing that Alethia's brother had been contacted, but showed no interest in the will. Since they weren't close, he wasn't expecting anything.

Nia couldn't understand that. She knew that Alethia and her brother were at odds over her marriage. She'd married his best friend and then when she filed for divorce, he had taken his friend's side and portrayed his sister as money hungry.

The result was that they gave her husband the divorce on the countersuit and she'd been left with no means of support. She'd found a job and lived in a room while she saved every penny she made. Someone she worked with bragged about the government grant her son had received for education and Alethia spent hours in the library and on the telephone until she found a program that covered her.

She applied and waited for months before getting the word that she had been accepted into a program that helped only if you became a teacher and accepted a position at an inner-city school for two years. After graduation, she spent her time in one of the toughest neighborhoods in California.

After two years, she'd moved to a private school and finally she'd worked her way into Stanford. It was there, she had her first taste of spending money. She no longer had to scrimp. She laughed when she told Nia how she'd piled on the pounds. She didn't care. Every time she looked in the mirror, she didn't see fat. She saw success. That's what she always said when Bree complained about her own weight.

Only Nia knew the story of her divorce and she'd

promised never to reveal it to anyone. That had created a special bond between them.

Nia, Bree and Julie listened to Frank and were astonished. Alethia had managed to build a net worth of almost one million dollars. She owned an apartment building, a house in Hawaii that she kept strictly as a rental property, numerous stocks, bonds and other property. The jewelry they all thought were paste copies was real. She left that to Bree, who had always admired it and the house in Hawaii. Nia had inherited the rest of the property. Julie got the stocks and bonds. Just to make sure that her brother didn't cause any trouble, Alethia left him one dollar. It would take them weeks before they would have everything sorted out.

The women went into the restroom and they were still in a state of shock. Alethia had never given them any reason to believe she was so successful. She couldn't use her personal fortune to fund the bank and they wouldn't be able to use it either. She couldn't take the risk of losing everything at this stage in her life.

They returned to Nia's office with red eyes, still sniffling. Brett had come to take them home. He'd been acting as their chauffeur, since he knew they did not belong behind the wheel of a car.

"Once you leave this room," Frank told them, "the will becomes public. It may also bring scrutiny to your finances. You were very close to Alethia and some will say that you knew about her wealth."

"You mean someone will think one of us killed her for the money?" Julie asked incredulously.

"All or one of you will be suspected."

That was almost more than Nia could bear, but she knew it was true. If someone was murdered, the police had to see if the money mattered too much to someone.

"What can we do?" Bree asked.

"Nothing, I'm afraid. The police will either find the person or leave the case open and go on to the next case."

# Twenty-five

Nia awoke early the next morning. She couldn't believe that she had gotten through the night without waking up in a cold sweat. Each time she would pray that it had been a dream, but it would all come back to her. The detectives, the media, the funeral and she would know it wasn't a dream.

Each time she had done that she'd cried into her pillow for several minutes before she pulled herself together and faced the day. Nia would then fling her arms and legs out and stretch across her king-size bed.

It may have been a fragment of her ruined marriage. She and Jared had shared a full-size bed and he always wanted to hold her as they drifted off to sleep. She'd felt suffocated and believed that was the first chip in their marriage. As soon as she bought this house, she had ordered two king-size beds. She imagined Brett was glad she'd done that since he'd slept in the guest room for the past two nights. His large frame certainly needed that much room.

All that had been said at the funeral was true. You had to take it day by day and the pain would lessen. She'd gone through this same thing when her parents had been killed. The pain did fade, but never completely. She knew that for the rest of her life there would be times when she'd wish that her parents or Alethia were there to share something important in her life. She had to accept that they would only be there in spirit.

Nia was grateful that Brett was still here. Julie had returned to Paris and Bree was in New York for a few weeks before she had to go back to Hawaii to finish her job. She felt alone in one of the most densely populated cities in America.

Nia finished her stretching exercises and went into the bathroom to take a shower. She slipped into her terry-cloth robe and went to see if Brett was awake. She found a note in his large scrawl. He had gone to get breakfast.

"Terrific. I didn't feel like cooking anyway," she said aloud. She returned to her bedroom and dressed leisurely. She still chose muted colors. Today she wore all gray—even down to gray lingerie with her gray, mid-calf dress. Nia sensed that any bright color worn too quickly after Alethia's funeral would find its way into the newspaper and make it appear she no longer grieved for her friend.

She had to admit that Brett was getting to her. When he had first arrived the night of Julie's wedding, she pushed him away, but he kept coming back. Alethia kept telling her what a good man he was and that she shouldn't let him get away a second time. Nia still wasn't sure if they were right for each other. She was a very different woman from the partner he once knew.

She heard the bell and thought it was Brett and opened the door to a barrage of reporters. The cameras flashed and she tried to close the door, but someone was leaning against it.

"What are the plans for the bank now that you're in charge, Ms. Sebastian?"

"Weren't you married to Jared Schuyler? Why did you break up?"

"Was Alethia Madison afraid for her life? Did she say anything to you?"

From the rear of the crowd, she heard Jared's voice yelling at the reporters to stop harassing her.

Suddenly the reporter who had been grinning at her as the others asked the questions was yanked off his feet and landed on the steps. Brett Faulkner had muscled his way to the door and now pulled it closed with Nia on the inside and him on the outside.

"Ms. Sebastian doesn't have anything to say. I suggest you get off her property before she calls the police."

"She's news and we have a right to ask questions. Who are you?" a man yelled.

"I'm the man who will break every bone in your body if you don't get off this property, now." Brett's voice was low, but he meant every word and the reporters knew it. She could hear them grumbling as they left, but they knew they were the ones who would be in trouble if the police were called. They were trespassing the minute they had opened the gate and come to her door.

Then she heard Brett say, "It's okay, Schuyler. I'll take care of her."

In the next motion he had opened the door, and entered the house. Nia impulsively hugged him.

He handed her a plastic bag with several foil-covered, take-out plates. "What was that all about?"

"I opened the door without checking." She waited for his reprimand.

"So those reporters were just waiting for you.

Damn! I should have seen that coming. I'll take care of it."

"You aren't going to mention that I shouldn't have opened the door without looking?"

"I wasn't, but since you brought it up, why don't you have a chain on that door?"

"I've been meaning to get one, but then I wanted to wait until I finished redecorating the living room—"

"Don't wait. Get the chain today. Never mind. I'll do it."

"Did I hear Jared out there?"

"Yeah, he was behind the reporters, trying to get through by being polite. I just put on my New York attitude and they let me through."

"Did he leave?"

"I guess so. Let's eat."

Jared Schuyler was two blocks away with the reporter Brett had pulled away from the door. The man was not a happy camper.

"You told me all I had to do was act like a reporter and keep her from closing the door. You didn't say nothing about the incredible hulk showing up." He rubbed his rib cage.

"Shut up. Here's your money. Take it and get out of my sight."

"I oughta get double."

Jared grabbed the man by his tie and pulled him down so they were face-to-face. "Don't press your luck. You didn't complete the assignment. I was supposed to be the hero of the day."

He held the tie until the man began to choke and then released him. He threw the money on

the ground and walked back down the street toward Nia's house.

"Man's crazy. This is the last time I'll believe a
guy who says I can make easy money." He snatched
the money from the ground and ran down the
street to his car.

Moments later, Jared rang the bell. He waited
and rang it again. He was about to press down for
the third time when Brett opened the door.

"I want to see Nia."

"Sure." He stepped back and Jared charged into
the room.

Nia was coming out of the kitchen. "Hi, Jared,
I heard you trying to help with those reporters.
Thanks. You aren't the type to get physical with
those people. You were kind of a fish out of water."

"I'm more of a ram in fish clothing," he said and
laughed at a joke only he understood. "I thought
you might need something. . . ."

"Don't worry, Schuyler. I've got it covered. Come
on, Nia. I'll follow you, just in case those people
show up again."

Jared could do nothing else. He watched them
leave and then went to his car. He'd get Nia back.
He had to have her back. He didn't care what his
mother said about her. No one left until he decided it was over. Alethia wasn't around now to
hold that little diskette over his head.


By the end of the day, Nia Sebastian had made
up her mind. She was going to tell Brett he could
go back to New York or Wyoming or anywhere but
stay here. She was becoming a magnet for danger

and she was afraid something would happen to him.

She sat behind the desk at the bank and ran her fingers down the schedule for the building to be finished. They had lost a few days because of Alethia's murder. Nia didn't intend to lose any more. She had to keep things together.

"Ms. Sebastian, we've had a few people who were going to be tellers resign," Charlotte explained. "So I had them put another ad in the paper. I don't think we'll have trouble replacing them. It's the training that will be the problem."

Many days, Nia thanked her lucky stars for a secretary like Charlotte. As soon as things were settled, she was going to mover her up to "administrative assistant." She didn't want to lose her. She'd graduated from Howard in D.C. and had come west to seek her fortune. She'd audited a couple of Alethia's classes and when the jobs were posted, she jumped at the chance. Nia considered herself lucky to have her around.

Two hours later, Charlotte stopped by to say good night.

"Don't worry if you see my car in the parking lot tomorrow morning. If I work too long, I'll stay at a hotel."

"I'm glad you'll stay at a hotel, but you've got to stop pushing yourself or you'll get sick."

"I just have to get through this week and then most of the hard stuff is done and we all can take it easy."

"Good night."

"Good night, Charlotte."

The workmen had resumed the project everywhere but in Alethia's office. They were going to leave that for last. When Nia had suggested it, she could tell the men were thinking along the same lines.

So many times during the day Nia wanted to run an idea by Alethia or ask her to pick a restaurant for lunch. She hadn't realized how much of her life involved her mentor.

Now she had to fight off those urges and remember she didn't have her mentor's guidance anymore. She just kept working until she was exhausted. As people stopped by to say good night, she had been working for twelve hours. Her eyelids were heavy and she knew she shouldn't get behind the wheel of her car. Tonight she was so tired she planned to stay in a hotel rather than go home.

She'd done this before and always carried a change of clothes in her car. She locked up and headed toward the parking lot. She smiled as she saw the Excursion parked next to her car.

As she approached, Brett opened the door and stepped out. All her plans to tell him to leave vanished. He was simply not a man who would run anyway.

"How long have you been waiting?"

"Since three. I thought you were keeping bankers' hours?"

"Those no longer exist."

"I figured you were pretty tired this morning and you shouldn't be driving. I'll give you a lift."

"Thanks. I was planning to stay in a hotel."

"Now you won't have to. Do you need anything out of the car?"

"Not anymore."

Brett came around to the passenger side and helped Nia get in the SUV. She stretched out her legs. It felt so good to be able to do that. She leaned back and closed her eyes.

They were halfway to her house when Brett spoke. "You're burning the candle at both ends."

"It's been very busy and I need it right now."

"You don't need to push too much. I'm sure Alethia covered everything."

Nia laughed. "You only knew her for a short time. How can you say that?"

"Believe me. She didn't come across as a woman who left anything to chance."

That was such a true observation. After Alethia's death, Nia was given her schedule and she was amazed at how many details it took to open a bank. The book was very detailed, but Nia wanted to make sure each item had been taken care of.

Nia kept her eyes closed for what she thought was a moment and the next thing she knew they were parked in front of her house.

"Where are your keys?"

She fumbled in her purse and then handed them to him. She waited while he inspected the house. Then he returned and lifted her down. She was groggy from lack of sleep. He held her as she walked because she was so sleepy her legs wouldn't function. When he reached the door, he lifted her into his arms and carried her into the house. She wrapped her arms around his neck to keep from falling.

Brett wondered if anyone in the neighborhood saw them and if it would look like they had just gotten married and he was carrying her over the threshold. He had to admit she felt wonderful like this. She trusted him again.

\* \* \*

Jared schuyler sat in his car, watching them. He slammed his fist against the steering wheel. He'd been so sure that Nia would come back to him if Alethia were out of the way. She was a rotten blackmailer and had gotten what she deserved. But instead of Nia running to him, Alethia had made sure that Brett Faulkner was back in her life. He knew they'd been partners, but now he was sure it was much more. Something that Nia had never told him about. He didn't care. He'd find a way to ease Faulkner out of the picture and then she'd have to turn to him for protection.

He drove home and was surprised to find his mother was still awake.

"Where have you been?" she asked.

"I went by Nia's to see if she needed anything."

"Did she?"

"I don't know. Brett Faulkner brought her home."

"Why do you keep running after her? She divorced you two years ago and she hasn't looked back."

"Alethia caused that. She never let us work through our problems. She just kept giving Nia a place to stay."

Daphne Schuyler shook her head. "Give it up, son. She's not the woman for you."

"I can't let her go. I'm going to bed."

Daphne sat on the sofa with her head in her hands. She'd tried so hard to keep the family name and the inheritance. Alethia had almost taken that away from them. Now if she could just make Jared see he was too good for Nia. He deserved someone who loved him. Someone who liked being a wife and wasn't interested in a career. In her day, it

would have been easy to find a woman who wanted
to care for a man, his house and his children. Now
women said they wanted to have their own money.
When she'd married into the Schuyler fortune, her
mother had danced for joy.

Once they were inside, Brett put Nia down and
held her for a moment until she got her bearings.

"Are you going to be able to get ready for bed
without help?"

"Yes. I'm just a little out of it. I'll be fine."

"I'll wait."

She was too tired to argue with him. She went
into the bathroom, removed her makeup and took
a lukewarm shower. Then she found a nightgown
and crawled into bed. As she fell asleep, she wondered if Brett would just take the guest room or
sleep on the sofa. She knew he was not going to
leave her.

Brett locked up and then found her best brandy.
He poured himself a shot and took it into the guest
room. He was getting used to sleeping here. Tomorrow he would just move in and see what she
said. She needed someone to watch over her. His
plan was to drop her off at work and then check
out of his hotel. If he moved in with her, he could
watch her more carefully. He wished he'd had his
uncle's training. Palladin Rush had been with the
Secret Service and would have picked up on things
that he had missed.

He took a shower, stretched out on the bed and
sipped the brandy. He set the glass down on the
table and the last thing he remembered was telling
Nia he needed a TV in his room.

\* \* \*

The next morning, Brett awoke to the smell of breakfast. He showered, dressed and then went into the kitchen.

Nia smiled at him. "Hello, sleepyhead."

"What time is it?"

"A little after six."

"How could you be so bubbly with such little sleep?"

"I don't know. I just am. Sit down. I'll fix you a plate."

He watched as she took a large plate from the china closet and loaded it up with bacon, eggs and grits. This had always been a comfort meal for them.

Nia was not a bad cook. He was surprised at how easily she moved around and prepared the meal.

"I've been thinking," she said. "You've been here more than you've been at your hotel. Why don't you just move in with me?"

Brett stared at her. "Move in with you?"

"Come on, we're old friends."

He couldn't believe he'd wasted time planning to move in and being ready for any kind of resistance from Nia. Now she was making the suggestion. He knew she wasn't talking about in the same bed, but he felt that once he got into the house, that would be easy.

"Why?"

"Because you will follow me everywhere anyway and if you live here, you won't have to make up any excuses for popping up every place I go."

"You think I'm following you?"

"A couple of times I almost caught you, but you disappeared behind something."

A cold chill spiked through Brett. He hadn't followed her, but someone had. He didn't want to alarm her and tell her the truth. He just let her think he was always around. Now he would be.

"I'm going to act as your bodyguard. I'll drive you to work, pick you up and I think we should go out to dinner a lot."

"That would give people the impression that you and I were . . . involved."

"So what? If you find Mr. Right, he can take over bodyguard duties."

"Yeah, right!"

Within days they had developed a routine they could both agree on. Brett didn't stay so close that she felt overwhelmed. She was grateful for the company.

# Twenty-six

Alethia was gone. The funeral was brief—as she
would have wanted it to be. The will was filed with
the probate court. Nia had made a decision about
her life. She and Brett would have to put their
budding relationship on hold. She had to complete Alethia's work.

She felt as if she was in the same position as
Trisha Terrence Faulkner. Brett's stepmother had
refused to marry Kaliq because of a dream she
wanted to fulfill. She'd purchased the bed-and-
breakfast and was doing nicely until her partner's
gambling destroyed the business and put her life
in peril. Four years had passed before they finally
got together.

She and Brett had already squandered time on
their individual careers. She didn't know if their
relationship could handle another crisis. How long
could she expect him to wait until her life was
right? He had his future planned. The ski lodge
would take years to become what he wanted. She
wanted to be with him when that happened, but
she wasn't naïve enough to think that Brett was
going to wait around while she got her life straight-
ened out. She could also hear her biological clock

ticking. How long could she wait to have a family? She was afraid if she asked him to wait he would say no. Now she was like an ostrich, putting her head in the sand and pretending everything was fine. If she could get the bank out of the way, she'd concentrate on what she wanted, a life with Brett.

Nia was torn between the love she felt for Brett and her duty to Alethia. She had so many things to do in her life, but she knew that in a weak moment she might give it all up for Brett and maybe regret it later. However, she could never walk away from Alethia's dream. She had to finish it. She just prayed that Brett would understand.

Alethia had given her so much. She wanted to do this single thing. Once the bank was up and running, she could think about her personal life. Unfortunately it might not include Brett. He had made it clear that he thought she should come back to Wyoming with him. She had no doubt she could get a job there, but somewhere in the back of her mind she knew it would make her miserable. It wasn't about a job. It wasn't about her feelings for Brett. It was about what made her feel alive. Wyoming wasn't her home anymore. Los Angeles had replaced it.

Nia had agreed with Kent's suggestion that she not stay in her home and had considered moving to a hotel. The murder was too fresh and the media was still hungry for anything that would sell newspapers. They would certainly camp out at her house waiting for her to leave for work or come home and then pounce on her. She needed time to concentrate. Theories were already popping up about the murder. One paper quoted an unidentified source as saying Alethia had fired someone and he swore revenge. Another paper printed it was just a random act of violence, and still another had another unidentified source claiming Alethia borrowed money from the mob and couldn't pay it back. It was putting the focus on the wrong things. The bank was for the neighborhood and that was who would benefit. That was why Nia had to see it through.

Brett tried to shield her but snippets filtered through. One day, Lisabeth Hemmings called her.

"Kent says you shouldn't stay in the house with all those reporters around. I was thinking that you might need to get away, and we have the house in Malibu. It's a fixer-upper, but you can stay there for a couple of months."

Nia laughed. She'd avoided Lisabeth because of the way she tended to rattle on, but the offer said there was more to the woman behind the blond-bombshell looks and the fact she could combine several sentences in one breath. Now Nia understood what Kent saw that everyone else had missed. He saw Lisabeth's soul and that's what he fell in love with. Nia promised herself she would get to know Lisabeth better.

Brett had helped her move some of her things to the beach house. She left her car in her driveway one morning and took a cab to work. She entered her office building and went straight out the back where Brett was waiting. He drove her to Malibu.

Kent had just purchased the house from a business associate. The Nilssons were moving to London and in the process of selling the house to Kent. Lisabeth wanted some renovations, so nothing had been changed. The furnishings in the house belonged to the Nilssons.

They had all of the furniture they wanted to keep shipped to London and the only things they left were a couple of twin beds in one of the bedrooms and a huge breakfront in the living room.

Nia had brought clothes, bedding, curtains and her computer. She didn't know how long she was going to stay. The wonderful thing about the house was when she opened the front door she saw straight through to the ocean. The first night she'd stayed there, she'd drifted off to sleep listening to the waves being tossed against the rocks. The next morning, she'd run on the beach until she was exhausted and then showered and fallen asleep. She was awakened by the doorbell. The house was dark, and she had to think for a moment about where she was. She found the switch on the lamp and managed to get to the door. She opened it to find Brett standing there with a bottle of champagne.

"What happened? I was about to kick the door in."

"Sorry, I fell asleep."

She saw flickers of passion in his eyes and looked down. She was wearing a blue-silk sleep shirt that was semi sheer.

"What time is it?"

"Just past seven."

"Seven! Oh no. I've been sleeping the whole day."

"Calm down. Your body needed it."

"I was tired. Now I'm hungry."

"I can fix that," Brett said.

He handed her the champagne and went back to his SUV. When he returned, he was carrying a large picnic basket.

"I think this has everything we need," he said as he handed it to her.

While he was gone, Nia had run into the bedroom and was wearing a robe that covered her completely. She took the basket in the kitchen and put it on the counter. When she opened it, she knew it was one of those specialty baskets that some restaurants prepare. It had a delicious meal for two, along with silverware.

"Let me freshen up and you set the table."

She darted from the room and Brett went to work. When she returned, she saw china, silverware and a dinner of Cornish hens, baked potatoes and apple pie. *If only this could last forever,* she thought. Brett left after dinner, telling her to go straight to bed. She did just that and slept through the night.

At eight the next morning, Brett showed up with breakfast in tow. Nia set up a schedule and whatever she completed, she would give to Brett and he would drop it off at the bank. Charlotte would put it in circulation and call Nia with any feedback or questions.

She'd been at the beach house for a week and Brett had called on her every morning and every night. He hadn't questioned Nia when she told him she wanted him to give her space.

"If you need me to stay just ask," he'd told her. He hadn't pushed. He'd just show up to bring her breakfast or dinner. It became a routine, and she was torn between wanting to get back to her own house and yet having so much fun working at the beach.

Brett had arrived for breakfast and after they'd eaten, he'd gone for a walk on the beach. Nia worked on the bank project. The project worksheet had been changed and she needed the newer version. She'd called Charlotte but, after a thorough search, they came to the same conclusion. Alethia had taken the disk home with her. As much as she dreaded doing so, Nia would have to go to Alethia's condo and get the disk.

She walked out onto the lanai. A tiny, white, wrought-iron fence surrounded the space. The furniture had been removed and since she wasn't going to be there much longer, Nia had no plans to replace it. That would be Lisabeth's job.

The thought of Lisabeth communicating with a decorator brought a smile to Nia's face. She could imagine some poor soul trying to stop Lisabeth's chatter so they could get the information they would need to transform the place. Nia liked it. It was an older structure that probably wouldn't meet building code standards now, but had been spared nature's wrath. The Nilssons were selling it because the last storm had done some damage to it, but Kent felt that once it was brought up to code, they would be secure. They were moving to London and didn't want to rebuild.

She looked up the beach and saw Brett. He'd run for a mile and was now walking back to the house. She could see his white shirt blowing in the breeze. It was open to the waist, showing off washboard abs. His red biker shorts revealing strong, muscular legs and thighs. He could be a pinup for any of the body-building magazines.

A couple of young women in very brief bikinis passed him and when he couldn't see them, both turned to take a good look at him. The young women probably thought he was in films. Most of the residents in this area were actors or directors.

Malibu seemed to attract them like a huge magnet. A beach house was also a symbol of success. And while many in the movie community owned houses, few got to enjoy them year round. They had other houses or apartments that were an easier commute to the studios.

Brett came up the stairs of the lanai and stood next to her.

"It's very nice."

Nia laughed. He was the only one she knew who could call a cottage on the beach in Malibu "nice."

"I guess so."

He could sense her mood change. "What's the matter?"

"I need something from Alethia's apartment."

"Do you want me to pick it up for you?"

She smiled. "I wish you could. It's the project worksheet and I would have to see it to make sure it's the last version."

"Do you want me to go with you?"

"Yes, I just . . ." Her eyes filled with tears and though she tried to fight it, one slipped down her cheek. "It's so unfair."

"The police will solve the case. It just may take awhile."

"Maybe. She was so close to her dream. In just a few days she would have opened the bank and . . ."

Brett took her in his arms. "I know, honey."

He knew that once Alethia's dream had been completed and she was running her bank, Nia would be free. Now they didn't know if the other people involved believed enough to keep the bank open until it became a fixture in the community.

He also knew that Nia's role had changed from supporter to the one spearheading the project.

"When would you like to leave?"

"Give me half an hour," she said.

While Nia was dressing, she decided to swing by her house and pick up some more clothes. She'd stay just another week in Malibu and then she would go to Alethia's place and get it ready. She couldn't live there and neither could Bree. She would sell it and set up a scholarship fund in Alethia's name.

She made a mental note to call Bree, who had gone back to her assignment in Hawaii, and Julie, who was back in Paris, and get their feedback and support.

Twenty minutes later, she walked into the living room and found that Brett was waiting on the lanai. He'd changed to a lightweight, beige-pinstripe suit. Living in New York meant seeing the seasons change and he obviously had to have a wardrobe to accommodate those changes. Since he'd driven from Wyoming, he could afford to bring more clothing than if he'd traveled by plane.

His long, black hair glistened in the sunlight. It flowed loosely around his shoulders as he brushed it.

"Need a hair dryer?"

"No, it's dry now. Usually after a shower, I have to use a dryer, but out here the sun took care of it."

He pulled a brush through his hair and with a seasoned move captured all the strands in a pony-tail and twisted a band around it. He tossed the brush in the duffle bag he kept in his SUV. Whenever he drove to Malibu, he brought a duffle bag and garment bag, just in case she asked him to stay. It was always best to be prepared.

It took them just under an hour to reach Alethia's apartment. Nia handed Brett the key and he opened the door and stepped inside. Nia followed him and flipped the switch by the door. Bright light flooded the apartment. The curtains were still drawn and everything was pretty much as Alethia had left it. The police had made a cursory search, not really looking for anything that changed their theory of a random act of violence. One of the detectives had passed out his business cards and suggested they call him if they had any evidence to the contrary.

The living room and dining room had been turned into a library. Alethia's tremendous collection had everything in it from the latest novels to rare books that were probably worth a mint. The shelves were packed tight and she still had so many books that there were stacks all over.

The bedroom had also functioned as a home office. Nia felt like a thief as she searched through the disks near the computer. There were only about ten and she quickly found the one she wanted.

She powered up the computer and it seemed to drag as the information slowly loaded in. "Oh, no!" she said.

Brett was in the other room when he heard her, but in a few quick strides was standing next to her. "What's the matter?"

"She has a password protection device on her system."

"Didn't she have one at work? Maybe it's the same."

"No, at the office we all have our personal passwords, but the computer-tech person can override the personal code and open the system. If someone quit, we had to have a way of getting into the person's system. The tech person can do that. I never expected her to have a code on her personal PC."

"So what can we do?"

Nia gathered the diskettes and dropped them into her tote bag. "I'll have to take them with me and pray that she doesn't have password protection on these."

"Do you want to look around for—"

"No. I don't want to look for anything else. I have to go to my house."

Brett could see that Nia was unraveling. She had continuously put off coming to the apartment. Maybe by the time she felt better, Bree would be back and help her.

He put his arm around her and they left the apartment. While Nia walked toward the car, Brett pulled the key labeled "Nia" from the key chain and slipped it in his pocket.

Just as they reached the SUV, Jared Schuyler appeared. He'd just come from playing tennis and hadn't changed from his tennis clothes. He still carried his large, oversize racquet.

"What are you doing here?" Nia asked.

"Don't get upset. I asked a neighbor to call me if you came by. I want to get some personal things for Mother."

"Maybe another time," she said. She couldn't

bring herself to go back into the apartment, nor could she let anyone else go in.

"Come on. You're here. It will only take a couple of minutes. Mother told me exactly where to look."

Nia shook her head. "I have to catalog everything and if you'll just tell me what it is, I'll see that Daphne gets it."

Jared caught her arm and pulled her toward him. "It's personal. So why don't you give me the key. I'll run in and—"

In a split second Jared had been turned around and was staring up at Brett. "Hey, I didn't mean anything. . . ."

"What's going on?"

"He wants to get something for Daphne and I told him that he couldn't right now."

Brett's black eyes pinned Jared to the spot. "So what part of that didn't you understand?"

Jared tried to pull away, but Brett tightened his grip. "Come on," Jared pleaded. "I was Alethia's godson. I'm not some stranger off the street."

"Brett, let him go," Nia whispered.

With a slight shove, Brett released Jared, who fell against the SUV. His tennis racquet dropped to the ground.

"What does Daphne want?" Nia asked.

"Never mind. I'll just tell Mother you're too busy trying to hold on to everything you can."

Brett took a step toward him, but Nia moved just as quickly and placed her body between them. "Come on," she said to Brett. "I'll call Daphne."

Slowly Brett turned and opened the door. He helped Nia into the vehicle and then walked around to the driver's side and got in. As they pulled away, Brett looked in the side-view mirror.

Jared scooped up his racquet and filled with rage, gripped the handle and slammed the head of the racquet against the ground with all the strength he could muster. Brett knew in that instant that a tennis racquet could be a deadly weapon.

# Twenty-seven

He waited until they were on the road before he asked about her marriage. "Was Jared the type who couldn't control his temper?"

"He had what I called tantrums. He especially liked to perform on the tennis courts. He would yell, toss his racquet, swear at the umpire, the linesmen."

"Did he ever bring any of that anger home?"

Nia turned to stare at him while he drove. "You mean was he an abusive husband?"

"Something like that."

"No. He wasn't. He wouldn't have dared try that at home."

"Why not? Men who can't control themselves in sports have the same problem at home."

Brett was absolutely right. Even though he'd carried on like a maniac on the tennis court, Jared had been the perfect gentleman off the court. His friends referred to his carrying on as his Jekyll-and-Hyde personality. Most of them joked about it.

Nia had found out about other women in his life. She knew that one had lived with Jared for a couple of years. She made it a point to meet the woman and talk to her. At first she was reluctant to talk about Jared and then she finally said, "Don't worry. His mother cleans up after him."

Only after her divorce did she run into the woman again. Nia was in a building, consulting with a client. They were going to look over some property, and she was waiting by the elevator for him. She and the woman said hello and then were silent until the woman said, "I heard you and Jared broke up. Did his mother see that you were taken care of?"

"She didn't have to. I've always had my career."

"Did you have to stop working until you healed?"

"Healed?"

The woman knew she'd made a mistake. She stammered about leaving something in her lawyer's office and hurried away. Nia's client was coming down the hall and nodded to her as they passed.

"Do you know that woman?"

"Not really. She must be on her way to see her lawyer. He has the office across from mine. He took her on as a client after she was in some kind of accident."

"Accident?"

"Yeah, her face was a mess the first time I saw her. She had some type of veil over it, but I got a glimpse of it. She must have gone through a windshield."

Nia knew then that she'd been right to leave Jared. She'd had only one incident with Jared's temper, and she told Brett about it.

"He tried it once. We'd been married a few weeks, and Daphne wanted me to go to a charity event with her. I said I couldn't. I thought it was settled until Jared came home ranting about me disappointing his mother. She'd told him when they were playing tennis. They used to be quite a team in mixed doubles. Anyway, he slammed his racquet on the table and knocked the food on the floor."

"And then what happened?"

"I left him. I grabbed my handbag and briefcase and walked out. Since I had given up my apartment when we got married, I went to Alethia's."

"She must have been furious with him."

"You could have fried an egg on her forehead. She was so mad she called Daphne. Within a couple of hours, we were all sitting down in Alethia's living room. I said I'd try again, but if Jared ever carried on like that again, we were through. I grew up in a house where my parents respected each other. I wouldn't settle for anything less."

"So did you leave him because he had another tantrum?"

"Yes. The next time was months later, but he threatened me. That time I didn't go to Alethia. I checked into a hotel and filed three days later."

Brett glanced at her before returning to watch the road. "Are you saying he never hit you?"

"Never. But I knew he would. Just the fact that he threatened to hit me meant that he had escalated from breaking furniture. I've had friends in abusive relationships. I know the signs."

"Most women wouldn't leave so early in the marriage."

"That's the best time to leave." Nia turned and looked out the window. "I think we're going to get some rain soon."

Brett knew she'd ended the conversation about her marriage. He also knew someone she cared about had been in an abusive relationship. It was probably Alethia, but if she didn't want to tell him, he wouldn't pry.

They pulled up in front of Nia's house and went inside. She retrieved some phone messages and put her cell phone in the charger.

Besides more clothing, Nia decided to take her laptop along.

"One computer isn't enough?" Brett asked.

"I want to work on the lanai sometimes and I can use my laptop."

"You're getting very comfortable in Malibu."

"I know. I think most people who move from cold climates think of living in Malibu."

Nia was in the kitchen putting together a snack package for her car. She tossed in candy bars, potato chips and sodas. The dry ice would keep things fresh for days. She wouldn't put it in the car until she was coming back home but she felt that would be in a few days. Then she joined Brett in the living room.

"We haven't talked about 'us' for a while."

Nia shook her head. She knew where he was going and she didn't want to talk about it. Nia was sitting in her favorite recliner and Brett was stretched out on the sofa.

"Let's wait."

"Let's not. I know you want to be with me, but you keep pushing me away."

"You want me to come back to Wyoming. You're planning to leave New York and go home. Wyoming isn't my home anymore."

"So we do what makes us both happy."

"What is that?"

"I don't know what you want. I want us to be

together. I still want my ski lodge. What do you want, the bank?"

Nia took a deep breath. She knew they would come to this. "I want to live in California. I really love it here. I don't know about the bank. I've been getting some rumors from Charlotte that they think I'm too young and inexperienced to step into Alethia's shoes."

"How can they think like that? Alethia groomed you for the job."

"She was grooming me. She thought we had a lot more time and so did I. I'm not sure what I want to do. I want the bank to be everything she wanted, but I don't have to be the one to make it happen. I like financial planning. Now I'll know to warn my clients about takeovers."

"It's not your fault. There was no reason to suspect anyone else wanted the company. Kent, Paul and Jeff have been holding their own. They're trying to buy back some of the stock that's still out there."

"What if they can't pull it off?"

"I'll find someone to play the white knight and ride in and save the day. Kent will survive. But now we need to see how *we* can have it all."

"Any suggestions?"

"We have a house in California. I guess it's going to be in Malibu. And we have a place in Wyoming. Come with me. Look it over and see if you can't live there part of the year."

"You're talking about a commuter marriage. They don't work."

"They don't work for *other* people."

"Are you sure you want to do this?"

"If it's what makes us both happy, why not?"

"We'll see."

"You have become such a skeptic since you moved out here. Maybe you're getting too much sun?"

"I'm not a skeptic. I'm a realist."

"Whatever. Let's go have something fancy."

"Like?"

"It's your town. Do you want to have dinner and then go to the beach house?"

"No. I'd rather drop this stuff off and get something around there."

They packed up the SUV and headed for Malibu. Since the reporters had stopped lurking about, Nia could return home anytime. She just felt like dragging out the luxury of Malibu a little longer.

By the time they reached the beach house, they had just enough time to shower and change clothes.

Nia selected a white shirt that reached her knees and had slits up both sides to go with her black stretch pants. She twisted her hair to the side and let if fall over one shoulder.

Brett wore a white shirt and black slacks with his black cowboy boots. They smiled as they met on the lanai for drinks. "We're beginning to think alike," he told her.

The restaurant wasn't too far from the house. Duke's Malibu was named after a legendary Hawaiian surfer, Duke Kahanamoku. The California restaurant was careful to stay true to the original one in Hawaii. Duke's Malibu was situated at the ocean's edge and had at least three hundred feet of picture windows on one side. It was fairly new to the area, but quite popular.

Nia had never been to the restaurant so when

Brett said he had reservations, she was thrilled. Her mouth watered from just perusing the menu. She finally settled on Huli Huli Chicken, which was barbecued with garlic, ginger and some wonderful spices that were a family secret.

Brett ordered the Herb Roasted Prime Rib.

"You are the worst thing for my diet," Nia said.

"If you'd rather stay home and cook, I don't mind."

"How about if you stay home and cook?"

"You might get tired of the same things over and over."

"You could borrow Trisha's recipe book."

His stepmother had been collecting recipes since she was very young and had a large three-ring binder filled with them. She also kept a computerized list of everything she would need to make Kaliq and Brett's favorites.

"I'm sure she would lend it to me. I'm just not sure it would taste the same if I made it instead of Trisha."

When the waiter came to suggest dessert, Nia shook her head. "I don't dare."

"I dare," said Brett. "I want a slice of that Hula Pie."

After the waiter left, Nia had to ask, "How do you know about Hula Pie?"

"I don't. Lisabeth Hemming suggested it."

"When?"

"A couple of days ago when I called Kent. He wasn't there, but Lisabeth was and I asked about a restaurant around here."

"She's an . . . interesting lady."

"Mmm, that's a long way from the woman who got on your nerves."

"I have to admit I was wrong about her. I wasn't wrong about her being a little ditsy, but she's got a good heart."

The Hula Pie arrived and Brett gave a low whistle. Macadamia nut ice cream was piled on a chocolate cookie crust and topped with chocolate fudge, whipped cream and a generous sprinkling of macadamia nuts.

"I think it's enough for both . . ." Brett didn't get to finish his sentence as he saw Nia grab her fork and begin to slice a section for herself.

They finished the pie and Nia closed her eyes and savored the last piece. "This is heaven."

"I'm going to have the chefs from the lodge come out here and sample this food. We can't duplicate it in Wyoming, but it might give them inspiration. It's nice but not Wyoming's style. Now how about it? Spend the weekend with me in Wyoming."

Nia thought about it. She'd only been to Wyoming once a year to place flowers on her parents' graves. She'd already done that for the year. Each time she returned, the pain came back. She missed them so much.

"I'll go with you."

"Great. Too bad we drove. After a meal like this, we need to walk a lot."

"I challenge you to a morning run," Nia said.

"I accept. What time?"

"Six A.M."

Brett laughed. "Are you trying to gain some kind of advantage? You don't expect me to drop you off, drive back to the hotel and get back here for a six A.M. run?"

"No. I don't. I expect to tap you on the shoulder and say, 'Let's go.' "

Brett's eyes darkened as the reality of what she was saying set in.

"Lady, you have yourself a real challenge now. Let's see if you want to get up at six tomorrow morning."

Once in the bedroom, Nia could not believe how bold she'd been. For the second time, she'd asked Brett to share her bed. She'd never done that with any man. Brett kissed her, and she forgot her momentary embarrassment. Brett seemed to know how she felt. He alternately removed something she was wearing and then something he was wearing. He started with her shirt and his boots. Then he removed her bra and his shirt. He continued until they were both naked.

"Nia, I've waited so long for you to be the one who asked." Brett's hands slid down her sides as she wrapped her arms around him. He groaned as they inched their way to the bed, neither wanting to let go or the spell might be broken. They lay on the bed, still holding fast to each other.

Brett's hand began to probe her softness, his fingers searching for and finding the tiny bud that would bring her to a higher plane. She arched to meet his fingers, relaxed when he took them away and then as he covered her body and brought them together in the world's oldest dance, she collapsed.

She needed him and she wanted him to need her as much. She began to use her hands and mouth to make him as happy as he was making her. No matter what their future held, tonight was a celebration of complete giving.


The next morning, all bets were off. They awoke to the gentle tapping of the rain. Brett drifted back to sleep, still holding Nia in his arms.

# Twenty-eight

The flight in had been perfect. They'd taken off a little late, but the pilot managed to make up the difference so there was no frantic run through the airport to make their connection.

Trisha was waiting for them and since they had opted for carry-on luggage, they didn't have to go to the baggage area. She wore a large hat that hid her graying curls. Her face was only slightly lined. She was dressed in the standard outfit of jeans and a shirt with the ranch name across it. The hat was to protect her hair. Trisha had no intention of coloring her hair but she didn't want it to get too dry. Her hair was quickly turning white, replacing the gray, but she didn't mind. Trisha's height and slender frame hadn't changed since the day she arrived at the ranch. She'd come to love the area, but she and Kaliq had made several trips to Europe. On their trip to France, she'd given him a tour of all her old haunts where she had studied and become a Cordon Bleu chef.

She hugged Nia and kissed her on both cheeks. "I am so glad to see you."

"Don't tell me that you've pulled out that old

recipe book from Paris," Brett teased. "I've got to watch my weight."

"Don't let him fool you, Nia. He loves my cooking and he only grumbles before the meal, never after it."

"I got that feeling when we went out to dinner."

Trisha did refrain from pulling out the old recipe book the first night they were there. She fixed fried chicken and potato salad, but she vowed she had to serve one special meal before they left. "I haven't had much practice lately and the two of you are definitely going to be judges."

They sat around the table when Nia made an announcement. "Brett can speak French. He must have learned it to surprise you, Trisha."

"I was so happy when he learned it, but I can't take the credit. It was a classmate who asked him to help her study. The next thing I knew he was forming little baby sentences. Now he talks to me in French sometimes."

"You forgot to tell me," Nia said.

"I thought I told you."

"No. I had to hear it when we had dinner in a French restaurant."

"Was he showing off again? He can't resist surprising people," Trisha said. "He didn't tell us about the resort he and his partners are going to build. He just showed up one day and dragged us out to tour the place."

"That's exactly what he was doing."

"Well, we can't have that," Kaliq said. "Brett, you behave yourself from now on."

"Okay, I won't lie to her anymore."

"Sure, that's what they all say," Nia said.

The ranch had changed so much since the last

time Nia saw it. There were actually cabins where there used to be a huge bunkhouse.

"Some of the boys asked if they could have cabins like Brett and we decided to remodel," Kaliq explained.

The ranch was even better equipped to handle Kaliq's wheelchair. He'd changed that also. It was now a motorized chair instead of the oddly shaped one with the wheels that leaned in and didn't have rests for his arms. He caught Nia staring at it.

"I decided to give up the macho act for comfort. My arms were beginning to kill me from all the pushing I was doing."

Nia was amazed when Kaliq told her about the different selections of wheelchairs. That there was a hierarchy, where the toughest had wheelchairs with no arms and had to be powered by the person.

Trisha took them to guest cabins that were side by side at the opposite end of the ranch from the main house.

"I hope you don't mind," Trisha said. "We weren't sure what the situation was, so we put you in separate cabins. They have a common door and . . . whatever."

"That's a perfect arrangement," Brett said. "We don't want anyone jumping the gun about our plans."

Trisha turned to him and waited.

He grinned at her and shook his head. "I'm not telling you anything. Wait until it's etched in concrete and then we'll tell you and let you make the announcement."

"Jesslyn and I have been hoping for something for a long time. We can wait a little longer."

He was home and it felt good. A few days with

his family was sure to recharge him. He hoped it would do the same thing for Nia.

Brett couldn't hold back a grin as he threw an arm around Trisha. "Guess what, Nia? She still doesn't know which comes first, dinner or supper."

"You know what I mean. I can't help it if my Eastern roots make me still say breakfast, lunch and dinner."

"After all these years?" Nia teased.

"Hey, I had a lot more years saying that rather than breakfast, dinner and supper. Just watch it or you'll be washing dishes as a penalty."

The cabins Nia and Brett stayed in were the kind that had an adjoining door that locked from both sides. They could remain as two cabins or the door could be open to make one large room. The older children preferred the single cabins. The younger ones who were a little apprehensive about being away from home for the first time, liked the doors opened.


Nia and Brett had not pulled the latch to connect their cabins when they changed clothes before joining Trisha and Kaliq. The night air was just a little cooler than Nia remembered. She found her old uniform of a big shirt and jeans comfortable, but tonight she chose a gray, cable-stitch sweater and slim black leather pants. She knocked on the adjoining door.

"Are you ready?" she called.

"Give me five minutes."

She went outside and waited for him. It was closer to ten minutes before he appeared in the doorway.

"I thought women were supposed to be the slow ones."

"Keep your pantyhose on, princess. I had to make a few calls."

"Hah! I'm not wearing pantyhose and boy, does that feel strange."

"Stop flaunting it and let's go eat."

"Not yet. Let's just take a little tour."

He caught her hand as they walked. He'd missed seeing open land. He'd bet there wasn't a single place in Los Angeles that had any more room to expand. It was true of New York also. He'd hopped on a plane and spent a few days with his family any time he felt the urge. One of the reasons he wanted the ski lodge was that it would bring him back to Wyoming. Now he had to convince Nia that it would be good for her also.

Brett had spoken with his assistant just before leaving Los Angeles. Ana Lisa had reviewed several requests for funding to open businesses, but most didn't want a partner. There was always a clause in the contract about buying an investor out so the business stayed in the original group's hands. What they didn't understand was that Brett was not a bank. He wasn't in the business of lending money and getting a percentage on his investment. Once he put his money down, he was a partner for life.

He was relying on his assistant more each day. She had a good eye for future profitable investments. She had especially liked the idea of the ski lodge.

Brett and Nia strolled around the property. Although she'd returned to place flowers on her parents' graves, she never came to the ranch. At first, it was because she didn't want to see Brett. Then after she married, she didn't want to remind Trisha and Kaliq that she was responsible for Brett's leaving Wyoming.

Now she had come full circle. Again it was a man who had made her run, but he was her ex-husband. She was back with Brett and while they were still trying to sort out their relationship, she was glad she'd returned. *The scenario is basically the same,* she thought. She wanted to live in Los Angeles and she hoped they would understand.

Trisha stood by the window and watched Brett and Nia walk hand in hand.

"I always knew they were right for each other."

"Terrific, now stop spying on them."

"I'm not spying."

"You're hiding behind a curtain, watching them. If that isn't spying, what is?"

Trisha turned to her husband. "Where is the romance in your soul?"

"I save it for you."

"That's not your soul talking."

"Who cares?" He laughed. "Get out of that window."

"Don't you want your son to come home with a wife?"

"Of course, I do. But you can't force things to happen. If they're going to be together, this time we just have to wait and see. If they decide not to be together, we're going to have to accept it."

"They love each other."

"Sometimes that isn't enough," he whispered.

Trisha knew he was talking about them. At the very time she had the chance to open Carlotta's

Kaliq had asked her to marry him. She wanted to fulfill her dream before she married and she had said no. Instead of a wedding ring, she developed Carlotta's. The bed-and-breakfast inn had done well, but a person from her past had come looking for her. He wanted to marry her and was furious that she didn't want him. He had tried to kill her. Kaliq had insisted that she come to Wyoming. But trouble followed her to Taharqa. There had been a showdown and the man had lost. Trisha had stayed in Wyoming and married Kaliq.

It had been four years before they met again and Trisha gave up the bed-and-breakfast. It had been five years since Brett and Nia had been together. Trisha shook her head. If there was one trait they all had in common, it was stubbornness. Each insisted on doing it his way and that's why it was so difficult to get together. The plus side of that was, once they made up their minds, no one could change them.

Trisha had pulled out all the stops with the meal. Tonight she served them spare ribs that had been marinated in caramel and coriander seeds, fried potatoes, and she ended the meal with a delicious dessert of poached pears in almond syrup.

After the meal and spending another hour just talking, Nia and Brett headed for their cabins. It had been a day filled with memories, but Nia noticed that the conversation had included falcons. Was Brett still afraid to try again or was it true that he had lost his touch and would never regain it?

"What's on the agenda tomorrow?" she asked.

"I need to do something very physical to work off that meal."

"How about a tour of the ski lodge I'm working on?"

"Sounds great. What time should we meet?"

"Let's leave here about nine."

As they reached her door, she turned, expecting a brief kiss from Brett. She stepped into his arms. He caught her wrists and held them at her side, then leaned down and kissed her long and hard. He crushed her against his body, then suddenly released her.

"I'll knock on your door."

"See you in the morning," she said and then kissed him back.

In spite of the searing kiss that she felt all through her body, she wasn't ready to give Trisha any more reason to hope for a wedding. She and Brett had a good physical relationship, but there were other things to consider and they hadn't even scratched the surface.

The next morning, when Brett knocked on her door, Nia was ready. She wanted to see the lodge that Brett had given such glowing reviews. Several of his partners in this venture were in town and checking out the place also.

He left Nia standing by the corral and ran in to say that they were going up to the main building of the resort.

The land was undeveloped, but soon the runs would be a reality. They would never put buildings up to ruin the view.

Brett also had another goal on this trip. He had

one more falcon that he'd trained, but had stopped taking out after the other one flew away. He was going to see if he could still whisper to the falcon and make it do what he wanted. Everyone knew that he'd been having trouble with the birds, and he couldn't come here and not try to regain his touch. He was going to prove that he knew what he was doing and make falcons part of his new life.

Brett and Nia used the ski lift to reach the summit. Then it was a short ten-minute walk to the massive Victorian house the Conrad group had decided to use as their office space.

While the outside of the house maintained the original structure, the inside was as hi-tech as it could get. The first floor consisted of the living room, dining room and kitchen. The radiant heat floors and high-quality appliances gave a new meaning to "roughing it".

Brett led her upstairs to his office, a spacious suite in the west wing of the building. The workmen were still busy installing the monitors that would allow him to see every section of the resort from behind the large mahogany desk.

"The other offices will be pretty much the same setup. We picked our own furniture, so that may vary, but we want to attract groups and families."

"It's beautiful."

He put his arm around her shoulders. "We are going to plan the best grand opening anyone has ever seen."

"After you finish the offices, what's next?"

"We haven't really decided on that. We knew we needed a base and this was it. Now comes the hard part. Selecting all the right people to bring it to-gether. Can you imagine, skiing down the slope with torches and one of the partners suggests a fire-and-ice ball?''

Nia heard the excitement in his voice and knew that he wasn't just putting up part of the money, he was tossing in all of his heart. Hot tears filled her eyes. She loved his dream, but there was no way she could abandon Alethia's. Had she lived, Nia could move back and live out Brett's dream, but not now. He was in the beginning stages of the resort. She was in the middle of the Freedom's Song bank. What would happen if their dreams collided?

They left the house and took the ski lift down to get Trisha's Jeep. As they drove away, Nia wondered just how long it would take before the place was up and running. Each of the partners had a task to perform and if they did what they were supposed to do, then all would be well. If anything went wrong, she didn't know what would happen to them. They were running out of time and each had to finish a dream.

They put the Jeep in the garage and walked to the main house. Trisha and Kaliq were on the deck. Brett's stepmother was sitting in his father's lap, the wheelchair securely anchored to the railing.

Nia considered Trisha a brave woman. She'd given up her bed-and-breakfast inn and moved to Wyoming. When she had first arrived, she thought she'd lost the inn she named Carlotta because of bad investments that her partner made before his murder. After the murderer had been caught, Trisha had the option of returning to Pennsylvania and reclaiming the inn. She refused. She now put her Cordon Bleu degree to work preparing meals for the little concrete cowboys that showed up every summer. Some of the boys now spent their winter break with the Faulkners.

When Nia was struggling with her decision about returning to corporate America, it was Trisha who encouraged her to try again. Nia was grateful because if she hadn't tried, she would have always wondered if she had wasted her talents. She now believed that the worst thing she could have done would have been to marry Brett at that time. They needed the years to mature and find themselves before they could be true to each other.

Now they faced another test. Was the timing wrong? Was this time to walk away from their careers and make a life together? She couldn't understand how love had come into her life and she would have to push it away again. How many chances would she and Brett be given?

The next morning, Nia awoke to see Brett fully dressed and holding the metal glove he used to train falcons.

"Where are you going?"

"To try to kill another demon. I have one falcon left. I've been afraid to take it hunting because I thought I would lose it."

Nia scrambled from the bed. "You just wait a minute, Brett Faulkner. You are not going out there alone."

"I'll wait."

Fifteen minutes later, after the fastest shower she'd ever taken, Nia dressed in jeans and a heavy woolen shirt. She put on socks and boots, and grabbed a heavier jacket to fight off the morning cold.

She joined Brett in the Jeep and he headed for the mountain. Once there, he prepared the falcon. He took a deep breath and removed the hood. He watched the falcon adjust to the light. He held his arm out and, with a strong command, released the bird. He watched as it soared high in the sky and then swooped down to the land and then up again. He gave a low whistle, one that Nia barely heard. They waited.

Nia stood away from him as they watched the falcon swoop down again and then up. She squinted as the sun blocked her view for a moment and then she saw the magnificent bird returning to Brett's outstretched arm. The falcon's claws gripped the mesh glove and he settled down. Brett slipped the hood over its head.

Nia waited anxiously until he put the bird back in its carrying cage. Then she let out a whoop that echoed through the mountains. She ran to Brett and he enveloped her in a huge bear hug.

"Thank you for having faith in me. I love you so much."

The magic was back.

# Twenty-nine

It was time to go home.

They got to the airport at 5:30 A.M. for the 6:40 A.M. flight. They should be in Los Angeles at 9:43 A.M. The flight left on time and the first leg of their journey home was only an hour away. They had a one-hour layover in Salt Lake City, and it didn't seem like much of a problem until they saw the board. A sudden thunderstorm had moved into Los Angeles and the flight would be delayed. Three hours later, their flight was announced. Another three-hour and one crying-the-whole-time baby later, they arrived at LAX and picked up Nia's car from long-term parking.

The flooding from the earlier rain meant they had to make a couple of detours, and it was another hour before they pulled the car into the driveway. They were bleary eyed, sleep deprived and angry. It took their remaining energy to call Kaliq and Trisha to let them know they were home, shower and fall into bed at one-thirty in the afternoon.

If this was any indication of what it would be like to try to commute on weekends, it was a dead issue. There was no way it would work.

They awoke later that night, showered and slipped on fresh clothes. Both of them were still suffering from sleep deprivation but famished as they stumbled into the kitchen. Brett set the table while Nia made a tuna salad.

"I should have known that the trip there was too good to be true," Nia said. "We can't think that a commuter marriage is going to work."

"I guess the only thing is to change that weekend idea. We can still make it happen."

"Right. I can just see me sitting in an airport with a screaming baby in my arms and everyone within fifty feet wanting to kill me."

"Okay. You made your point. But, honey, I swear by the time you have the baby, this ski lodge thing will be finished and we'll live in one state. I promise."

"Which state?"

"I . . . I don't know. You might be ready to be a stay-at-home mom."

"What if I'm not? What if I really love my job and I want to work?"

"We'll cross that bridge when we come to it."

"That's why so many marriages don't last. People think things will work out all by themselves."

"I don't want to have this discussion now. Let's get some rest and talk about it later."

Nia wanted to pound sense into him, and she needed to do it now. If she waited, she just might let him talk her into something she'd resent. It was obvious, but he wasn't planning to be the one to move. The office he'd chosen at the lodge was gorgeous. She'd fallen in love with it the minute he opened the door.

Then she had to admit she was still upset about

the flight, and she should just let it go. There would be another time to bring it up, and she would have to stand her ground. No matter how much she loved him.


The return to Los Angeles also meant returning to work. Nia threw herself into Alethia's plans for the bank. The charter had been granted and they were almost ready to open the doors and greet their first customers.

By Friday, she was running on adrenaline. She was tired, but still wound so tight she couldn't fall asleep easily. Brett had been terrific and so understanding. While she pressed on at the bank, Brett set up the plan to fight the takeover Jared had launched. He adjusted to her moods, and she began to look forward to coming home to him.

Charlotte buzzed her and announced Bree was on line one.

"Hey, girlfriend, when did you get back?" Nia asked.

"Two days ago. I was so tired all I did was sleep the first day. Then I was groggy the next."

"That's not like you."

"I know, but I'm ready now. What do you say to a girls' night out?"

Nia hesitated for just a moment and then heard hearty laughter on the phone.

"I guess I should have called Brett and asked him if you could come out to play."

"Brett does not control my life."

"Uh-huh."

"You are the only person I know who can say volumes without real words."

"So he's still hanging around. Is he still at a hotel?"

Nia felt her face burn. "No, he isn't."

"Okay. Call the man and see if he has plans for tonight. If he does, we can make it some other time. If he says he doesn't have anything on the burner, let's have dinner. Call me back."

"I'll talk to you later."

After she dropped the receiver back in the cradle, she thought about the old times. She, Julie and Bree would do a three-way call at lunchtime and decided in fifteen minutes what to do for the evening.

During the time she was married, Nia couldn't always join her friends. In fact, Daphne tried to arrange something for each moment Nia had available. There were so many clubs she wanted her to join, teas she wanted her to attend and charity events took up the entire weekend.

At first Nia had tried to please her mother-in-law, but she missed her friends and began to refuse. That brought on a lecture from Jared about the "right" way to do things. It was the beginning of the end of their marriage. Once Jared let it be known that he expected her to give up everything in her past, including her friends, Nia grew more determined to avoid being pigeonholed.

She stopped attending anything that wasn't appealing to her. She arranged her nights out with the girls to match Jared's nights out with his friends. The stronger she grew as a person, the weaker the marriage became. When she filed for divorce, her friends knew and his friends were totally out of the loop.

Nia called Brett on his cellular phone and was surprised at how quickly he answered.

"Do you have plans for tonight?"

"Nothing etched in concrete."

"Bree and I are getting together tonight so I'll be home late."

"I think I can manage to find something to do, but why don't you spend the night?"

Nia's eyes widened. "Are you sure?"

"I think it's a good idea. You probably need to hang out with your buddies every now and then."

She remembered that they had never gotten a key made for Brett. "Lee, my neighbor, will be able to let you in. I'll give her a call and I'll tell her to let you hold on to the key until you make a copy."

"Uh, okay, see you tomorrow," he told her.

Nia called Bree and told her what Brett suggested.

"He's a doll. You better hold on to him."

She didn't answer because she and Brett had agreed to wait until after the Bryant Electronics thing was over before they sat down and talked about their future.


When Brett got off the phone he knew he'd missed the perfect opportunity to confess that he had removed her key from Alethia's key ring. It didn't seem to be a major crime, but he wasn't sure how Nia would see it.

If she was going to be out, he'd take the time to do some more investigating of her former family, Jared and Daphne. Something there might help him understand why they were so determined to take Bryant Electronics from Kent.

* * *

Their girls' night out was an old custom developed when Nia, Bree and Julie were in college. They celebrated the end of the semester by catching up on all the movies they'd missed during the school year. Most of the movies were on video, so they each popped into the video store and rented five movies each and spent the weekend munching on popcorn and commenting on the hits they hated, while silently viewing the ones they liked.

After graduation, they continued the ritual when they wanted to unwind after grueling work schedules. Only they rotated the hosting duties.

Tonight was a modified version of that time. Nia was glad she still had her emergency-trip suitcase in the trunk of her car. She gave Charlotte some last-minute instructions to prepare for Monday's meetings. Then she drove to the video rental chain and spent a few minutes browsing before selecting an old Hitchcock movie. Nia drove to Bree's and parked in the visitors' space in the garage and retrieved her overnight bag from the trunk. Then she heard a sound. Her heart pounded as she looked around. Nothing. She heard another noise and turned back to see the guard making his rounds. Nia breathed a sigh of relief. She'd become so jumpy lately, and she was sure it was because she'd spent too many hours working.

Nia approached the concierge, who recognized her and called Bree. Nia and Julie had teased Bree about the high-rise apartment when she first purchased it. They gave her all kind of scenarios of the four elevators going out and she'd have to walk down to the first floor. But the breathtaking view at night of the city from the twenty-fifth floor was not to be denied.

When she opened the door, Bree's full figure was encased in a huge towel.

"Give me fifteen minutes to shower and change—" Nia began.

"Not yet. I've got something special planned, and all you'll need is this." She held out an extra-large towel.

The concierge buzzed and Bree picked up the phone. "Great. Send them up."

"What are you up to, Bree?"

"It's something I do after every trip when I'm all tense. I can see you're burning the candle at both ends. We both need something to make us feel good. So I didn't rent any tapes. I ordered something better."

"What is that?"

"I'm not telling. Wait until the guys arrive."

"Bree, I know you were always the one to do something differently, but I'm not sure I want to participate."

"You don't have any choice."

She wasn't going to argue with her friend. She would just go in the guest room and watch her video.

The bell rang and Bree strolled to the door and opened it. "Come in, gentlemen."

Nia turned to see two men who looked as if their hobby was body building. Each of them had a medium-sized backpack and each had a folding table. She made a face at Bree for not telling her what she'd planned.

The two were strictly business as they arranged the tables and accessories. Nia slipped into the bathroom and emerged wearing just the towel her friend had given her.

The next hour her muscles were rubbed, kneaded and pounded. It was sheer heaven.

"Now take a good hot shower and you should sleep like babies," one of the men said as they left.

The condo had two master bedrooms, so Nia went into the guest bedroom, showered, slipped into a nightshirt and joined Bree in the living room.

Bree was wearing a very long, hot-pink shirt with long side slits and matching stretch pants. She was shoeless and her toenails were painted in the same shade of pink.

"When did you start this?" she asked Bree.

"A couple of months ago. I met a woman on the plane and we started talking about business travel and how to unwind. She told me about these guys and I tried it out when I came back from Chicago. I felt so good the next day I wanted to scream it from the rooftops."

Nia yawned. "I'm going to turn in now. See you in the morning."

"I lied. I did rent a tape and we can watch it tomorrow. What time is Brett expecting you?"

"Late. He's got a lot on his plate with the ski lodge and Bryant Electronics."

"Ski lodge?"

Nia yawned again. "I'll tell you tomorrow." She went into the bedroom and crawled into bed. Her last thoughts that night were of the times she, Bree and Julie used to flip a coin to see who slept in a real bed and who got the sofa bed in the living room.

\* \* \*

The next morning, she felt terrific. She opened her eyes, remembered where she was and what had happened. She knew that Brett had a spa area at the lodge. She'd have to tell him to make sure a masseuse was on call twenty-four/seven.

She showered and put on another large sleep shirt before heading to the kitchen. Nia didn't know if it was the massage, but suddenly she was famished.

She raided the refrigerator and found fresh fruit. She made a large salad and then added yogurt.

Bree staggered into the kitchen. "Morning is not my time," she said and headed for the coffee-maker. She rustled in the cabinet until she found the coffee.

"Shame on you. Give up that caffeine."

"One day when I can face mornings."

Nia used a serving spoon to lift her share of the salad into her bowl. She nibbled slowly. "I've been eating out too many nights."

After making the coffee, Bree drank half a cup before spooning the salad onto her plate.

She tasted it and nodded. "Not bad."

"You have all the makings in your refrigerator. Buy a book that tells you the other combinations you can do with fruit, tuna, vegetables. Healthy stuff."

"I can't help myself. I'm shopping at the farm-ers' market for all the good stuff and then I finish and go right to a butcher and get a steak."

"You are hopeless." Nia always encouraged her friend to eat healthily, but never to diet. Bree was a happy plus-size and she didn't feel that being skinny would do any more for her. She had a very full life, but each time she met someone who Nia and Julie thought was "the one," it never seemed to work out.

Nia called Brett and they talked for a few minutes. He and Kent were meeting for lunch and Brett wanted to know if it was possible for her to invite Lisabeth over. She groaned, but promised to call her.

Nia made the call and, although she lived twenty minutes away, Lisabeth arrived an hour later.

"Thank you for inviting me. I hate it when Kent gets in his all-business mode. What are we going to do?"

Bree waited until Lisabeth wasn't looking and made a face at Nia. They put in the first movie and then wondered how their little blond friend was going to handle watching Bree's choice, *Shaft* with Richard Roundtree.

They watched as Lisabeth blushed at the shower scene, but got into the story after that. As the credits rolled, she turned to her new friends.

"I hope we can do this again. I'd like to see this movie again and then the new one with Samuel L. Jackson. Did you notice the original didn't have the Empire State Building in it?"

"That's right. It wasn't completed until long after the movie was made." Nia suddenly felt she'd been a little harsh in her judgment of Lisabeth. They made some popcorn and then watched Nia's selection, Hitchcock's *Vertigo*.

They debated the ending. Nia thought the point was that Jimmy Stewart cured his vertigo at the expense of Kim Novak's life and would never be happy. Lisabeth thought he should be concerned with finding his friend who got him into all the trouble.

The afternoon turned out much better than Nia had expected. They probably would include Lisabeth the next time they got together. They said good-bye to Bree and took the elevator down to the garage.

"I'll call you, and the next time we can go to Malibu," Lisabeth said as she headed for her car.

Nia was on the freeway and still thinking about how Lisabeth had fit in when she felt the first bump. She looked in her rearview mirror and saw a black SUV right on top of her. The second bump sent her out of the lane and the third tapped her car just enough to make it spin out of control. She tried to hold on to the steering wheel and keep the car on the road. She failed. With the final bump, her car shot through traffic and onto the shoulder. The car skidded up an embankment and halfway up the hill. The car slid down the hill and back into traffic before she could get it under control. She pulled off the highway. She was shaking too much to continue driving. She was ever so grateful that almost everyone carried a cellular phone. She was crying as she gave Brett her location.

Brett parked behind her and got out. She threw her door open and was out of the car and into his arms.

"Come on. We can leave your car here."

"No. I can drive it as long as you follow me."

"Are you sure?"

"Positive."

When they got to her house, he rushed her inside. "Did something happen with the other driver?"

"What do you mean?"

"Is this a case of road rage?" He remembered reading about California drivers being shot and beaten up because they cut someone off or beeped their horn.

"I don't think so. The driver didn't say anything. Just kept bumping my car. I was so scared."

"Did you get the license-plate number?"

"No. I was just trying to keep from hitting anyone else."

"Don't worry. You're safe now."

He managed to get them into bed. She was shaking so badly he thought he might have to take her to a doctor. Finally, she settled down and fell asleep.

Brett didn't sleep. He watched over her instead. He didn't tell her that he, too, was afraid for her.

# Thirty

Brett and Nia relaxed in bed, reading the Sunday papers. Neither of them was actually reading. Brett was thinking about his phone call to Palladin the night before. He'd found a white knight for Bryant Electronics. Palladin was flying out to L.A.

He put the newspaper down and turned to Nia. She hadn't turned the page she was supposed to be reading for ten minutes. She'd been remote since they'd returned from Wyoming. He didn't like the idea of a commuter marriage, but he didn't see any other way. They had each worked too hard to achieve success, and neither of them was willing to give that up.

"What's bothering you?" he asked.

"I feel so bad. If Kent loses the company, it will be my fault."

"It was a sound business decision. This whole thing is personal. Schuyler doesn't want the company. He wants to hurt you, and he knows that Kent's your friend."

"Alethia considered Kent one of her 'kids', even though she didn't meet him until he drove me back here. She encouraged him to take a chance on using part of his trust fund to buy the company."

"Kent said Jeff found the company. Were they close friends?"

"Not really. Jeff doesn't come from money like Kent and Paul. He worked a few years before going back to college and then he worked part-time and went to a city college. He transferred to Harvard as a senior and that's where they met."

"He's not too friendly."

"Sometimes he gives the impression he thinks he's better than most because he's worked harder. He only got Kent and Paul for partners when he realized he couldn't afford to buy the company alone."

"And he went along with the deal?"

"He didn't have a choice. I think he's really mad with Jared."

"We've got to get this show on the road. I'm going to make a few phone calls."

Nia stretched and swung her legs from the bed. "I'll get dressed and fix breakfast."

"Great. I'll get dressed and eat breakfast. I might have to spend the night bringing Palladin up to speed."

"I understand. I just want this to be over and I want Jared out of everyone's life."

He leaned forward and took Nia's face in his hands. "Don't worry. We're not going to let him win." Brett planted tiny kisses on her face, then on her neck. "You are so beautiful."

Nia giggled.

"What's that about?"

She ran her fingers through the hair on his chest. "I am amazed that you've changed so much.

I thought that venture-capitalist people spend their time in front of a computer, figuring out what companies were ripe for takeovers."

He rolled her over and ran his knuckles down her spine. His strong fingers kneaded her shoulders.

"Are these the hands of someone who spends the day staring at a computer screen?"

"Mmm. I'm not sure. Keep doing that for a few more minutes."

"You are so tense, Ms. Sebastian. However, I have the perfect remedy."

"I think I know what you mean," she said and laughed.

She slowly turned until she was staring up at him. His eyes were cloudy with passion. He leaned down and kissed her. Her heart raced as the tingling sensation spread over her body. She lifted up and pressed her soft body against his hardness.

"Brett," she whispered. "Now. Please now."

For a while there were no other problems. They were just two people celebrating the joy of being in love.

It seemed that it had only been hours since Brett had called Palladin Rush, and already his uncle was on the way. Nia knew it would have been the same if he'd called his father. Brett had thought long and hard before he placed the call to Palladin. At one time he'd thought of stretching his growing empire very thin and acting as Bryant's white knight, but it was better to call someone he trusted. Brett saw the company as a good deal, but the ski lodge was something that could fulfill something more. It would give him the best return for his investment. He had to hold on to that.

Nia watched from the window as Brett backed his SUV out of the driveway and headed for LAX to pick up the man he thought of as his uncle. Palladin had booked a hotel, and he and Brett would spend the night there as Brett brought him up to date on the situation.

A slight shiver slid up Nia's spine as she thought about the man who had agreed to bail Bryant Electronics out. If Jared thought Brett was intimidating, she knew that she wanted to be in the room when Jared met Palladin.

She'd called Jared a bully and she wished she could be there when he met his match. Unfortunately, she was not on Kent's payroll nor was she part of the white knight team.

She showered, slipped into a housecoat and applied her facial masque. Now she could relax for a few minutes to let the masque harden before she rinsed it off and applied her night moisturizer. She put on some soft jazz and stretched out in the recliner.

Since Brett had moved in, Nia had been paying more attention to business than herself. This was the time to do all those little maintenance things women needed to do. Tonight he would stay at the hotel while he brought Palladin into the loop.

She picked up the folder on the resort and began to leaf through it. There was a picture of all the partners. Seven very gorgeous men. She made a mental note to make sure all her single friends went to this resort.

The phone rang and she was surprised to hear Trisha's voice.

"Hi, Nia. Is Brett around?"

"You just missed him."

"Oh, well, I had a call from one of the skiers and he wanted to know when Brett would be able to meet with them."

"I was just going over the brochure."

"It's really going to be different," Trisha said. "Brett and his friends are sure that they could turn a profit in a couple of years."

"So Brett really wants this resort."

"He's been driving all of us crazy talking about it, showing us plans, faxing his partners."

A commuter marriage seemed to be the way to go for them. The reunions would be spectacular, but the times apart could be devastating. She didn't understand why love had to be so hard for her.

Brett stood in the waiting area as the plane disembarked. He knew his father was right. The only way to flush out the murderer was to take away the prize. In this case, according to Alethia's notes, that would be Bryant Electronics.

He had to hide a smile as he saw passengers casting furtive glances at the tall, broad-shouldered man he called uncle. At six feet, four inches, and more than two hundred pounds, Palladin Rush would certainly stand out in a crowd. However, it was his hair that caused the looks. Palladin's dread locks hung below his shoulders. He had one piece of carry-on luggage.

The men hugged and gave the handshake that black men do when they meet.

"Thanks for coming," Brett said.

"I'll do what I can to help with this business situation, but you know that I'm here as a spy for the women?"

Brett laughed. "Trisha and Jesslyn are still playing matchmaker."

"So, do they have something to cheer about?"

"Maybe."

"Don't tell them that. 'Maybe' sounds more like yes than no."

"The problem with them is that anything I say sounds like a 'yes,' but Nia and I have a lot of things going on in our lives."

"If you and Nia don't work out, they'll feel as if you deliberately misinformed them. Believe me. They will go for your jugular."

"Well, I have to keep them in suspense until this deal is finished. Then we'll tell them what we have planned."

"That sounds as if it isn't something they want to hear."

"You're right. Let's get to the hotel and see if we can eliminate the business problems, and then Nia and I can work on the personal ones."

The men walked to the SUV and climbed in. Brett spent the ride to the hotel bringing Palladin up to date.

After checking in, they went to the suite and settled in. Palladin called home and spent a few minutes talking to his wife.

The men were leafing through the prospectus when Palladin looked at Brett.

"I do have one question."

"Go."

"Are you asking me to help you with some kind of vendetta?"

"I want to help Nia. She thinks it's her fault. Her ex has nothing to do with it for me."

"Are you sure?"

"Positive. Nia explained that they had to hold on to enough stock to keep the majority. They didn't understand and let too much get away. Schuyler moved in. Now, I don't really care that the man is her ex. I do care that she thinks she let a friend down."

"I think I have enough to work with," Palladin said. "You don't have to spend the night. I'm sure there's something you'd rather be doing."

"Thanks. I'll call you in the morning, and we can have breakfast."

"Now, that's a problem. I'm functioning on New York time, so why don't I get some sleep, run some more figures and see what our next step should be? I'll call you. For now, go make my wife and Trisha happy."

Palladin winked at Brett and he got up to leave.

"I think you and Dad are closet romantics. Jesslyn and Trisha don't hide it, but it's not a bad idea."


An hour later, Brett pulled into Nia's driveway. She peeped through the blinds and saw him. When he reached for the bell, she opened the door. She groaned as she saw the shocked look on his face. She was still wearing the masque. She'd been so sleepy she'd forgotten to rinse it off.

"I thought you weren't coming back tonight. I thought you were going to stay at the hotel. I . . ." she stammered.

"Sorry. I just thought I'd rather be here with you."

"Well, you'll just have to wait until I . . . wash my face."

Nia strutted into her bedroom with as much pride as she could. Even as she continued into the master bath, she could still hear Brett's laughter.

Brett used the guest bath to shower and put on the bottom half of his pajamas before going to Nia's room to wait for her.

The masque was a little more difficult to remove because she'd waited so long. After splashing her face with warm water, she held a washcloth over it for a few seconds, then gently removed the residue. Then she cleaned her face with astringent before applying her nighttime moisturizer. Nia opened a drawer in the cabinet under the sink and selected a soft, black-satin sleep shirt that was four inches above her knees.

It was only a few minutes before she appeared in the bathroom door. Her dark hair was pulled back and her freshly washed face glowed. He turned back the bedclothes on her side of the bed and waited until she slid in beside him before he touched her. She ran her hands over his bare chest. There was something she needed to tell Brett but it slipped from her mind when his lips caressed hers.

She and Brett had been friends in the past, but that was before either of them knew what it was like to give everything and expect nothing in the act of love. Now that they were older, it was true that experience brought wisdom.

The roller-coaster ride was just beginning as their

desire for each other increased. His kisses became deeper, harder, yet too intense to stop.

Kent had picked the Four Oaks restaurant in Bel-Air for their meeting. The menu offered a wide variety. Brett decided on roast beef with needle fries, while Kent chose the quail with pecan-apricot-mushroom stuffing.

"I'll have to suggest this to Nia," Brett said. "It should take us about a year to go through this menu."

"So I guess that means you'll be around."

"Not necessarily."

"So what did you think of Bryant?"

"You've got some strong numbers running around there. I like it and I understand why Schuyler does."

"My partner, you know, Jeff, found it. He's really pushing for us to keep it."

"Why did Schuyler suddenly start giving you a hard time?"

"I don't know. It was out of the blue. One day we're taking over and trying to reorganize. A few days later, we get the notice that Schuyler has acquired enough stock to make a run for the company."

"I know you need help," Brett told Kent. "You can't get out of this without help. You need a white knight to come in and make life difficult for Schuyler."

"I think Alethia was hoping you would serve in that capacity."

"I know, but I'm involved in a major deal and I can't handle it," Brett explained. "So I found them someone who will help you."

"Thanks. Why are you doing this?"

"For Nia. She asked me to help her finish Alethia's projects and you were one of them."

"I've got to tell my partners something. We can't go forward until this is settled."

"Let's set up another meeting tomorrow with them. Is that too much of a rush?"

"No. We'll meet in my office tomorrow for lunch."

The two men finished their meal and talked about other things before going their separate ways.

Across town Jeff Michaelson entered Daphne Schuyler's office through her private entrance. He joined her for her version of "high tea." Every day at this time she locked the door to her office and told everyone to stay away. Most of her staff thought she was taking a nap. It was the perfect time for her to meet with people she didn't want others to know about.

She sat at her small conference table and nibbled on watercress sandwiches and scones. The lavender jacket that matched her skirt had been tossed on the beige loveseat.

"Are your partners trembling in their shoes?"

"They were until today."

"What happened today?"

"I got a look at Kent's appointment book. He scribbled something about a possible 'white knight,' and that he was meeting him for lunch at Four Oaks."

"So, of course, you dropped by."

"I didn't let them see me. He was having lunch with Brett Faulkner."

Daphne's mouth turned to a sneer. "The Faulkners are well off and could possibly see this as a favor to Kent."

"I tossed the waiter a few bucks. Kent set up a meeting at our office for tomorrow."

"Are you going to attend?"

"No. I've got to check on another project that my partners don't know about. I'll just say something happened with one of my kids."

"Don't you think you should be at this meeting?" Daphne could not believe the man. Just because his partners were losing their battle didn't mean they didn't have to be watched at all times. She needed to know if there was the slightest chance they would find someone to bail them out.

His voice hardened. "No. I have this other deal and it's too hot to lose. I'm going to need it when you and your son take over Bryant. Besides, Kent will call me and tell me everything that happened."

"Why don't you want them to have the company?"

"Ha! Why should I own a third when the whole company should be mine?"

She watched as his mouth tightened and twisted to the side.

"I asked for a loan and what do they do? They weaseled their way in so they could be my *partners*."

"Well, you won't have to worry about them. Jared will replace Kent."

"What do you get out of this?"

"What do you mean?"

"You could buy any company for your son. Why are you helping me with this one?"

"I'm settling an old debt."

"I don't understand."

"You don't have to. Just keep your ears open and keep me informed."

Jeff knew he'd been dismissed and didn't press the issue. He left the same way he had come in. Now Kent and Paul would know how he felt when they wormed their way into his business deal. He scanned the area before getting into his car and driving away.

Daphne watched him from the window in her office. Men were so arrogant, she thought. They didn't know how many times women used them. Jeff didn't know that Nia Sebastian was her target. Her ex-daughter-in-law was in for a rude awakening. She would have to set helplessly and watch Jared take over her friend's company. Daphne had waited a long time to teach her that no one walks out on a Schuyler and gets away with it.

# Thirty-one

Nia sat at her conference table, reviewing her schedule for the next day. She'd canceled two meetings and rescheduled three others. She needed time to review Alethia's notes. She was just locking up when Charlotte stopped in.

"I'm glad I caught you. When the men moved the furniture, this file was behind the cabinet." She stepped forward and handed Nia a manila envelope with her name written in Alethia's large script.

"It's probably something she meant to give me but fell off the top of the cabinet."

"I don't think so. It was *taped to the back* of the cabinet."

"Taped?"

"Exactly. I didn't look inside. I just felt it might be important."

"Thanks. I'll take it home with me." Nia tried to act nonchalant as she slipped the envelope into her briefcase. She wanted desperately to know if it was important, but felt it was better to view it privately. She and Charlotte chatted a few minutes before Nia left for home.

* * *

In the Century City offices of Bryant Electronics, Palladin Rush leaned back in his chair and tossed the file on the desk. He and Brett had discussed the company most of the night. He'd read Brett's report on the company and agreed that it was solid, healthy and ripe for a takeover.

Now they sat with two of the men who owned Bryant. After being formal for the first hour, as Kent and Paul had nervously answered Palladin's questions, the men were now on a first-name basis.

Kent and Paul had invested too much money to think of losing it and at this time would try anything. They were sure Jeff would also. They just didn't know where he was at the moment.

"You've done a great job."

"I've gotten us into a battle," Kent replied. "I'm not sure we can hold on to our business. We're fighting off a hostile takeover because I let too much of the stock go when we went public."

"No one's blaming you," Paul said. "We would have gone under a long time ago if you hadn't been so diligent in bringing us into the twenty-first century. Now we're attractive enough for a suitor. I just hate that it had to be Daphne and Jared."

"I understand this isn't really over Bryant Electronics," Palladin said.

"No, it's a little more personal," Kent confessed. "I'm sure Brett filled you in on the details, but let me just say that we're not the first company to feel the Schuylers' wrath. If you act as our white knight, you will have made a lifelong enemy."

"I'm not worried about that. I like what I see. Now I must warn you, once I acquire a percentage of the stock, I'll be your partner for life."

"You mean we can't buy you out later?" Paul asked.

"Exactly. Once I become a partner, that's how it works. I'm a venture capitalist, not a miracle worker, nor am I in the charity business. I'm very careful about how I invest my money and I expect a good return on it."

"Well, what's one more partner?" Paul said.

The men shook hands and talked about calling their lawyers to draw up the legal papers.

"Oh, one other thing," Palladin said. "Let's keep a low profile on our deal and let the other team put their cards on the table first."

"Sounds good to me," Paul said.

Brett looked at Palladin and then turned to the men. "I know this is going to sound strange, but don't even tell your other partner who's bailing you out."

Since their situation was desperate, they agreed to just say they had a white knight and would not lose the company.

After they left, Palladin said he was glad that Brett added that last term.

"Something bothers me about Jeff. I can't put my finger on it, but if my partners were taking a meeting, I'd make sure I was there also," Brett said.

"Let's go talk to your lady."


Just before Nia reached her house, Lee flagged her down. Nia pulled over.

"Please, can I borrow your car? My agent set up this audition and my car is still in the shop. I just have to get to the beauty parlor."

Nia laughed and handed Lee the keys. It was

then she noticed Jared's car sitting in front of her house. She walked over to his car. She stood on the sidewalk and waited.

"Nia, we need to talk. Get in. I promise it won't take long."

"We have nothing to say to each other."

"Come on. It's important."

"What is it?"

"Get in and I'll tell you," Jared said and smiled.

Nia turned, opened her gate, and marched up her walkway. By the time Jared could get out of the car, she was at the front door. She put her key in the lock and turned just as he was about to open the gate.

"Does the word 'trespassing' mean anything to you?"

He stopped. "Nia, this is ridiculous. Just because your boyfriend and I are on opposite sides of a deal, doesn't mean we can't be civil to each other."

"What do you want?"

"It's not for me. It's Mother. She wants to talk to you about the beach house. The one you liked so much."

"I'm not in the market for another house right now," Nia said.

"It's about *your* beach house," Jared told her. "She can get the owners to give you a good deal. Please just think it over." He then got back in his car and drove off.

Nia had forgotten about the manila envelope until she was putting her briefcase away. She took it out and sat on her bed while she stripped off the tape and dumped the contents on the bed. Several yellowed newspaper clippings fell out. One was a picture of Daphne leaving the hospital after Jared's birth. Another covered the funeral of Jared's father. There were a few more clippings of the Schuylers and some of Nia and Alethia at business functions. Nothing seemed important enough to hide.

Palladin and Brett were still in the meeting with Kent, Nia thought. Bryant Electronics was making money, but there were other companies that were just as ripe for a takeover and worth much more. Of course, the others didn't belong to the friend of the woman who jilted her son.

The bank had opened three days before but Nia had not participated in the festivities. The newspapers covered it and so did the tabloids. The unsolved murder was again grist for the mill. Each day Nia buried herself in work and waited for the stories to be replaced with other gossip or breaking news stories.

Nia tossed clothes in the washer and set the dial. She had just enough time to do one load before she had to get to the bank. In her position as acting CEO, she'd had to spend quite a lot of time checking records and keeping the bank solvent. Sometimes when there was any scandal with a bank, people panicked and began switching their money to another bank. Since the earlier run on the bank, things appeared to be settling down and some of the clients had returned. They were accustomed to the employees of the smaller bank knowing who they were and what they liked. She wanted to be sure that the customers would be comfortable with the change.

The dryer stopped and Nia began separating and folding the clothes. She remembered how she and Brett had done the laundry together. He was a man used to taking care of himself and didn't think of

it as "women's work" as Jared had. She had confused age with wisdom when she assumed that
Jared was better for her than Brett. She would
never do that again. She'd tried to get Brett to see
the good side of Los Angeles, but he still had his
love for the space Wyoming provided.

She heard the SUV pull into the driveway. Palladin and Brett had returned. She opened the back
door and waved.

They waved back and talked to each other for a
few minutes before entering the kitchen.

"I wasn't sure you were home. I didn't see the
car," Brett said.

"Lee borrowed it. How did it go?" she asked.

"Kent and Paul seem to be on the same page
but Jeff kept throwing monkey wrenches into the
mix."

"What is he doing?"

"Asking questions about breaking up the partnership. He wanted to know if they could split up
the company and then get back together at a later
date."

"Can they?"

"No. If they try it Jared will make his move and
they will not be a united force so he'll win."

"It's amazing what's happened to the people who
have crossed Daphne Schuyler. I know she's a
widow, but what exactly happened to her husband?" Palladin said.

"I have something to show you," Nia said. She
went into the bedroom and gathered up the clippings.

She gave them to Brett. "Charlotte says they were
taped to the back of a file cabinet in Alethia's office."

"Why would someone keep what amounts to society clippings hidden?" Brett asked. "Maybe there's something else that ties this together. What about her husband? It doesn't say what he died of."

"He passed away from cancer a couple of years before I married Jared." Nia saw the muscle tighten in Brett's jaw. So did Palladin.

"What are you thinking?" Palladin asked.

"I think we'd better find out more about how her husband lived and died."

"I think you're right, but I've got to call Jesslyn. I'll use my cell phone."

"Don't be silly, use the phone in the living room," Nia told him.

After Palladin left, she turned to Brett. "Is it a problem for you that this deal involves my ex-husband?"

"Not at all," he drawled. "It's just every time I hear his name I wonder why he wasn't a better husband. How could he always take his mother's side?"

"He wasn't a better husband because I wasn't a better wife. I thought he was the answer to all my problems. I was marrying a wealthy man who encouraged me to have a powerful career. I didn't know until after we were married that Daphne planned to groom me to fit into the family business. I wouldn't quit my job."

Brett winced. He couldn't believe he'd been so strongly against something she loved. It must have been his need to feel in control at that time. The career was no longer a problem for him, but he hoped that they would find Alethia's murderer before he returned to Wyoming. He hated the thought that by association Nia's life could be in danger.

"Daphne tried to talk me into being part of the family business, but mergers and acquisitions never interested me. She, on the other hand, loved the idea of taking over a business, building it up and then selling it for a huge profit."

"So you and Alethia provided resources to save the businesses and Jared and Daphne wanted them to fail and sell out."

"That's about the size of it. Would you like something to eat?"

"No, thanks. Kent's partner kept us well supplied with food during the meeting."

"It's obvious Paul isn't watching his weight."

"Well, he'd better get started."

"What are your plans for the rest of today? I have to go to work for a couple of hours."

"I don't know. Let me check."

He walked into the living room. Palladin's back was to the door. Brett heard him talking to his wife.

"Are the boys giving you a hard time? I miss you," he said. "Let's get away for a weekend when I get back."

Brett didn't mean to eavesdrop, but it was something about a man who'd been married more than fifteen years talking to his wife about getting away together. He'd heard his father and stepmother say the same thing. He realized that was what he wanted. Trisha had given up her career to become partners with his stepfather. Palladin and Jesslyn had two houses, one in Pennsylvania and one in New York, but they were never separated. In fact, he didn't know anyone who had a commuter relationship.

How could he and Nia have the same closeness if they were going to be separated by a time zone?

Palladin said good-bye to his wife and Brett snapped out of his reverie. "Nia wants to know where we'll be for the afternoon," Brett said.

"I know this is hard for her, but I'd really like to check out Alethia's place."

"The police didn't find anything."

"Sometimes something ordinary holds a clue."

They went into the kitchen and asked Nia for the keys to Alethia's house. The question caught her off guard for a moment, but she nodded and went to get them.

Nia rummaged through her tote bag until she found a rectangular key chain with Alethia's name on it and several keys. "I haven't been able to bring myself to go over there. I know I have to do it soon."

She pointed out the keys that would open the front door and the closet where Alethia kept her important papers. Maybe something would tie back to the newspaper items.

"I'm surprised that she didn't keep much in her safe deposit box," Brett said.

"I suggested that once and she said what if she needed something when the bank was closed," Nia explained.

"She should have made copies." Palladin said. "Then she could have the originals in the safe deposit box. Did she ever say why the papers were important?"

"No. You have to understand that Alethia came from a background where secrecy was important. She was raised by her father. He paid for her brother to go to college, but felt she'd get a degree, then just get married so it would be a waste.

She never told him about the scholarship she got. She just moved out and never looked back."

"Did they ever reconcile?" Brett asked.

"No. Her father considered what she did a betrayal and no one notified her when he was sick until it was too late. Her brother is still around, but when I called him, he didn't seem to care."

"So she left him one dollar and you her estate," Brett said.

"Mmm, she was a smart lady. She knew if she didn't mention her remaining family they might contest the will. She covered all the bases," Palladin added.

"That's the kind of woman she was." Nia felt her throat closing and the tears coming. She turned and busied herself with the laundry.

"I'll call you when we're on the way back," Brett said.

As she said good-bye to Brett and Palladin, she remembered her cell phone had signaled it was low and needed to be recharged. She returned to her bedroom, searched through her tote again and pulled out the cell phone. She put it in the charger before she showered, and changed clothes. The doorbell rang. She was relieved to find Lee waiting for her rather than Jared.

Her neighbor looked quite professional with her hair in a French twist instead of her usual ponytail. Her blue linen dress was also a far cry from the tattered jeans she always wore.

"While I was under the dryer, they called to say my car was ready." Lee gave a dramatic sigh. "I filled your tank and I replaced the potato chips I ate. I like your idea of having supplies in the car. I'm going to do the same thing."

"Thanks. I didn't get a chance to ask you earlier. How did the other audition go?"

"It was postponed until next week," Lee said. "I have to go back to talk to them," Lee said and laughed. "I need the exposure, even if it's only a weird TV movie. I need to pay a few more bills."

"Good luck."

"Now I have to convince a producer that I'm the woman who can handle a low budget. Gotta run now. Frank's coming over for dinner."

"So long."


Brett and Palladin drove to Alethia's condominium in West Hollywood. She'd lived there since she became a tenured professor at Stanford. It was one that had a two-car parking space and they pulled in alongside of her Buick Century. Brett made a mental note to remind Nia that she'd have to decide to sell the car or keep it. Palladin waited at the door for Brett. He hadn't called Nia to tell her what they were doing.

Once inside, Brett turned on the lights. The apartment had been closed too long and was hot and musty. He found the air conditioner's switch and turned it on. The radio was playing. Evidently no one had turned it off since the police completed their investigation. The weatherman had been talking about another rainstorm. This one might be worse than the last. It made Brett think about the rest of the night. He could drop Palladin off at his hotel and get back in time to have a nice quiet dinner with Nia. It might even finish the way their last quiet dinner had, with lovemaking as the dessert.

The computer appeared to be in need of repair. The screen was dusty, the monitor wasn't plugged in and the CPU was across the room. He and Palladin spent a few minutes assembling all the pieces and attaching the connections.

He turned on the computer and waited. The screen lit up and he hoped that the information on the hard disk would shed some light on Alethia's business dealings. Nia had mentioned she had several irons in the fire if the bank didn't work out.

"Uh-oh," he said.

"What's the matter?" Palladin asked.

"I need a password."

"That's unusual. Most people don't need a password on their home computers, unless they have inquisitive roommates."

"So Alethia Madison may have a secret life hidden in here."

"What could she have used as a password?"

They tried her name, initials, even her telephone number, to no avail.

"Brett, she'd probably used something that's easy to remember. Something that was important to her." He snapped his fingers and leaned over the keyboard.

The screen opened.

"See, I told you. It would be something very important to her," Palladin said.

The password was "Nia."


Nia was about to leave for the bank when the phone rang. Lisabeth Hemmings' voice was just a whisper.

"I can't get Kent and I'm stuck in Malibu. I'm afraid. My car won't start."

"Afraid of what?"

"The storm."

Nia sighed. Lisabeth was probably near panic and Nia had to help her. "I think everyone is still in the meeting. I'll come pick you up."

"Maybe you should just get in touch with—"

"I'll be there before you know it."

She hung up, grabbed her purse and ran out to her car. Lee had been chatting with another neighbor and called to her.

"Did I leave my makeup kit in your car?"

Nia opened the door and looked around. The small case, that could only have housed a lipstick and powder sponge, was on the floor under the driver's seat. She retrieved it and took it over to Lee.

"Thanks, my purse fell off the seat and I just missed it. Are you going to the bank?"

"I was but a friend is stranded in Malibu and I'm going to pick her up."

"Do you think you should? I heard the weatherman say that a really bad storm is headed our way."

"Don't worry, Lee, I'll be there and back in a couple of hours."

Nia turned and walked back to her car. She'd been driving ten minutes when she realized she'd left her cell phone in the charger. Hopefully Lisabeth had hers.

A light rain had started by the time Nia reached Malibu. She pulled into a parking space in front of the beach house and ran for the door. She knocked and when there was no answer, she turned the doorknob. The door wasn't locked.

She walked in and slowly called Lisabeth's name. "Run! Get the police," Lisabeth screamed.

Nia took another step into the room where she could see Lisabeth. She felt someone behind her. As she turned, she caught a glimpse of something as it crashed against her head. Then everything went black.

# Thirty-two

"Nia . . . Nia."

She heard her name, but could not move. Shards of pain pierced her head. Someone called her name again. Slowly, she opened her eyes. The unfamiliar room came into focus. She was at the beach house. Lisabeth had called her for a lift.

Nia looked around the room. It had been reduced to rubble. Porcelain fragments of what had been the thimble collection were scattered across the room. Paintings were missing from the wall and the china closet was lying on its side. The rain hadn't stopped.

She should have waited for Brett. She should have realized the normally talkative Lisabeth was not talking about the storm when she said she'd been left alone at the beach. Nia pulled herself into a sitting position.

"Nia . . . please wake up."

Lisabeth! She saw the woman pinned under a beam that had fallen from the ceiling. She was trapped. She looked up and saw another beam sagging. Nia's brain began to focus on the real problem—survival.

"I'm okay. We've got to get out of here."

"Thank God! I thought you'd never wake up. I thought you'd be unconscious and we'd drown and you'd never know." Lisabeth began to sob. The thin beach coverup she wore over her bikini did nothing to keep her warm. Her teeth chattered loud enough for Nia to hear them. "Daphne left. She said . . . we'd only last an hour."

They had been warned about the dangers of the unfinished house. *"It's close to the ocean and the delays in building put it in danger of falling if there's a bad storm."* They had to get out of the house. She dragged herself over the beam and tried to push it. It didn't move.

"How long ago did she leave?"

"I don't know. I can't get this thing off of me. We're going to die. Daphne wants us dead and she always gets what she wants. . . ." She pounded her fist on the beam.

"Lisabeth! Calm down. We can't get out of here unless you get yourself under control."

"But we—"

"Shut up!"

Lisabeth stopped talking and moving. She looked at Nia. It was as if she'd been awakened from a nightmare and didn't know where she was or what was happening.

"I'm sorry, but you were getting hysterical. We have to think. We have to get out of here."

"I don't think there's anyone around to help. I heard Daphne tell someone that we were just leaving. I think it was the police."

The house shifted and the beam pressed against Lisabeth and she screamed in pain. A lamp fell to the floor and smashed into thousands of pieces.

Nia's head throbbed, her stomach churned, but she had to help Lisabeth.

"I'm going to see if anyone is still around who can help. Sometimes the police and rescue squads swing by again because they know people don't always leave when they're told."

Nia wanted to give Lisabeth a ray of hope, but deep inside she didn't believe that anyone could help them. The house had not been protected enough and the storm had hit early. Only Mother Nature could wreak this type of havoc on man.

If the beach-house renovation had been completed, their chances would have been better. She held on to the front door as the rain battered against her. She looked for flashing lights that would signal that a rescue team was in the area—nothing. She couldn't hear anyone calling for help or checking for stranded homeowners. They had probably made one sweep and assumed that everyone had been evacuated. She returned to try to help Lisabeth, but the truth of the matter was they would probably have to wait out the storm and pray they would still be alive.

Brett and Palladin began reading the files. Most didn't make any sense.

"We're going to let Nia sort this out," Brett said. He opened the desk and found a zip diskette and copied the files onto it.

Palladin turned on the television and heard about the storm. They showed pictures of rescues from the last time California had a storm. He turned the TV off and continued searching.

Palladin found some documents hidden behind a picture of Nia and brought them over to Brett.

"Alethia Madison loved Nia like a daughter."

"I know. She didn't have any children and so Nia filled that void," Brett said.

The men shut down the computer and locked up.

By the time they got to Nia's, the weather reports were predicting bad storms. They didn't see her car in the driveway. When they entered the house, to see if she'd left a note, Brett saw her cell phone on the charger.

"Any idea where she'd be?" Palladin asked.

"She's probably at the bank."

Brett picked up the telephone in the kitchen and dialed the bank. No one had seen her.

"I have a bad feeling about this," he said. "Maybe Lee knows where she is."

"Lee?"

"A neighbor. She's an aspiring actress."

Brett ran next door. He was stunned to learn that Nia was in Malibu. He rushed back and told Palladin.

"I can tell you think we should go there," Palladin said. "I saw some rescues and it could be dangerous."

"She might try to wait out the storm there and that's the last thing she should do."

"She's lived here a long time, wouldn't she know what to do?"

"She hasn't spent that much time at the beach. All she talks about is her consulting career and the bank."

"Then I guess we'd better get there quick," Palladin told him. "I saw a couple of evacuations going on."

"Call Kent and tell him what's happening."

Palladin made the call and then had to convince Kent not to try to make it to Malibu.


Brett cursed the traffic as he swerved around stalled cars and stranded people to get onto I-10. He drove west on the Santa Monica Freeway. Normally the drive would take about forty-five minutes, but with the rain, wind and heavy traffic, it would be much longer. The radio announcements about more rain on the way scared him. He thought about the danger Nia was in. He pounded on the steering wheel with his fist.

"Calm down," Palladin told him. "We'll make it. You're starting to drive like Jesslyn."

As he hoped, that comment took Brett's mind off Nia. "Your wife is an excellent driver."

"She is until she gets nervous, upset or angry. The she's a crazy woman."

"I only saw her get like that once," Brett said. "When Ethan got hurt."

Palladin laughed. "I don't know how she managed to get to the hospital without getting a ticket."

They drove in silence for a few minutes. Then Brett thought about Daphne.

"Are we really sure Daphne killed Alethia?"

"It's always amazing what money will make people do," Palladin told him. He'd watched his mentor sink to the depths because of greed. He'd felt shocked and betrayed by Mac. "The evidence says yes, but there's a wild card in this mix."

"Jared?" Although Brett said the name as if it was a question, he knew that was the only other possibility. All the other players in the game—the bank, the backers, the community—would have used the law to push her aside. Only someone who had a personal vendetta would have killed her in this way.

"Alethia helped Nia get herself together after the divorce. He might have felt that Nia would have come back to him. It's been obvious from the time I got here that he didn't like Alethia." Palladin remembered the pictures in the newspapers at his father's funeral. Jared had seemed to be relieved, not sad. He wondered why Alethia held on to those papers.

"Nia wouldn't have gone back to him. She believes in learning from the past, not repeating it."

"What about repeating the past with you?"

"We're not repeating the past. We aren't going to be business partners. We're going to be married."

"Does Nia know that?"

She will. I'm going to tell her right after I ring her neck for running off without me."

Both men knew the conversation was just keeping their minds occupied. There was a possibility that the police would start closing the roads and they wouldn't be able to make it to the beach house.

"I'll give Nia a chance to look at the notes before we call in the police. She might get a different take on them."

"I hope we make it before it starts raining too hard."

As soon as the words left Palladin's mouth, the sky opened up and rain pounded on the SUV.

"Any other time that would have been funny." Brett grimaced. "There's rain gear in the backseat. It's in that blue box. Would you get it out? We're probably going to have seconds to get the women out of there."

Palladin gave a low whistle when he saw the supplies in the backseat. "What, are you expecting to be cut off from civilization for a couple of years?"

"Nia and I were going camping with Kent and Lisabeth."

"And you needed all the comforts of home? I thought camping was about roughing it?"

"You haven't met Lisabeth. Her idea of roughing it means the servants stay home and you have to cook." He wondered now if they would ever have the chance to fulfill that camping promise. "Women! I can't believe Nia just took off. She just had to do it her way."

"One day you'll accept the fact that strong women are always going to do what they want and we have to let them." Palladin chuckled.

"I don't know. . . ." Brett sighed and pulled the SUV into another lane, hoping to lessen the travel time.

Palladin knew that both he and Kaliq had fallen in love with and married strong women. When Brett had lived with the Rushes, the gentle type never lasted, no matter what he said. It wasn't in his nature to have a passive wife. In fact, the best thing going for them at the moment was Nia's resiliency.

\* \* \*

The women sat in the living room, frustrated by their lack of brute force. They had given up on moving the beam. Now they just listened to the rain and prayed.

"Why would anyone want to live this close to the beach?" Nia asked. "Storms seem to hit here first."

"Yeah, but on the good days it's like heaven." Lisabeth laughed. "If . . . *when* I get out of here, I'm going to rethink this idea. Concrete, clay, heavy traffic and office buildings are beginning to look much better to me."

"I might go back to Wyoming."

"Really?"

"I don't know. Brett thinks we can have a commuter relationship, but I'm not sure. I do know if this deal with the resort goes through, he'll be spending a great deal of time there."

"You'd give up your career for him?"

"Wouldn't you?"

"I don't look at other men anymore. I am a married woman," Lisabeth said. "But if I weren't married, I'd live on top of Mount Rushmore for that hunk."

The women laughed. Nia looked at the lanai. The metal fence around it was leaning farther away from the house. She remembered the workmen had left ropes that they'd used to pull sections of the roof up.

"Nia, what's the matter? What are you staring at?"

"I've got an idea." She crawled to the unfinished section of the house and got the rope. She began to wrap it around the end of the beam.

"What are you doing?"

"I am finding a miracle. I think the railing is going to fall off the lanai."

"And that's a good thing?"

"If my plan works, yes. If it doesn't . . . we won't think about it not working."

Nia finished wrapping the beam and then crept out to the railing. The rain pounded down on her, but she managed to use the rope to keep her balance. She looped the rope between the fence's railings and wrapped it over and over. Then she made her way back to Lisabeth.

"Listen carefully," Nia told her. "The next time the house shifts, the railing will go and it should pull the beam enough for you to get out."

They waited for what seemed to be an eternity before the shift happened, but when it did, the fence gave way and pulled the beam toward the opening.

Lisabeth scrambled free and the two women headed for the door. Just before they reached it, the house shifted again and another beam fell. This one separated the two women, tossing Nia back into the living room. Lisabeth screamed as she saw Nia sliding toward the opening. If she fell into the ocean, she would be lost. Lisabeth tried to grab Nia. She caught the sleeve of her shirt, but it ripped from the shoulder. She only held the sleeve and Nia was slipping away. The ocean roared in and knocked Lisabeth back. The gate went over the side of the balcony.

Then the door shattered and Brett's tall frame filled the doorway. Palladin was right behind him. He picked Lisabeth up. Her fingers dug into his clothing.

"Nia's over there," Lisabeth whispered.

When the men turned, there was nothing. No sign of Nia. Brett's heart stopped. She must have been dragged out into the ocean.

"She had the rope and she tied it to the fence."

Brett charged over the debris and followed the rope. He looked down. Nia was clinging to the fence. She was too exhausted or too terrified to make any noise.

"Nia," he called. "I'm here. I . . ." there were no words. He caught the rope and pulled. Nothing happened. There was only one way to save her and yet it would be the last thing anyone would consider.

He prayed she heard and understood him. If she held on to the railing, it worked against what Brett was trying to do. Another time, it might be all that kept her from the ocean's pull, but right now it was her worst enemy. She would have to put complete trust in him and he wasn't sure she even heard him.

He pulled the Swiss army knife from his pocket. He opened the knife and cut the rope. Now he could wrap the rope around his waist.

Palladin returned, but another beam fell and smashed a hole in the floor. "It's not going to hold both of us, Brett. Try to wrap the rope around one of the pilings."

Brett fought the rain and wind and did what Palladin suggested. He walked around the column so he could eventually use it as a pulley. He then walked to the edge of the balcony where Nia still clung to the fence railing.

"I can only pull you up if you let go of the fence," Brett called over the storm. "Can you hear me? Let go of the fence."

He saw her head move; then slowly she held up both hands. Using all his strength he pulled the rope. It tore the skin from his palms and he felt the blood trickle like water. As he reached the middle of the room, Nia's head appeared above the balcony edge. He pulled until she was lying on the balcony. Then he threw the rope down and ran to her. He lifted Nia over his shoulder in a fireman's carry and rushed from the house. He reached the SUV and put Nia down. They heard what sounded like an explosion and turned. The beach house tilted and slid into the ocean.

Brett hugged Nia tightly and then pushed her away as he said, "You never listen to me. I said, wait for me. But no, you had to do it your way."

"Don't yell at me."

"Hey, can you two lovebirds wait a couple of hours to have this fight? They're going to close the rest of the road pretty soon."

Brett climbed behind the wheel and Nia took the passenger seat. She took the robe and towel Palladin offered and thanked him.

As Brett backed into the street, they took one last look at the shambles of a house that had once been the envy of so many. Then they drove away.

Palladin had given Lisabeth a heavy terry-cloth robe to cover herself and a towel to dry her hair. "Thank you," she said. "Does my husband know where I am?"

"Yes, he does," Palladin told her.

"He didn't come with you?" She bit her lip, trying not to cry.

"It isn't that he didn't want to come with us. We convinced him this vehicle would be better equipped to reach you and as soon as we can, we'll give him a call."

"I'm sorry I yelled, but you don't know what it was like to know you were in danger and not being able to contact you," Brett told Nia. "We couldn't even call the police because they were busy with the evacuation."

"I accept your apology," Nia said stiffly. She paused and then the anger dissipated. "How did you know we were still there?"

"I was hoping you weren't. I really wanted to get there, find the house empty and you in one of the shelters. What a mess. The telephone lines were down, so we couldn't even call."

Lisabeth began to cry, more from relief than pain. "It was Daphne," she sobbed. "She tried to kill us."

"I know," Brett said. "We found some things on the computer that implicate her in Alethia's death."

"Did you call the police?" Nia asked.

"We didn't want to make a mistake. We need you to look over the records to see if they made any sense."

Two hours later, Nia, Brett and Palladin were gathered in her living room. The printout from the hidden diskette had told of an ongoing feud between Alethia and Daphne.

The picture that had puzzled Brett and Palladin was very clear to Nia. The circle that said the baby was full term could destroy Jared.

"What's the big deal?" Palladin asked. "They met in July, got married in August and Jared was born in January of the following year. So she was pregnant when they got married."

"She's always maintained that he was a premature baby."

"Right. I agree with Palladin. It's not what they wanted, but it happens. . . . Wait a minute," Brett said.

"Now, if he wasn't a premie, she was pregnant a month before she met her husband," Palladin said.

"And if he's not Schuyler's, then he's not the legitimate heir to his fortune."

"That's what Alethia meant when she told me not to worry about Jared. She was holding this over his head."

For a moment, Nia wanted to cry. She'd always looked up to Alethia and now she'd learn that her mentor was a blackmailer. "What do we do next?"

Palladin understood. "We can't just march into the police station and tell anyone that."

"Why not?" Nia said. "It's true."

"You can testify about her attack on you, but not Alethia's murder. Jared had as much reason as Daphne. They'll probably work out a story and without proof . . ."

"So I guess I'm asking the same question," Nia said.

"We look through these papers until we find something. If we don't, then we'll have to go with the attempt and hope the police can tie her to Alethia."

"Where's the yellow Zip diskette?" Nia asked.

"We brought everything here."

"I know she had one that she said was all the information she would ever need."

"Nia's right," Brett said. "She said that I should look for it if anything happened to her."

"Suppose I drive over to her house and look for it . . ." Palladin offered.

"No, wait." Nia jumped up and ran into her bedroom. She returned with a box. "I got this a couple of days after . . . after . . . but I was afraid to open it."

She slid it into her computer and waited for the index to appear. Only a few seconds passed before it was on the screen.

# Thirty-three

Nia removed her jacket and folded it next to her while she examined the files from the hard drive and diskettes Brett and Palladin had found once they'd broken the code. She glanced at the clock. It was seven-thirty at night. With all that had happened, she thought it was much later. Then she realized it was only a little after three when she had arrived at the beach house.

She began sorting through the information. Alethia was such a detail-oriented person there was much that didn't matter. Nia had to wade through it all to find the files that could possibly reveal something someone would kill for.

It was all there. Document after document on everyone. Although she knew that they were looking for information on Daphne, the first file Nia opened was her own.

To her relief the data only started after her divorce from Jared. She would have been crushed if Alethia had kept notes about her for anything earlier. It would have meant that she planned to use her in some way, for that was exactly what happened to everyone else she kept files on.

"She tried to protect me without telling me."

"Why did she contact me?" Brett asked.

Nia made a quick keystroke to do a "find" for Brett's name. The entry was about Brett's first big business deal. The second was the fact that he had acted as a white knight for a friend whose company was in the middle of a hostile takeover.

"She knew you were a good businessman and the best way to attack Jared was through business. That's why she asked you to save Kent's company."

She printed out the file and gave part of it to Brett and the rest to Palladin.

She didn't tell him that there was another file with his name on it. While they reviewed the print-out, she moved the second file from the diskette to the C-drive and then put in a blank diskette and saved it. She slipped that one into her jacket pocket.

As they perused the diskette index, Nia found something odd. A file for only one of Kent's partners—Jeff Michaelson.

"Why only Jeff?"

They opened the file and read his bio and how the partnership had formed. The only thing mildly unusual was that he had been part of a deal with Jared before Kent. He was just another partner. He had not been a good businessman and when he was first approached about the electronics firm, he didn't have enough money to be part of the deal. Nothing seemed sinister, until his financial records came up, and they stared at the screen.

"So that's why," Nia said as she read the information. Alethia had recorded a telephone conversation with Daphne where she talked about having a mole in the perfect place.

"I guess we'd better talk to Kent and Jeff," Brett said.

"I agree. He didn't seem to have anything to liquidate, so where did he get the money?"

"Aren't we going to tell the police about Daphne?"

"Not yet."

"Why not? She tried to kill Lisabeth and me."

"I know, sweetheart, but I think she may have killed Alethia. Wouldn't you rather have her arrested for that crime than the attempted one on you?"

"Of course." Tears came to her eyes when she thought about Alethia. Everyone was convinced that she had surprised a burglar and he had accidentally killed her. That in itself was a horrible way to die, but now it appeared someone had deliberately taken her life. Someone, whom she let into her office that night, killed her. Someone she trusted or thought she could control.

"It could have been Daphne."

"Or Jared. What if he killed Alethia and Daphne was protecting him by getting you and Lisabeth out of the way?"

"This is getting to be a truly tangled web. Why can't we call the police?"

"We need the motive. Why did someone kill Alethia?" Palladin asked. "Keep searching through those files."

After another few minutes, they hadn't discovered anything else and decided to go see Jeff Michaelson. Perhaps he could shed more light on what was happening.

Brett called Kent and explained that other problems had appeared and there would be a delay in calling the police. They explained their suspicions and asked if he wanted to talk to Jeff with them. Kent declined. Lisabeth was still frantic so he opted out of going with them to Jeff's. "If he is the one that's been making these deals harder than they should be, I'll never do business with him again."

"What will you do? Spread the word about him?" Brett asked.

"No. I don't want to do that. It might hurt his kids."

Brett retrieved Alethia's address book and leafed through it until he found the listing he needed. He placed a call to Jeff and set up a meeting.

"Stay here," Brett said to Nia. "We're going to have a little talk with Jeff."

Nia said nothing. However, when the men went to retrieve their rain slickers, she was right behind them.

"Nia . . ."

"Don't even say it, Brett. Alethia sent me the diskette. She wanted me to know what was going on around me."

Brett looked at Palladin for support, but got none.

Not long after that, they stood in front of Jeff's house.

It was a two-story colonial. He'd purchased the house after his divorce so when his children visited they would still have their own rooms. Nia remembered him proudly showing her their pictures when they had first met.

It was after nine when they got to Jeff's house. He didn't seem surprised to see them.

"Come on in," he said. "Can I get any of you something to drink? It's the butler's night off so I'm fending for myself."

They knew he didn't have a butler. It was his way of being sarcastic, but they didn't understand why.

His guests declined but Jeff poured himself a shot of scotch. They introduced him to Palladin. The men did not shake hands.

"I bet I know why you're here," Jeff said as he sipped his drink. "You finally figured out why Jared could run circles around you with Bryant Electronics.". He turned to Palladin. "You must be the white knight that will make everything bad go away."

"Since we all know what this is about," Brett said, "why did you do it?"

"You don't have enough time in the world to listen to all the reasons. Why don't I just tell you about Daphne? She came to me with a proposition. She found out that everything connected with Bryant Electronics had come from me."

"She just asked you to help her get the company for her son?" Nia asked.

"She knew they stole it from me and she said she'd get it for her son and he would make me a silent partner."

"I don't understand how you could do that to your friends," Nia said.

"They weren't my friends. We didn't come from the same background and they never let me forget it."

"So you sold them out?" Brett added.

"You think you're so smart. You're all alike. Rich, spoiled, eased into Ivy League schools. I knew I was smarter than Jared, Paul and Kent."

"What are you talking about? You graduated from Harvard just like Jared and Kent."

"Sure. But I had to live through three years of city college. While they were making contacts from the first day of school, I was trying to work during the day and go to college at night. I had to work my way into their little clique."

"You should be proud of what you did."

"Did you know that acquiring Bryant Electronics was my idea? The old man didn't know what he had or what it could become, but I did. I just didn't have the money."

"So you called Kent and Paul."

"Right. They made me a partner and thought they'd done something fair."

The bitterness tinged every word—the venom and the need to destroy the men he felt cheated him. "I wanted someone to give them trouble and I dropped a few hints to Alethia. I was hoping that you would come in and see that it was a great deal."

Palladin nodded. "You wanted the 'white knight' to like the deal so much that he would step in and push Kent and Paul to the side."

"Right! Too bad you didn't. Too bad you became friends instead of enemies."

"So you leaked information through Daphne to Jared."

"Another set of people who didn't have a moment's struggle. She thought she was so smart. I played them up and down and they never caught on. If this thing with Alethia Madison hadn't happened, you guys wouldn't have dissected this deal."

"So why were you so gung-ho to help them take the bank away from Alethia?"

"Hah!" He gave a bitter laugh. "Sorry, guys, that credit doesn't go to me. I never cared about the bank, but it's a compliment that you think I was capable of manipulating so many people."

He walked over and began to throw logs in the fireplace. It was as if he had gotten a sudden chill knowing that this would be the last deal he would work on with Kent. He knew it had come to an end and he was prepared. The only thing that shocked him was the time it had taken. In only a matter of a few weeks, Nia and Brett had gotten to the heart of the situation. It didn't matter that they weren't looking for it. It only mattered that they recognized it and followed through.

"I guess Kent will destroy me."

"No, Jeff. He isn't like that," Nia said. "If you had been honest with him, I'm sure things would have turned out differently. Kent isn't out to steal dreams. He likes making them come true."

"Yeah—yadda, yadda, bring out the violins."

"He's a very smart businessman and dragging you into court would be detrimental in the long run," Palladin answered.

"So what's it going to be?" Jeff asked.

"He's going to ask you to bow out of Bryant Electronics."

"Now he's really stolen everything."

They were heading for the door when Brett turned and said, "I'd like to give you some advice. You can use your brain and find another great deal, or you can keep believing that you're some kind of victim and let it destroy you."

"Don't give me advice, Brett. My wife left me because she said I was obsessed with this deal. Now I don't have a deal or a wife. You people don't know what it is to struggle and lose someone you love." He whirled and slammed the glass into the fireplace, shattering it, much the same way he had his life, without a single thought.

\* \* \*

Brett, Nia and Palladin left him. Palladin got in the backseat and promptly fell asleep. They would wake him up when they got to his hotel. Then they would also try to sleep. Tomorrow would tell the tale. If the police believed them, Daphne would be questioned about Alethia. If they still didn't believe Alethia was murdered, Daphne would be arrested for what she had done to Nia and Lisabeth.

"He's never going to change is he?" Nia asked.

"You can't heal the world," Brett said. "There will always be people out there who blame anyone and everyone for their failures."

"Yeah. He's so used to playing the victim he didn't even see the chance he had to win big," Brett added.

"Now can we call the police?" Nia asked.

"Absolutely, honey. I don't know how much of this they'll believe."

"Then let's only give them enough to make them question Daphne."

"Think she'll tell them anything?"

"Who knows?"

They dropped Palladin off and drove to Nia's.

The house was dark. They stopped in the mud room to shed the rain gear and boots. Nia stayed there as Brett entered first and went from room to room as he checked the doors and windows. He stoked the fire to life in the master bedroom. They were tired yet not sleepy. Their adrenaline still pumped so strongly they would be unable to rest.

He returned and assured her that they were safe. He doubted that Daphne even knew that Nia and Lisabeth had escaped. The woman was so sure she had eliminated the last of her trouble that she was probably sleeping like a baby.

"Get ready for bed. I'll be in shortly," he told her.

He stopped in the kitchen and selected a bottle of Merlot. The full-bodied wine should relax them. He grabbed two wineglasses and joined Nia in the master bedroom.

Just as he thought, she was staring at the ceiling, unable to turn off her thoughts. She sat up when she saw the wine. He handed her a glass and she smiled. He poured the wine for her and then for himself as he got under the thin blanket.

Having only a thin blanket most of the year might take some getting used to, he thought. He'd never lived anywhere that seasons didn't change dramatically.

They tapped glasses as he said, "To our future." Then they sipped the wine. One glass was all that Nia could handle, but Brett had another. He put his glass down and turned out the light so only the fire illuminated the room, and snuggled under the covers.

"How sleepy are you?" he whispered.

She answered with a faint giggle.

"This isn't funny. We've been through all kinds of hell tonight and right now the only thing on my mind is how much I want you."

She turned to face him. "I know how you feel. I want you too."

Brett knew that she wasn't talking about romance. She didn't need to be coaxed or lured. Tonight she needed the kind of hot sex that made one feel alive and so did he.

"You are so sweet. I don't know how I let us stay

apart for five long years." He brushed her lips with his, then kissed her long and hard.

She kissed him back, then pressed her nightgown-clad body against his so she could deliberately feel his growing desire.

They wriggled apart just long enough to shed their clothes and again she pressed herself against him. Now it was perfect. Skin to skin. No thinking. No talking. Only feeling.

His lips left her face and quickly found other parts of her body to savor. Each whispered meaningless words as passion responded to passion. The tip of his tongue stroked her neck, then down to her breasts, then her belly. A sharp spike of need shot through him as he thought about the possibility of them creating a child. He'd told women that he wasn't the husband type and yet he could not just live with Nia without the piece of paper that would bind them. He'd also told women that he had no desire to become a father. He now knew that wasn't true. He wanted to father Nia's child. He wanted the bond that would tie them together forever. He wanted a reminder of this night for the rest of his life.

They had never made love like this before. Not together, not with anyone else. She could feel him deep inside and, although she knew it was impossible, she wished they could spend a lifetime like this, and if not a lifetime, at least a week.

Everything that had happened to them had been wiped away by their love. No matter how they thought about why they were just allowing their bodies to talk, Nia knew that it could only happen because they loved each other enough to give everything. She'd let him see how much she needed

him. She'd never done that before, nor had he.
They were so perfectly matched. She would do
whatever it took to be with him, even if she had
to walk away from Alethia's vision.

"I can't believe that we did that twice," Brett
whispered.

"Twice?"

"Maybe more," he said and pulled her back into
his arms.


The next morning, Sergeant Bailey listened to
their story and reviewed Alethia's notes with Nia
and Brett. Palladin would join them later at the
board meeting at Bryant Electronics.

"I hate to break it to you, but it's mostly circum-
stantial," the sergeant said.

Nia's heart dropped. It was what she had been
afraid of all along. "So you're saying that Alethia's
note about Daphne on her way over doesn't place
her at the condo that night?"

"Suppose she was on her way. Suppose she got
a flat, a phone call, changed her mind, any and
all of the above. We can only say that she was supposed to be there. Nothing puts her at the scene.
Sorry."

"So she's going to kill my friend and get away
with it?"

"If she's the one who did it. Now we can pull
her in for what happened to you. We'll check to
see if she made any 911 calls on your behalf and
if not, that's our best chance."

Nia caught Brett's hand. "I can't believe this."

"Now there is one thing, miss," Bailey added. "I
can have her picked up and if she thinks that we

can prove more than we can, she might fold and tell us everything."

"I have an idea," Brett said.

Bailey warned him that it might not work, but to catch a murderer he was willing to try. They left the station still afraid that Alethia would not be avenged.

They picked up Palladin, Kent and Lisabeth, briefly explained what they were going to do and headed for Bryant Electronics. When they got there, they were surprised to find the dowdy Marlene sitting in the reception area. She pointed out the room and went back to her desk.

# Thirty-four

"Gentlemen," Daphne Schuyler addressed the board members, "since my son succeeded in putting together the people who can save this business, we intend to let it be known that we are taking over and making some changes. One of them will be to make Jared the new C.E.O. and there's nothing you can do about it."

"Don't you think we should give Hemmings a little more time?" Paul asked.

Jared leaned back in his chair and stared at the man. "Even with more time, he won't be able to save this company. He doesn't have the capital and you know it."

"Have you tried to contact him?" Daphne asked. "I bet you haven't been able to reach him all afternoon."

Paul cleared his throat, and murmured that he'd been unable to contact Kent or Jeff. "I'm sure he's on the way. When we talked last night, he was very confident about finding someone else."

"Still think you can find that white knight and bail yourselves out of trouble? You haven't been able to reach Hemmings and you're his friend as well as his partner," Daphne said and laughed.

"Doesn't that tell you something? Doesn't that tell you that he's failed and he's too embarrassed to even show up?"

Before Paul could respond, the door opened and Kent Hemming and Brett Faulkner stepped into the room.

"What are you doing here?" Jared was genuinely surprised to see Kent and Brett. He was even more surprised to see the large man with dread locks with them.

"I don't think this meeting should continue until all of the principal players are accounted for," Brett said. Let me introduce a new principal—Palladin Rush."

Kent walked over to the empty chair at the head of the table and sat down. Brett and Palladin took seats at his side.

"Good to see you, man," Paul said to Kent. "Where's Jeff?"

"That's a whole 'nother story. I'll tell you later. Sorry I couldn't return your calls. I was deep in negotiation."

"Later we'll talk about the heart attack you almost gave me." Paul turned to Daphne. "Now we can get this meeting started."

"You have no right to be here," Daphne said. Her voice was suddenly high pitched. "How can you do business at a time like this?"

"At a time like what?" Kent asked.

Daphne gasped as she saw Lisabeth and Nia come in. "Now you two definitely don't belong here."

Even though she knew she was safe, Lisabeth could not look at Daphne. Nia was different. She stared at the older woman until Daphne turned away.

"What's going on here?" Jared demanded.

"Allow me to shed some light on the situation. I'm Palladin Rush. I'm what is known as a 'white knight.'" He grinned at the contrasting term. "Kent Hemmings and I have worked out a deal."

"No! You can't just come in here and say that you sold the business to someone else, Hemmings. We had this all sorted out. You can't change the rules this late in the game. Mother, I thought you said everything was taken care of and we controlled the company?"

Daphne put her face in her hands and just shook her head. Jared looked around the room. "So you think you've won the battle, but we will win the war."

Nia shook her head and wondered how this man could have fooled her. He had seemed so strong when he swept her off her feet and into marriage. She'd left Brett because she thought he was too young, only to find a man her own age who was still a child trying to please his mother.

"Your mother has much more to worry about than your little power struggle," Nia told him.

"You and Mother never got along. You're so jealous of her."

"I'm not jealous of her. I feel sorry for her. Attempted murder?" Nia said. She turned to Daphne. "You were supposed to be Alethia's friend."

"Alethia? How could she be my friend? She was a common. She'd managed to work her way into a power position, and I used her until she tried to destroy my son. She dared to say that she was going to ruin Jared's career. I couldn't let that happen."

"Mrs. Schuyler," Brett said. "It's best if you don't say anything else. The police are on the way."

"Don't give me orders, young man." Daphne's voice became more strident.

"Mother. He's right. You shouldn't say anything."

"Very well. I have very powerful attorneys who will destroy you for those accusations."

"Excuse me," Marlene interrupted them. "The . . . uh . . . police are here to see Mrs. Schuyler."

"Nia, I can't believe you're doing this to my mother. Just because you couldn't make our marriage work, you're on some vendetta."

"I'm on a vendetta!" Nia's eyes narrowed and her fingers curled into fists. "We found the computer disk, printed out your mother's little plan to make you a mogul and gave a copy to the police."

"Last night your mother tried to kill Nia and Lisabeth," Brett added.

"Liar," Jared sputtered. "She has no reason to harm them."

Two plainclothes detectives entered the now overcrowded room. They identified themselves and asked for Daphne.

"I'm Daphne Schuyler. How may I help you?"

The detectives approached Daphne. "Ma'am, you'll have to come with us," one said.

*"No!"* Jared shouted. "Wait until we contact our lawyer."

"Don't worry, son," Daphne said, then turned to the detectives. "I'll go with you. I want to straighten this out immediately." Daphne got up and stormed out of the boardroom. The detectives and Jared were right behind her. As they reached the reception area, Daphne clutched her chest and began to hyperventilate. She staggered over to the window.

"She has a heart condition. She needs her pills," Jared yelled. He managed to get them out of her purse. Daphne took the bottle and opened it. "I need some water."

"I'll get it." Jared went back into the conference room.

Nia remembered that once before Daphne had taken the medication without water. *She must be stalling for time,* Nia thought. *She must be so afraid of what is going to happen. She might not be able to make it through a trial.*

Daphne was hidden from the others by the girth of the two policemen. One of them called out, "Don't."

At first, Nia thought the woman had tried to escape, but then she saw the men lower her to the floor. Then one picked up the telephone on the receptionist's desk. "Emergency! A woman is having a heart attack at Bryant Electronics." He gave the address and dropped the receiver into its cradle.

Jared returned with the water and rushed to his mother's side. "Where are her pills?"

"She threw them away," the detective told him.

"Oh, my God!" Nia gasped. Now she understood. Daphne hadn't tried to escape—she'd thrown away the only thing that could preserve her life, her nitroglycerin pills.

Everything around Nia seemed to be going in slow motion. She saw people moving and heard voices, but she couldn't distinguish what they were saying. An ambulance arrived and the paramedics tried to save Daphne, but everyone knew that once she tossed the pills through the open window, she had sealed her fate.

Nia waited outside with Jared until the paramedics put his mother in the ambulance. She was gone, but Jared hadn't accepted that yet. "You're wrong about her, you know," he said. "She would never hurt anyone. Alethia was her best friend. One day the truth will come out." He climbed into the ambulance and the attendants closed the doors.

Everything on Nia hurt. She was so tired. She just wanted to sleep. Maybe she wasn't that tired. Maybe she didn't want to think about what had happened in only a few days. She waited until Brett pulled the SUV around. The police had agreed they could give their statements the next day.

As soon as she got in the car, she closed her eyes and tried not to think about all the questions that would never be answered. She'd been running on pure adrenaline. The exhaustion from the previous night finally took over, and she slept.

Brett took surreptitious glances at Nia as he drove back to her house. It would never happen again. He made a silent vow that he would be there anytime she needed him. Palladin had offered him the position of legal counsel for Bryant Electronics, and he might as well take it. Nia loved California, so that was where they would be living. He caught his reflection in the rearview mirror and laughed at himself. He could have made this move five years before and avoided a lot of pain. Nia was right when she said he wasn't ready, but having lost her once convinced him he never wanted that to happen again. Now all he had to do was convince Nia. They had just agreed to have a long-distance relationship. Other couples hade done it, albeit few successfully. She'd never believe he was willing to move to California, but she'd get used to the idea and he'd get used to California. He thought about his stepmother. Trisha had seemed like a city girl who wouldn't be able to handle the isolation of the Wyoming area his father called home. Now she loved it. She still made frequent trips to New York, but that was more to see her best friend, Jesslyn Rush.

Daphne had committed suicide to avoid the consequences of her actions. She did it all because Jared couldn't fight his own battles. She'd paved the way for him. Every time he wanted something—from the partnership at the law firm to the CEO of the bank. Even Nia had been selected for Jared without his knowledge. Daphne had orchestrated many lives and now that she would not be around, Brett couldn't gather any sympathy for Jared. People had to make their own mistakes and live their own lives. They couldn't expect their parents to make everything right for them.

As the sun set, Nia awoke and as her mind cleared she burst into tears. Her marriage and divorce and career had been a lie. She lay in Brett's arms and sobbed for Alethia, Jared, and even Daphne. After she slept for several hours, she was more in control.

Jared kept the funeral as private as he could, but the curious and the reporters showed up. People attended more out of a strange sense of loyalty to the woman they knew and not the one they were reading about in the newspaper.

Brett and Nia spent the next few days answering questions from the police and avoiding the reporters who were on a feeding frenzy. One of the city's most powerful women was dead and the people wanted to know every sordid detail.

"Next comes the 'tell all' books," Brett said one night.

"What makes you think there will be books?"

"I heard a few comments by the reporters at the police station. They don't know the whole truth, but they know enough to sensationalize this."

"I hope Jared can handle it."

The deal of course, had taken on a different life. Although Kent no longer had to worry about Jared, he realized that his company was still vulnerable. Palladin was still going to become a partner in Bryant Electronics. He would leave the "hands on" to Kent and Paul, but insisted on selecting one member of the board.

Jared would have to wait three years before his trust fund would kick in, but now he was an heir to his mother's estate and it made the trust fund a very small part of his net worth.

That night Nia and Brett watched the coverage on the news. "She was my mother-in-law for almost two years. Why couldn't I see what was happening to her?"

"You know the saying about not being able to see the forest for the trees? You saw her as this strong, invincible woman, but she was only strong when she could use her money and influence to get whatever she wanted. She really believed that she could get away with murder until the police arrived. What happened to Alethia's notes?"

"Darling, you are a lawyer and that means you don't need to know everything."

"Tampering with evidence could get you in a lot of trouble."

"It's only evidence if there was going to be a trial."

"You really mean I don't want to know."

"Right. Everything is going well for the ones Alethia and Daphne left behind and that's how it should be."

"Kent and Lisabeth are vacationing in Hawaii."

"Hawaii? That's a great place for a honeymoon."

Nia still had reservations about a long-distance marriage. "We'll see," she told him.

Now that Palladin Rush owned Bryant Electronics, Nia suspected Kent was relieved.

"Nia, what about the money?"

"What money?"

"Jared's trust fund."

She shook her head. "People are speculating that she killed Alethia to keep her quiet about the take-over. They don't need to know the truth."

"Jared gets to stay very rich. He could live quite well on what his mother left for him. Do you still care about him?" Brett kept his tone matter-of-fact, but Nia saw his jaw twitch.

"He needs the money. It's all he has. It's all he will ever have. He's just not capable of handling his finances. I hope he hires some good people to do that. He'd better pay more attention to Marlene."

"Marlene? His secretary?"

"Yes, for reasons that are beyond me, she's in love with him."

"You're making that up."

"No, I'm not. She was just too soft for Daphne."

"Are you going to give him a little prodding?"

"No. I don't think we'll be seeing a lot of each other. What we had is gone."

Brett relaxed. He could tell she was ready to start a new life. He just hoped it would be with him. He was torn between blurting out his feelings and waiting until she at least suggested he stay in California.

She waited for him to suggest she come back to Wyoming. When he didn't, she waffled between feeling relief and being angry that he didn't even try. The courage to ask him to move to California was slowly fading.

One morning as Nia and Brett were having breakfast, they seemed to be skirting around the real questions that needed answers.

"I've never asked, but how did you know I was in Malibu?"

"I talked to Lee. She was worried about you," he said.

Nia didn't see how this commuter marriage they were planning would work. Spending four or five hours on a plane wasn't her idea of happiness. She hadn't told Brett about the bank's plan to give her Alethia's position. It would be in an acting capacity at first, but if she proved herself, she would become the C.E.O.

Finally, Nia decided to push him into a decision. She might not like the results, but she had to do it and she didn't want to wait around to find out the answers.

"They've asked me to stay with the bank and there may be a C.E.O position in my future," she told him.

"I think you should go for it."

"Well, I'm not sure. It might interfere with our commuter plans." She waited for him to ask her not to take the job. If he only asked her to go back to Wyoming with him, she'd give it up. She could find something there.

"She certainly groomed you for the spot. I think she was hoping that you would someday. I've watched you, and I have to admit you're good."

"I know, so I gave you another chance and you were too chicken to take it."

"You wretch. Don't think I'm not going to make you pay for that. I wanted you to ask me to come back to Wyoming."

"I couldn't do that. You love it here. I want you to be happy. I love you."

"I love you too. I can't believe you just sat there when you knew I needed an answer. I'll make you pay for that too."

"I'm sure you will. Dad and Trisha are going to be a pair of happy campers. Let's have the wedding in Wyoming."

"Let's call Trisha and Kaliq right now!"

"No. Let's call them later." He kissed her and added, "Much later."

# Thirty-five

The rains eventually abated and the newspapers and television stations constantly showed pictures of the damage. The Hemmingses' beach house was a total loss. Kent had the funds to rebuild, but the permits for demolishing the house and rebuilding from scratch would be a long time coming. Lisabeth had recovered nicely from her ordeal, but was taking private self-defense lessons just in case. She confessed how badly she felt about not being able to think when they were trapped in the beach house.

When she and Kent returned, Lisabeth called Nia to tell her they would begin another project.

"With all the safety precautions Kent is talking about, our children will be out of college by the time it's finished."

Although separated in age by more than a decade, Lisabeth and Bree had bonded quickly and soon Julie would be paying them a brief visit, while Jack worked in the home office before returning to Paris. Nia's home and heart were really in Los Angeles. She and Brett had agreed on a commuter lifestyle with promises of never being apart for more than three weeks. Los Angeles would be home.

Nia had talked about her plans during a three-way conversation with Julie and Bree. Each had urged her to give it a try. She agreed with them that happiness could be fleeting. She'd thought that Jared was strong, but it was just a facade. He let his mother push him into things he couldn't handle and then allowed her to bail him out. Brett would never be like that. She was lucky and she should just accept that.

"Then if it doesn't work and you decided to go back to Wyoming, at least you know you tried," Bree told her.

"That's right," Julie had added. "Give it every chance possible."

Brett slipped away while Nia immersed herself in her phone call. Two hours later, he entered the offices of Schuyler and Schuyler. It was quite a different place from the one that had existed when Daphne ran it. Now very masculine tastes permeated the space. The flowers that once sat on everyone's desk had been replaced by dark brown carpets and rich mahogany cabinets. Jared Schuyler had eschewed his mother's taste for that of his competition, not realizing that he'd made it a cookie-cutter image rather than being innovative. He knew how to manipulate people, but not how to make himself stand out in a crowd.

Brett carried a briefcase with potentially damaging information, but since he wore jeans and a shirt, his visit appeared casual. He had come to settle things with Jared once and for all.

Heads turned as he waited for Marlene to press the buzzer to release the small gate. If he really wanted to get in, it would have been quite easy for him to step over it.

Everyone in the room knew who he was from the newspaper accounts of his rescue of Nia and Lisabeth.

"Is that the new man visiting the ex-husband?" asked one of the secretaries.

"Uh-huh. I'd like to be a fly on the wall for that conversation," said another as she gave Brett more than a cursory perusal.

"Get back to work, ladies," Marlene snapped as she made her way from her office and headed toward Brett.

He didn't recognize her at first. Marlene's dress had also changed. Gone were her thick glasses, replaced with contacts. Instead of the loosely fitting dresses he saw before, she now wore a black designer suit with a black-and-white camisole.

*Sexy,* he thought. He wondered if Jared noticed the change, or perhaps had been responsible for it. Nia had told him that Marlene was in love with Jared and for a brief moment he thought about doing her a favor and telling her thick-headed boss to take a closer look at her.

Brett smiled to see this woman half his size thinking she could really stop him if he wanted to see her boss.

"I . . . I have to check with him. . . ."

"Don't worry. He's expecting me." Brett smiled. Jared had another woman ready to protect him. She, like the others, didn't realize how tough Jared Schuyler was, nor how ruthless he could be if he didn't get what he wanted.

Her eyes said she didn't believe him, but before she could pick up the phone, Jared appeared in the doorway.

"Come on in," he said to Brett. Then he turned

to Marlene. "No calls unless the building is burning down."

Despite the puzzled look on her face, she nodded and returned to her desk. Brett noted the change in Jared's demeanor. Now that he was the person making the decisions, he seemed stronger, more decisive. That only reinforced what Brett believed.

They entered the office and Jared motioned to the small conference table on the other side of the room. Brett walked over and sat down in a beige leather chair next to the black one at the head of the table.

"I have to admit I was surprised to hear from you." Jared joined him at the table after Brett refused his offer of coffee.

"So it was your curiosity that made you take the meeting?"

"What do you want? Haven't you done enough to my family?"

Brett decided to put the man out of his misery. He opened his briefcase and pulled out the file and tossed it to Jared.

"What's this?"

"This is the most powerful weapon in the world, the truth."

Jared looked at the plain manila folder as if it might explode if he touched it. "I hate riddles. What's your point?"

"Everything you need to know is in there."

Reluctantly, Jared opened it and began to peruse the documents. He closed the folder after only reading two or three pages. "What do you want?"

"Nothing much. I want you to stop your little revenge plot against my wife and Kent Hemmings."

They weren't married yet but he knew that it would rankle Jared.

Brett noticed Jared wince when he heard the words "my wife."

"If you remember, Brett, it was my mother who had the vendetta against women who she felt hurt me."

"You can do that tap dance for anyone else but not me. I looked at those notes that Alethia made. Each came from a talk she had with your mother. The only way your mother would even have a clue that Nia and Lisabeth were her enemies was because you played on her feelings. You've known a long time that you weren't the true heir to the Schuyler fortune."

"I suppose you can prove that?"

"It's amazing what people say when they're joking around. Remember when we were at the party? Nia called you a fish out of water and you said I'm a goat in fish clothing."

"All of your papers say that you were born February 20, which would make you a Pisces, the fish. Only the papers in Alethia's safe said you were born January 8, which would make you Capricorn, the goat. But you know that. You are not Schuyler's son."

Jared's hands trembled as he ran his fingers over his face. "I don't know what you're talking about. What has that got to do with anything?"

"Don't play dumb at this stage. You know exactly what I'm talking about. You've used your influence all over the city to block the acquisition of the bank. First you tried to stop Alethia's success. That's why she called me. She didn't really care if I bailed Kent out or not. She knew if I thought

Nia was in danger, I'd stay here. She didn't count the length your mother would go to protect you."

"Don't say anything about my mother."

"You used her to get through life and then when you didn't want her around you told her that Alethia was interfering with your takeover project because Nia wanted her to do it."

"Alethia and my mother were friends."

"No, they weren't. You heard what your mother said. She only used Alethia."

"I didn't expect Mother to kill anyone."

"I believe you. However, you knew she'd confront Alethia about the documents. If Alethia knew, you weren't entitled to any money from the Schuyler estate."

"You can't prove that."

"I'm not trying to prove it."

"So what's the point. You have the papers that clearly show Jared Schuyler was not my father. What do you want?"

"I want you to call off your friends and leave the bank alone. Nia wants to fulfill Alethia's dream, and I want Nia happy."

"What if I don't? My mother was Schuyler's legal heir and I'm hers."

"I know legally nothing can be done, but scandal sheets love this kind of stuff. If you were in show business, this might catapult you into instant stardom. Unfortunately, your business exists because people trust you. The truth about you pedigree won't break you, but what do you want to bet that all those private clubs you belong to decide to revoke your membership? All the whispers about your theft of a fortune could go on for years. People might invite you to dinner—but to do a deal with you?—I don't think so."

The silence in the room was almost palpable. Jared knew Brett was right. He'd always prided himself on being with the right crowd. There was no way he would be accepted if they learned his inheritance was questionable.

"So how many copies of these exist?" He tried to hide the trembling in his voice by speaking at a lower pitch.

"That's the only complete package. Everything in it is a matter of public record, so I can't say that someone won't stumble on the information again."

"This is from Alethia's safe."

"Right."

"Then I guess we have a gentlemen's agreement."

"I think you mean we have an understanding. Neither of us qualifies as a gentleman right now. Just remember that I am as protective of Nia as your mother was of you."

"Nia doesn't know anything about this meeting?"

"She's not the type to coerce anyone."

"I should have taken better care of her. She's a very special lady."

"I know." Brett didn't need a document to claim her as his wife, even though that would come later.

"I see."

"Good."

Brett closed his briefcase and stood. He ignored Jared's outstretched hand and walked out of the office. Marlene was sitting at her desk. He could tell she'd been watching the door and looking for any sign she might need to call the police. He thought again about what Nia said about Marlene being in love with Jared. She needed to find someone with a heart. It might be better if Jared didn't find out how she felt. He'd only find a way to use her. He really didn't deserve the woman.

Brett made a couple of stops before going home. First, he found a bookstore that specialized in law books. Then he stopped at a jeweler. He pressed a buzzer that opened the first door and then walked down a long narrow hallway. He knew he was being watched by a security team as he entered the reception area. An older man was waiting for him.

"Mr. Faulkner," the older gentleman said. "Please come with me." He led Brett into another smaller area. On the table in front of Brett were the rings he'd designed when he first came to Los Angeles. Then he'd been so sure of the outcome. He had assumed that Nia would realize that she loved him completely and give up California to come back to Wyoming, where they could live and raise a family. Later, he wondered if he would be purchasing wedding rings that no one was going to wear.

Now he was sure they would be together. He wanted a family and so did Nia. They didn't have much time as her biological clock ticked away—or so she'd been telling him for the past week. Now, he just had to convince Nia he knew what he was doing.


When Brett got home, he found Nia dancing around the house in her bare feet. She flashed a big smile when she saw him.

"What, besides being married to me, can make you so happy?" he asked.

She wore a purple sleep shirt emblazoned with yellow letters that proudly proclaimed I AM WOMAN.

"Watch that. You're always talking about me being married to you. I think it's time you admitted that you should be happy since you will be married to me."

"You are absolutely right. I am happy about that. What else has you dancing?"

"I just had a call from the board. They've decided that they will buy the building, and Freedom's Song bank will be a reality."

"Where do you fit in the picture?"

The smile left and she walked over and took Brett's hand and led him to the sofa. He sat down and she curled up in his lap. "They asked me to stay and act as an advisor to the person they will select in about a month."

"So what's the verdict?"

"I'm not sure. I like my consulting business but I also like the bank."

"I think it's going to be the bank."

"I think you're right, Brett."

"I don't know. My business is expanding and I might not be able to meet our agreement. What if something big happened and we're separated for three weeks? What if you couldn't travel? What if I couldn't travel?"

"You're right. I mean whose career would take precedence? I guess there's only one way to solve that problem." He opened his briefcase and gave her the bag with the bookstore logo.

As she studied Brett's face, Nia wasn't sure she wanted to know. She slowly pulled the oversize book out and then frowned. It was a reference guide for taking the bar exam.

"What's this about?"

"I'll have to take the bar exam again."

"Why?"

"I'm not licensed to practice in California and since I'm going to be living here . . ."

Tears came to her eyes, and at the same time she wanted to burst into laughter.

"You wretch! You let me think that we were going to have this commuters' marriage?"

"I confess. I wanted to know how much you were willing to give up for me. I'm selfish that way. The truth is, we should think about whose career takes precedence. For us, it's yours. It happens to some people. They're just born in the wrong state. You are a California woman. I can accept that. Besides, you have the opportunity to be part of something that is so right and that could give so much to the community by helping them finish Alethia's work."

She jumped up and glared at him. "When did you decide all this? What about Ana Lisa?"

"I think I always knew it but, of course, I had to do things my way until I almost lost you. You were right. You needed to be where you could do the most good. That's here, not in Wyoming. So I just adjusted my original plan slightly. Instead of dividing my time between New York and Wyoming, I'm going to operate from here."

"And?"

"Ana Lisa will be my partner and she'll handle things in New York."

"I have to . . . did anything ever happen between the two of you?"

"No way. She made it perfectly clear it was business and I respect any woman who is almost as tall as I am and has a black belt in tae kwon do."

Satisfied with that answer, she nodded.

"We'll have to get married when the kids aren't there. Now that they've expanded the program, that might take some doing."

"A couple of kids from New York who were in the first group are coming to live on the ranch. They really loved falcons and when summer camp was over, they went home and continued studying them."

"In New York?"

"Well, my skeptical friend, there are falcons in New York who are actually trained to frighten birds out of the path of the jets taking off from Kennedy Airport. It's amazing that if one of those got sucked into the plane engine, it could cause a crash."

"So now that they are going to be working on the ranch, Kaliq and Trisha will be able to visit anytime. Fantastic. What do you think?"

Brett put one hand on her waist and slipped the other one in his pocket. "I think we should make it official the old-fashioned way."

He showed her the black velvet box and with a flick of his thumb opened it. Nia gasped.

"It's beautiful," she whispered. "Not exactly conventional, but beautiful."

In the box was a small silver band that looked like a falcon in full wingspread. In the center of the ring was a marquis-shaped diamond.

Brett released his hold on Nia long enough to take the ring and slip it on her trembling finger. "Now it's official."

"It's beautiful. You designed it, didn't you?"

"Yes. I wanted something that was special to both of us."

He leaned forward and kissed her ear, then her throat. He shifted her so she was facing him. She put her arms around his neck and pressed her lips to his.

"We are so lucky. Did you know that there is a dance that describes us?"

"Really," he said as he stood up with her still in his arms.

"I can't remember the name, but a couple dances together and then they separate and dance with other people and then they get back together."

"That sounds about right. But, darling, you are never going to dance with anyone but me again."

Brett walked to the bedroom and gently placed her on the bed. She trembled a little when he joined her. He gently slipped the nightshirt over her head and tossed it on the chair next to the bed. As quickly as he could tear his clothes from his body, he added them to the chair.

Shards of excitement shot through every vein of her body, and she relaxed even more as they traveled the magical path that only true lovers knew. Whenever Brett made love to her, it was the same and yet different. Each time she felt she was on the top of a roller coaster and experienced the sudden drop. Her heart pounded, her breath grew short and she was in the place that allowed her to be completely uninhibited as he moved on top of her.

She pressed her fingers against his back as he surged deeply inside her. She opened her eyes and watched him losing control and felt exhilarated knowing that she was responsible for it.

"Nia, we are never going to let anything separate us again. I love you so much."

"I love you too." She didn't say it, but she loved the idea of belonging to a family again. She hadn't realized how much she needed to be part of one until she began jotting down the people she would be inviting to the wedding. Before she could voice those feelings, she felt him growing hard again.

He drove inside her until she was lost. She closed her eyes again and just enjoyed being loved. Her every nerve ending was aware of the intense pleasure, her every movement causing that pleasure to spread to another area of her body.

Soon all the control that Brett had been so proud of vanished and he, too, forgot everything except the woman in his arms and how much pleasure she brought to him. He drifted off to sleep while clutching her tightly to his chest.

Later that evening, as they sat across from each other at the dining room table, he broached the subject that had been gnawing at him.

"There is one thing we have to do soon," he said.

"What is it?"

"Buy a larger house or check with building codes to see if we can add on."

"And what would you like to add on?"

"Closet space. When I bring my summer wardrobe here, I'm going to need more room."

Nia began to laugh so hard she could hardly talk.

"You pompous little . . . I thought you were going to say we need room for a nursery."

"That too."

It was the next day before they told family and friends they were getting married.

# Thirty-six

A few minor details had to be worked out before they made their announcement, so they quietly went house hunting. They decided on an old home in the quiet community of Bel-Air. It had three bedrooms. Nia said her whole house could fit into one of the bedrooms. Two rooms would be converted to office space for each of them. There was also a separate guest house that they planned to renovate and make wheel-chair accessible for when Kaliq and Trisha came to visit.

After the purchase, Nia put her house on the market and then they told their family and friends their plans. The decision surprised everyone, but it was right for them.

"I can't believe you," Bree screamed into the telephone. "I no sooner get back to Hawaii and settle in than you get engaged. When's the wedding?"

"In three weeks," Nia said and braced for another scream, which came in a second.

"Why the rush? Is there something I should know?"

"I am not expecting a baby, if that's what you mean."

"That's exactly what I mean. Well, that's good. What did Julie say?"

"She said I didn't give her enough time."

"Was she as angry as I am? You can't do this to us. You know we want to plan a big party for you."

"Bree, the wedding is in three weeks in Wyoming."

"Oh, I am not even going to respond to that, girlfriend. I'll see you in a couple of weeks."

"Okay and buy a blue gown, maid of honor."

"You are too much. See you soon."


Later that night Brett and Nia had a good-natured argument over the song for their first dance.

"There's only one song for us, when you consider our history," Nia told him. " 'At Last.' "

"Honey, are you kidding?"

"No. What's wrong with it?"

"Nothing. It's not just going to be our first dance."

They talked about a few other songs but finally settled on "I Swear."


Her wedding was only two weeks away and Nia lay in bed with the printout that Alethia had on Brett. He was in Wyoming, handling another phase of the ski lodge project. She hadn't looked at the printout because she was afraid to find something that could be used for blackmail. Could he have an illegitimate child? Could he have bilked someone in a scheme?

Now she felt she could handle it. She took a deep breath and opened the folder. The first page began with Brett arriving in New York and beginning NYU. Ten pages later, she closed the folder and smiled.

She picked up the telephone and pressed the automatic dial. A minute later, she heard Brett's sleepy voice.

"Hello, darling," she whispered.

"Nia, is something wrong?"

"No. I just thought I'd call you and tell you how much I love you."

"I love you too. What time is it?" He paused and she knew he was looking at the clock. "Honey, what's the matter with you?"

"Brett, I was lonely."

"Me too. So why don't you let me get some sleep and I'll be home in three days."

"Make it two."

"I will if you let me get some sleep."

"Goodnight, darling."

It hadn't been easy to tell Kaliq and Trisha that while the wedding would be in Wyoming, he and Nia had chosen to make California home. Trisha coordinated the wedding with a bed-and-breakfast inn nearby.


Nia wanted to do something different to celebrate her engagement. She called her friends, told them her plans, and all agreed it was just the thing to do. A week before the wedding, Nia treated Trisha Faulkner, Jesslyn Rush, and her bridesmaids—Julie and Bree and her administrative assistant, Charlotte—to a three-day trip to a spa in Wyoming. They indulged themselves with massages, facials, manicures, pedicures and a few special treats. Bree, Trisha and Jesslyn opted for a reflexology treatment. The theory was that all the nerve ends are in the feet and the masseuse worked on those nerves. They all swore the treatment was all that it was meant to be.

Nia and her friends stayed at Brett's house while he moved to one of the cabins normally used for the inner-city kids who spent the summer at the ranch.

Nia, Julie, Charlotte and Bree were sitting in front of the two-story fieldstone fireplace. The furniture was massive, since Brett was much taller and larger than any of them.

"This is beautiful," Julie said as she stared at the beamed ceiling.

"My favorite is the guest bedroom. I mean when I climbed into that huge bed last night, I was in seventh heaven. I'm going to buy one just like it." Julie saw Nia's face and asked, "What's the matter?"

"I know when Brett expanded the house he was hoping for lots of children. I mean the place has seven bedrooms. That's not going to happen with me. I want a career."

"Don't worry about it," Bree told her. "You can always adopt children."

"Absolutely," Julie said. "It's something that Jack and I have talked about too. Right now, his company is going to send him somewhere else. We don't even know yet."

"That's awful," Nia said, her mind no longer on her situation.

"It's the way his company works. I'm seriously considering not having children. Anyway, who said if we'd married young, we'd have children?"

"Julie, other people have made that decision and it works for them," Bree said.

"I know, but let's face it. If I were younger, I'm sure I'd feel differently."

"Or we could have married young and had a child that was so baaad," Bree suggested.

"Uh-huh, my kids are going to be little angels," Nia said.

"You wish. They're going to be just like you. Headstrong, difficult, demanding," Julie warned.

"Hey, what do you mean by that?"

"That's how it goes for women who find Mr. Right too late for children," Bree added.

"I guess we'll just have to see what happens," Julie said.

"Hey! Let's not get maudlin. We have a lot to be grateful for, so let's think of something to do."

They decided to raid Brett's refrigerator. He'd just purchased a couple of gallons of ice cream the night before. They spent the next three hours making sundae concoctions. By the time Trisha called them to come to dinner, they were too full to do anything but push the food around on their plates and then have Trisha wrap the food up so they could take it back to the cabin.

"We are never going to do that again," Bree said.

"We certainly aren't going to do it before the wedding. I mean we spent three days at the spa and now we're trying to undo all that hard work," Nia said.

"Remember what Alethia used to say about us?" Bree asked.

"One of you—No trouble. Two of you—big trouble. Three of you—disaster time," they said in unison.

They laughed and went to bed in anticipation of a very big day very soon. This was the very best time for each of them.


Brett, Kaliq, Palladin, Vance and Ethan Rush were having a male-bonding session. They had talked about the details that would make this wedding special.

"I don't know if I want all this junk," Vance said. "My friend Jimmy says his parents eloped."

"It's not up to you," Ethan told his brother. "It's up to the girl."

"Well, she'll just have to know that I'd rather elope."

Brett, Palladin and Kaliq exchanged knowing looks. They had planned their lives and then met women who made them change their minds. One day, Vance would learn just the way they had.


Fifty people had descended on Kaliq and Trisha's home. Just as Nia wanted, only family and very close friends would share this time with her. Ana Lisa, Kent and Lisabeth couldn't make the early festivities, but arrived the morning of the wedding. Nia kept everything simple to give her friends time to meet her new family.

"I wouldn't miss this one," he told Brett. "You finally got what you wanted."

"With a few compromises."

"That's always going to happen."

Brett appeared to be the perfect host, but every time he and Nia were alone, he'd tell her what would happen when their time of celibacy was over.

He whispered graphic promises that made her blush. She spent one night not even looking at him for the entire meal.

The night before the wedding, as they were saying good night, she stepped back and whispered a promise to him. As she was getting in the car, she heard him mutter something about a very cold shower and hot revenge.


Brett and Nia had made their wedding arrangements so quickly they hadn't given their friends a chance to give a bachelor party for Brett, nor a shower for Nia.

Jack flew in from Paris three days before the wedding. Kent, Lisabeth and Ana Lisa arrived the day before the wedding. Julie's mom and dad drove from Las Vegas, where they had decided to live. They were seated by Ethan and Vance Rush. As ushers, Nia had told them they could decide what they would wear. Later she confided to Brett she hoped they didn't show up looking like they were headed for a rock concert.

She had worried for nothing. The twins were showing their personalities were entirely different. Ethan wore an elegant black Gucci suit, while Vance caught the eye of all the young girls at the inn with his choice of black slacks and chevron jacket from his current favorite designer, Nicole Farhi. Living in New York and attending one of its most prestigious prep schools had given them style at an early age. Just fourteen, Ethan was six-feet tall, just an inch shorter than his twin.

As they dressed for the wedding, Nia tossed on her robe and took a moment to step outside on the balcony and say a few words to her parents and Alethia. They had wanted her to find happiness and now she had it, and they weren't here to enjoy it with her. As she whispered her thanks for their love, a warm breeze surrounded her. It lasted a moment and then cool air replaced it.

When Nia walked back into the room, she found two frantic women. Bree and Julie were in their bridesmaids' dresses.

"Didn't you hear us call you?" Bree asked.

"When?"

"About two minutes ago," Julie answered. "We knocked and didn't get an answer. Then we realized the door was unlocked so we came in."

"Yeah, and we called you."

"Sorry. I was on the balcony."

"Come on, let's get you ready," Julie said.

They helped her into her dress.

"I absolutely want you to throw the bouquet to me," Bree instructed Nia.

"Someone get a tape recorder. No, get a video camera!" Julie cried.

"Don't be smart! I just think if you two were lucky in the marriage department, I might have a shot at it."

Nia had chosen a Richard Tyler wedding gown in a deep ivory. The long dress did not have a train, nor did she wear a veil. Nia took a last glance in the mirror and then nodded to her friends that she was ready.

Julie was the matron of honor, and Bree the maid of honor. Their dresses were the same shade of pale blue, but each wore a style that suited her figure. Julie's dress was form fitting and sleeveless. Nia watched Julie's slender figure as she walked ahead of her to the altar. Bree was next, and her dress had long sleeves and the cut allowed her full-figured frame to sway gently with the music.

Although she had had several volunteers, Nia had elected not to have anyone give her away. She carried something old: her parents' wedding rings around her neck. The something new was the pale ivory body suit under her wedding gown. The something borrowed was a thin silver bracelet from Trisha. Her something blue was a blue-and-silver pin Alethia had left her.

Tears welled up in her eyes as she looked down the aisle and saw Brett, the man about to become her husband. In many ways she had come full circle. Five years ago, she had had the chance to stand in this same spot, but her heart knew she wasn't ready and so she had broken contact and carved a new life. Now the man from her past was her present and her future. She didn't know how many people ever got a second chance, but those that did understood how fragile love could be and how to care for it forever.

Brett and his father, who was also his best man, waited at the altar. They were so handsome in their black tuxedos and black ties. Nia remembered a time when Brett would have climbed in his truck and driven away before anyone could get him into a tux. Now he was among the few men who actually owned one.

Brett smiled as he watched her come toward him. His throat closed up and he had trouble swallowing. She was so beautiful. He glanced down at his father. When Nia left Wyoming, Brett thought he would never allow himself to love that hard again. That seemed an eon ago. Now he waited for that same woman and knew he loved her more than ever.

After Nia and Brett recited their vows, and the minister pronounced them husband and wife, Kaliq read a Native American prayer:

Now you will feel no rain,
For each of you will be shelter to the other.
Now you will feel no cold,
For each of you will be warmth to the other.
Now you are two bodies,
But there is only one life before you.
Go now to your dwelling place
To enter into the days of your togetherness
And may your days be good and long upon
　　the earth.

Then everyone went to the inn for the reception. When it was time to throw the garter, Brett made a big show out of spinning Nia around in the chair before kneeling down and slipping the garter down her leg. He danced around, did a couple of spins and tossed it over his shoulder. There were a couple of shrieks from the crowd. Brett turned around to see Vance Rush twirling the garter around his finger.

Jesslyn Rush turned to her husband, "I think we better keep a closer eye on our sons."

# Epilogue

On New Year's Eve, Alethia Mary Sebastian Faulkner made her entrance into the world, screaming and fighting, much to the delight of her parents. They had agonized over the fact that they would probably have only one child. She carried the weight of four families on her shoulders. Alethia— Nia's mentor; Trisha—Brett's stepmother; Mary— Nia's mother; and Faulkner.

Brett stared down at Nia, too choked up to say anything. He leaned forward and kissed her forehead. Her eyelids fluttered, but she was too tired to open her eyes. "Poetic justice," she whispered.

"What's poetic justice?"

"I read the file that Alethia had. You were quite a ladies' man before we got back together," she said. "Now you have a daughter and one day the Hugh Hefner of the twenty-first century is going to show up on your doorstep to take your daughter out."

"He's going to have a very short playboy lifestyle if he's one minute past curfew. You never told me you looked at any more of the files. What else did you read in that file?"

"I learned all of your secrets."

"For example?"

"I shouldn't tell you. I like that puzzled look on your face. You must be very guilty about something."

"What do you think that is?"

"Well, it could be that the only time you took Ana Lisa to dinner, you forgot your wallet and she had to pay."

"Oh, man. I remember the look on her face when she realized I wasn't kidding. Fortunately I pay very well, so she had enough for both of us."

"Mmm. One day I'll tell you another secret from that file, but right now I just want to rest."

"I can certainly understand that."

They laughed and he kissed her forehead before he left the room. People had told him that women were beautiful during pregnancy, but he felt they were even more beautiful after. Nia's skin was clear and glowing without any makeup. An hour had passed from the time Brett stood in the delivery room and held his minutes-old daughter, shared a brief moment with his wife and joined the other fathers at the nursery window as each pointed out his child with a sense of bewilderment. He went to his Excursion, retrieved his cellular phone and sat in the passenger seat as he placed a call to New York. His parents were celebrating the New Year with Palladin and Jesslyn Rush.

He knew they had him on a speakerphone in Palladin's study. He could hear the music and laughter in the background, and he remembered how the happy crowd moved from one room to another. A year ago he and Nia had been part of that crowd.

This was the first year he'd missed being in New

York for the New Year since college. His partners
had kidded him about it. Tonight his reason had
been much more exciting than great food and interesting people. He was a father. Just as Palladin
and his father had told him, there was no greater
joy.

Being with Nia was opening up new worlds and
he wondered why he didn't realize he could have
both a business in Wyoming and a life in California. When Nia was almost killed at the beach
house, it had been the turning point. He'd almost
lost her, and he never intended for that to ever
happen.

"Hi Dad, Trisha. I just called to—"

"Your timing is a little off." Kaliq said. "We've
already brought the New Year in here an hour ago
and yours hasn't happened yet."

"My timing would only be off if I called to wish
you Happy New Year. I didn't."

"What's wrong? Is Nia okay?" Kaliq's voice
dropped to a whisper.

"Nia's fine and so is your granddaughter."

Silence. For a moment Brett thought he'd been
disconnected.

"Nia wasn't due for another three weeks," Trisha
screamed.

"Well, my daughter didn't know that," Brett
countered.

"Give us a few hours to get there," Kaliq said.

"You don't have to hurry."

"Are you kidding? My first grandchild, and you
think I'm not going to hurry? I knew we should
have come there for New Year instead of Christmas.
I'll see you soon."

Brett talked to Trisha, but could hear Kaliq in

the background shouting that he had a new grand-daughter. He heard Ethan's voice. "Vance, we're uncles." He could also hear the toasts and cheers from the other members of the Rush family.

"How's Nia?" Trisha tried to keep the concern out of her voice, but failed miserably. A first pregnancy at thirty-seven could be difficult and that was one of the reasons she and Kaliq had planned to be with Brett and Nia.

"She's fine. She came through without a problem."

"Wonderful. I believe we're going to have to be the two sane minds now," Trisha warned him.

"It's a good thing the stores are closed."

"Well, that doesn't seem to matter. Palladin just turned on his computer and the Internet has a million stores opened twenty-four/seven just waiting for buyers."

Brett groaned. He thought about the baby shower Nia's friends threw for her just days before and wondered if there would be room in the nursery. In a few days, deliverymen would be lined up at his door.

"Oh, Trisha, I think this little girl is going to be very spoiled. I guess I'd better talk to them."

"Maybe we can talk them into buying only one item each." She turned to see everyone gathered around the computer, calling out prospective sites to check out. She heard Kaliq call out a couple of websites that looked interesting. "Maybe not."

By the time Brett joined Nia in her room he had accepted congratulatory remarks and advice on newborns from Palladin, Jesslyn, Vance, Ethan and several party attendees that he'd never met.

He was surprised to see she was awake. He wasn't surprised that now that she was awake, she'd changed from the white cotton gown she'd selected to wear while giving birth. She now wore a pink silk gown with a white lace neckline.

"So when can we expect them?" Nia asked.

"If I know my father, he's probably on the phone now trying to get a flight out, but I told him not to hurry."

"In other words, they'll be here tonight," Nia said and laughed.

Brett was still choked up from the experience of seeing a life he'd helped create come into the world. "I think a lot more men should watch a birth. It's an awesome experience."

"So you have a newfound respect for all the moms out there, huh?"

"I guess. I don't know what to do next."

"The first thing you can do is take all that football equipment back and get something for a little girl. I warned you that I didn't want to know whether it was a boy or girl and you just assumed it would be a boy."

Brett grinned. "Yeah, I was a little presumptuous. I'll return it and get a tennis racquet or soccer ball or maybe boxing gloves."

"Excuse me?"

"Women today are into all kinds of sports and while I don't think football is the game for her, there are others."

"Well, I suggest we wait until she decides what her female mind tells her."

Somehow he knew his daughter would be as stubborn as her mother—and her father. If he hadn't been persistent, he would never have found the love he once lost. He leaned forward and kissed her. "But, honey, that's what we men do all the time."

# More Sizzling Romance from *Jacquelin Thomas*

# More Sizzling Romance From
## *Marcia King-Gamble*

\_\_**Reason to Love**    1-58314-133-2    **$5.99**US/**$7.99**CAN

\_\_**Illusions of Love**    1-58314-104-9    **$5.99**US/**$7.99**CAN

\_\_**Under Your Spell**    1-58314-027-1    **$4.99**US/**$6.50**CAN

\_\_**Eden's Dream**    0-7860-0572-6    **$4.99**US/**$6.50**CAN

\_\_**Remembrance**    0-7860-0504-1    **$4.99**US/**$6.50**CAN

---

Call toll free **1-888-345-BOOK** to order by phone or use this coupon to order by mail.

Name_____

Address_____

City_____ State_____ Zip_____

Please send me the books I have checked above.

I am enclosing     $_____

Plus postage and handling*     $_____

Sales tax (in NY, TN, and DC)     $_____

Total amount enclosed     $_____

*Add $2.50 for the first book and $.50 for each additional book.

Send check or money order (no cash or CODs) to: **Arabesque Books, Dept. C.O. 850 Third Avenue, 16th Floor, New York, NY 10022**

Prices and numbers subject to change without notice.

All orders subject to availability.

Visit our website at **www.arabesquebooks.com**.

# Arabesque Romances
## by *Roberta Gayle*